Over my Obsidian Heart

LA CAÌDA DUET
SIERRA MARIE

Trigger Warnings

This book contains trigger warnings. Please take a moment to look over them for your own mental health. This book delves into a few deep topics, but first and foremost I am a huge advocate for mental health awareness, and this book does get graphic. Trigger warnings include:

Depression
Trauma
PTSD
Emotional Abuse
SA
Traumatic Birth
Substance Addiction
Kidnapping/Abduction
Suicidal Ideation
Attempted Suicide
Overdose
Bullying
Asphyxiation
Graphic Sexual Content

Graphic Violence

Torture

Stalking

Forced Marriage

Slut Shaming

Murder

Cursing

This novel is an interpretation of my knowledge of mental health struggles and by no means whatsoever do I want anyone to feel like I am taking from their experiences or downplaying anything specific. Depression is a debilitating monster that affects many and feels like it literally corrupts one's mind.

It also can snowball into other thoughts and feelings, so please if anyone ever feels like suicide is the answer, I implore you to seek help. The National Suicide Hotline is 1-800-273-8255 and will be there for you.

Life is hard and can be downright mean. I just want you to know as my reader that you are not alone if you ever feel even an ounce of what Amelia feels throughout this story; her struggles are not unique. CPTSD is also something I have been learning about, and it is amazing what the mind does to protect your body, but it's also incredibly insane the memories our bodies hold onto and remember.

My main character struggles with CPTSD throughout this novel, and I wanted to bring awareness to the struggle. We are all in this together, from one healing heart to another. Please know that life is better with you around.

"For anyone who has had to ask themselves why me? This is where we turn why me into try me."

CHAPTER 1

The Crushed Obsidian Pebble

MANY PEOPLE SAY that when we die, there is a bright light that reaches our eyes. It overtakes our entire vision in a blink, and then there it is—the other side.

Some say that our loved ones stand there waiting for us, while others say that we have to wait at the pearly gates to be evaluated. No one has one description that correlates with another when it comes to describing it.

Is it heaven? Is it hell? Is my family waiting for me, or is the grim reaper ready to show me the way to the flames?

Five…

Four…

Time ticks slowly and quickly all at once. I don't see a bright light, though. I see darkness clouding my sight.

The dark haze on the outer portions of my vision is growing heavy and slick as it starts clouding over my eyes.

My limbs want to rest forever, and my heart can barely beat as it too starts to welcome eternal sleep.

Three…

Two…

Many say there is a moment where guilt takes over like quicksand. But the trick with quicksand is not to struggle.

You're supposed to stay still and gather your thoughts on the most appropriate way to get out of a shitty situation. Deliberate moves, unhurried decisions, and you won't quickly sink.

That is exactly what I did with *this* decision. I slowed down and thought about every action—my every move.

I pondered which path to take that would be the best for me. Not the easiest, not the fastest, but purely the best for me.

One…

This world was something I clearly wanted no part of.

How am I supposed to live when every fiber of my being wants everything to end?

How am I supposed to smile when all I want to do is cry? How am I supposed to face the people that cause me nothing but pain when all I want to do is beat them to death with my bare fists?

Why should I even have to face any of it at all? Because I simply just don't want to.

My eyelids grow heavy and finally close. I can feel every nerve ending throughout my body start to relax and shut down as the drugs make their way through my system.

My mind is the only thing I don't want to deal with anymore and yet it is the last thing to seem to have any energy at all.

Slowly, they trickle down…

The memories start to fade like a picture caught on fire, but I don't smell the flames.

Smoke muddles my brain, and nothing makes any sense anymore. My thoughts too fade, finally.

Goodbye.

Zero.

"Amelia, open your eyes—Amelia!" Concern laces the voice; it's one I recognize.

"She may not be completely there. We don't know the extent of her injuries. There could be permanent damage," a rough, deep tone filters through the haze. This voice I do not recognize.

Beep, beep, beep.

Where are those beeps coming from? They slowly start speeding up, becoming closer together.

I push through the thick gray haze that is clouding everything. Suddenly, a bright white light burns my eyes as I attempt to peel them open with the small amount of strength I can muster.

I gasp out and immediately close them. There's that stupid white light. My eyeballs feel like they are on fire, and pain pierces through my skull, causing a muffled groan to escape my throat.

"Amelia! You're awake. Oh, honey, you're awake!" The shrillness in the woman's voice crashes through my brain.

Suddenly, a large pop shudders through my mind, and everything becomes ten times louder.

Beep, beep, beep.

"Her blood pressure is 72 over 43, her heartrate is 153. I need another line; she is burning up! Where is my Tylenol?!" a young woman's voice ricochets through me on the right—demanding attention.

"What is her temperature?" another soft feminine voice asks from somewhere to the left. The nasally tone immediately reminds me of my aunt.

"105.4—place more ice packs!" the demanding woman's voice answers, barking out orders.

"Is she going to be okay?" There's that voice I recognize

again. It's her voice, my best friend Lacey. Why is she here? What is going on?

Suddenly, I feel a sharp stab of iciness in my groin, my armpits. Why is everything so cold?

"Right now, we need to stabilize your friend. Once we have her stable, I will come and update you on everything. Does she have parents we can call?"

Don't tell them about them. Say no, Lacey. I can't speak out loud, and I try to swallow and realize something is clogging my throat. I try to swallow again, and panic starts to rise within me as I realize I have a tube in my throat and I'm choking. I am awake and choking.

"It's okay, Amelia, it's okay! We're trying to help you stay still," someone urges.

I didn't realize I had any strength to move at all, but my arms and legs start to jerk as I try to reach for the damn tube in my throat. I've gotta get that out! I'm choking!

"Don't touch that," the woman reprimands me. "She needs more sedation. Pull—" I can't hear anymore as I try to push against the hand holding down my own.

Let me go! I want to scream, but unable to speak I just scream in my mind. *Please, don't hold me down!*

Panic is a harsh adrenaline that gives no mercy as it tackles your mind. Panic tackles your thoughts, your processing, your heartbeat, and your fight or flight stance. What do I do, what *can* I do?

I can't be held down again—I can't. A small sting trickles throughout my arm, sending me on further alert.

But then the familiar dark haze returns. I feel the heavy claws pulling me down, down, down. I can't fight them off. I have no strength. Is this what is happening? Am I going down to Hell?

I hear the sobs of Lacey as everything starts spinning down the drain. I become weightless and begin to float through the darkness.

I am the darkness.

CHAPTER 2

When Life Turns Upside Down

Amelia

Two Months Prior

"I AM NOT some girl on the corner that you can just put up for sale, Mom!" I yell.

I stare at my mother, all five-foot-five of her standing there in a too-small blue crop top with a tan stain on the left side hem, booty shorts ripped and long dirty blonde fried-brown hair reaching mid-length on her shorts, and her signature smeared burgundy lipstick with a Marlboro cigarette hanging out the side of her mouth.

Her almond eyes I inherited narrow with anger as the blue becomes bright and hot. Her arms cross over her chest, her lips curling in a sneer.

I used to feel that glare in my soul as it penetrated through me. Luckily, I inherited my "father's" hazel eyes, and I learned to become desensitized to that withering look. I glower right back.

Mom scoffs, "Oh, shush, you are not being placed on the

corner, Amelia. Why do you always have to go straight for the dramatics? Huh?"

She blows out a puff of smoke, the protruding smell of cigarettes filling my nostrils. I have learned to hate this smell with everything in me. The stench curls around every sensory nerve I have, and the day I get out of here I promise that horrible smell will be nowhere around me.

"Oh, okay so not giving me a choice on who I can be with—date, marry whatever—is not selling me out? How much was I worth to you, Mom?" I challenge. "How much time was used to negotiate this apparent contract between the two of you? Huh!"

Tears start to cloud my vision, and I do my best to swallow them down. I don't want her to see me cry; I don't want her to have the satisfaction of being able to affect me again.

I turn and slam the cup back into the sink full of soapy water behind me. I had been washing the dishes trying to pick up the trailer when she came in flouncing through the door with what was supposed to be "great news". I haven't had a choice with much in my life at all, but who I decided to run off with into the sunset should have been at least one of them!

Taking a deep breath, I look up at my reflection in the window. The light from the dining room dimly lit behind me allows me to see the dark circles underneath my hazel eyes. My long brown hair is thrown up into a messy bun on top of my head—the curls I got from who knows who—are reacting to the humidity and uncontrollable at this point.

My high cheek bones have slightly sunken in from the nights I have gone without food lately so my sister could eat from what little I made from the diner down the road. Sacrifice, all the sacrifice I give just for her to come in and stomp all over it.

Twenty-three years of my life I have given in this damn

cycle. If it weren't for my little sister, I would have packed my shit and been out of here a long time ago.

Mom smirks. "I guess you get a small bit of the dramatics from me, dontcha? Ah." She smacks her lips as a smile stretches her face. "No worries, hun, no need to be scared of this one, okay? I told him he couldn't hit you—no hitting! No hands on that pretty face."

I turn and stare at her, my mouth gaping open in shock. She thinks she is being *motherly* right now. That she is doing me a favor by making sure whatever man she set me up with won't beat the crap out of me like some of the deadbeats she brings back home do to her.

"No hands on the face making you money in your pocket, huh?" I whisper out, no longer having the ability to yell or fight.

Being an adult doesn't mean shit, does it? Having a druggy deadbeat mother will always pull me down, will always be a disadvantage to me.

Her lack of awareness of how I feel about her news astounds me. She sits there finishing off her cigarette on our little beaten-down round dining table. We're missing one of the chairs thanks to her grabbing it and slamming it into the back of one of the assholes she brought home who tried to move from her to me.

At least, I pray that's why she hit him: defending her daughter. I was thirteen at the time and had started to blossom more, and it was getting attention.

I may be skinnier than average because of the amazing diet I've been maintaining all these years, but my breasts took the hit coming in at a triple D. Yay me. Breasts draw attention, and men like breasts. I, however, started hating them long ago.

Mom picks her nails absentmindedly as I hold on tight to the counter. My blood starts rushing at the idea that just sprang to my mind.

"I am just going to leave. I am taking Andrea, and I am leaving, Mom. This isn't some sixteenth century bullshit where you can decide who can have my hand in marriage. I am not having it—it isn't happening." I dry my hands on the small faded yellow hand towel and push my shoulders back, emphasizing my decision. We will struggle, but I'll figure it out.

Mom starts with a small chuckle that turns into a full-blown hyena laugh, and the alarm bells in my stomach start to go off.

I stare at her as she snuffs out the cigarette in the glass holder and she grabs her Bud Light beer can beside her. She slightly chokes on the sour taste before locking eyes with me and giving me a wolf-in-sheep's-clothing smile.

"Oh, honey, this isn't just some random John on the corner. I scored you the tippy top of the food chain. He runs the mafia on all the west side of San Juan County, and I may have told him that if you didn't agree to marry him that your *sister* would do." She shrugs her shoulders.

I feel all color in my face drain away. Red-hot anger simmers deep in my belly as it rises up toward the base of my throat. I can feel the slick coat of acid ready to erupt through my mouth as I stare at the woman willing to sell off a twelve-year-old child.

I cannot read the emotion in her eyes as she breaks the stare-off we were conducting between each other, but I pay no mind to the fake sincere bullshit she tries to pull over my head.

"I will hide with her. They will never find us," I seethe through clenched teeth.

I try to think of the money I have set aside; it isn't much, but it can put us on a train to a bigger city so we can hop on another one and get states away before they can try to find us.

The wheels turning in my mind make me dizzy as I try to think of how much money I will have for food until I can find a job or a place for us to crash at.

Mom snorts. "He is the *La Caìda*, Amelia, don't you understand? Barnette Reyes runs the whole damn thing. It's his, baby. He is nobody to mess with." She shrugs, like that's supposed to make it better.

My fight or flight nerves come to a screeching halt at the mention of Barnette's name. Fucking Barnette—I know that name. Well, know *of* that name.

The stories that circulate about how ruthless and crass he is. He is known for not giving second chances and not putting up with anyone's shit. He has the cops in our small town on his dime and our only reputable lawyer in his pocket. I saw him in passing once, and that was enough to decide to keep off his radar.

"Why?" I try to swallow the breakdown I want to have, but the emotion clogs up my throat I want to cry, I want to scream, and I want to break everything in this goddamn trailer.

Mom just waves me off. "Listen, just help your mama out, okay? I owe some people money, alright?"

My hysteria filters out in laughter, and now I match her hyena laugh. It is always about money with her. Always about getting caught up in the wrong crowd and doing shit she knows she shouldn't be doing, but anything to catch that high.

She purses her lips, scolding me, "Stop that foolishness. You need to go shower and freshen up before he gets here." That sobers my hysterics up real quick.

"He is coming *now*?" I yell in disbelief.

Her glare radiates through me at my tone, as if she is angry at me. The nerve, the nerve of this fucking woman!

I take a step towards her as she stands, knocking the chair

down behind her. She may be drugged up, but she is street smart, and she's quick. She can also sense a fight when it's about to happen, and for the first time in all my years on this shitty earth, I want to hit her.

I take another step towards her and can feel the rage shaking my body as the adrenaline courses through me.

Disbelief…

Shock…

Anger!

And underneath it all? Hurt. I am so tired of this woman who is supposed to love me hurting me instead.

"Fuck you!" I scream, my heart pounding in my chest.

What's the point in holding all this in? This isn't the first time we've had a yelling match, but I usually wrap it up for the sake of Andrea. I don't want my temper getting her in trouble too, but she isn't here right now.

Mom's lips curl back from her teeth. "Fuck *you*! You ungrateful brat! I am doing you a favor! He is the top of the food chain, baby, you will want for nothing!"

Something in me snaps at her accusing me of being ungrateful. I feel it like a coil that's been spun way too tightly in my head. I hear the break before my entire body trembles at the feeling of it.

I'm on the floor on top of my mother before I even realize I flew at her and knocked her down.

She and I smack and punch each other. Like two lionesses wanting to dominate to come out on top. She pulls my hair back, yanking my neck to the side, and I swing blindly, aiming for her face she relies so much on for her sales.

We scuffle, and she is just barely able to swing me off and pin me underneath her. I buck my hips, trying to throw her off of me as she takes a couple swings at my eye and jaw.

I don't feel any of the hits; I just feel pure *rage*.

I manage to get a punch in, briefly blinding her before I shove her off of me, and I quickly pin her back down. For the first time in my life, I understand the term 'blinded by rage'. It is hot and sticky magma in my veins.

The door to the trailer bangs open and slams into the wall so hard the doorknob sticks into the wallpaper, and both my mother and I freeze as we look at the three men who just entered into the doorway. The living room looks even more tiny in size with the three of them in it.

I immediately recognized the one in the middle. Barnette.

He stands there taller than normal as I straddle my mother on the floor, my chest rapidly rising and falling as I attempt to catch my breath.

His dark blue eyes are framed by his caterpillar eyebrows and sharp cheekbones. His black hair is carefully slicked to the side as he stands there in his blue jeans, brown suede shoes, and a black collared button-up long-sleeve shirt. His skin is sun-kissed tan, and his lips are tight and framed by his short, stubble beard.

He is clean and casual—and he *does* radiate wealth and "fuck around and find out".

I gulp down at the intensity of his gaze. He looks angry, and my attention is immediately drawn to the man on his immediate right who has a smirk playing on his lips.

His teeth slightly show through his full lips. His dark brown eyes sparkle with amusement as his soft brown softly curled hair lays lazily against his forehead. He stands with his hands in the pocket of his dark jeans, and thanks to his blessed caramel skin, the red shirt fits him well and doesn't wash him out.

Ink peeks out from the cuffs of the shirt, but my attention is drawn right back to the smirk on his face. Fuck them both! I sneer at his amusement, which causes him to chuckle softly.

"Do I even want to know what is going on between the two of you?" Barnette asks calmly.

I shove off my mother, leaving her on the floor staring up at the men open-mouthed like a fish out of water. I pull my shoulders back and wince slightly as I try to cross my arms, pain starting to seep to the surface. My adrenaline, however, is still pumping and influences my ability to speak.

"We were having a disagreement about the arrangement that was made behind my back." I keep my eyes locked carefully with his.

He may be the big king around here, but this is my home, my life, and I don't feel an ounce of fear standing up to him now. It may be stupidity, it may be adrenaline, or it could be a good mixture of both.

Barnette takes a small step towards me, but his two lackeys stay put. He sighs, "Ahh, I see your mother just now told you about this."

He glares down at her, his eyebrows scrunching in disapproval, and my mom quickly snaps out of whatever trance she was in and stumbles to get up.

"You had a month to tell her," Barnette reminds her.

It takes every ounce of control in my body not to hit that bitch again. I almost pull a neck muscle as I swing my head towards her.

"A month!" I grip tightly onto my arms to keep my hands from reaching out to her. Mom looks at me sheepishly, and I can see the movement in her throat as she tries to swallow down a gulp.

"I've been busy," she snaps at me, then looks at Barnette and gives him her porn-star smile. "I am so sorry, hun, it must have slipped my mind until today. I know she looks a little scrappy right now, but she is feisty, and you will have fun!"

The jab at my appearance stings hard in the middle of my chest. She has never given me much of a compliment, and I think *feisty* is the kindest thing she's ever said about me, but her insults still hurt.

Her lack of love still hurts. I can hear them like an echo in my brain on replay.

"How is someone supposed to love you while you look like your dad?"

"Your own dad doesn't even love you!"

"You aren't smart enough to go to college. Try to learn to fix your face and work the streets."

"You won't achieve anything greater than this place. These are your roots, girl, run with it."

"No one will ever love you like me; I am preparing you for this harsh world. Toughen up!"

Her words spin and spin in my head. I stumble back and grab onto the table, hoping it's strong enough to hold me up.

I can see slight movement as Barnette's second-in-command takes a half step towards me, but Barnette lifts his hand and stops him as his gaze latches back onto me.

He is like a leech wanting to take everything from me, but I don't have much to give.

"Are you seeing stars?" What an odd way to ask if my head is spinning. His lips are in a tight line as he waits for my answer.

"No," I answer a bit roughly and then clear my throat. "I see a man in my living room that I want nothing to do with."

His eyebrow shoots up in surprise as Mom lets out a gasp.

"Amelia!" she reprimands. She turns towards me, about to give her world-famous speech about how we don't talk to men with attitude or sarcasm, when Barnette takes two seemingly big steps forward and smacks my mother across her cheek.

I gasp aloud as she grasps her face, using the wall to hold herself up. The unexpected action stuns both of us.

"You are done, Ramona. No more words out of your mouth. You already didn't follow the rules, and now I have half a mind to turn my back on our little arrangement and leave you to deal with the consequences," he snaps.

To that, my mom starts to whimper and shake her head over and over. She must have really barked up the wrong tree to look so scared.

He grabs her roughly by the chin, making her head stop shaking back and forth. She looks absolutely pathetic with tears wetting her face, smearing her caked-on mascara in small dark streams down her cheeks. Her skin, already pale on a normal day, is bleached white as she grasps on top of his forearm with an iron-tight grip.

Her smeared burgundy lips are puckered out and caked with blood from the busted lip I gave her. But I see the fear in her eyes, and even though she has put me through hell and back, seeing the raw terror there turns my stomach. I back up around the table slowly.

Barnette's head whips to the side. I was unaware he was tracking my movements, and I freeze mid-step.

Don't show him fear. Don't show him fear. Don't show him fear, I chant in my head as I hold myself steady, staring him back down.

The air in the trailer is hot and sticky with electricity, and I desperately want to get out of here. I want to run, grab my sister, and get the heck out of dodge. The urge to vomit suddenly hits me fiercely at the thought of my sister. I turn and look at the clock and see it is ten past two. Fuck!

"Now *there* is the fear I was looking for," Barnette comments as he lets my mother's chin go and steps towards me.

I narrow my eyes and harden my expression at him, and he has the audacity to chuckle at the change.

"Someone is going to be home any minute now, and I know my future wife here has such a soft spot for her little sister, doesn't she?"

Everything in me goes rigid as he uses my one weakness against me. Then I hear the soft steps on the porch as my little sister gets home from school.

"Meli?" her soft voice echoes through the house as she looks into the open doorway.

I can't even imagine what she thinks she's seeing. Mom and I are covered in blood, and there are three big scary-looking men in the trailer. She never learned to stay silent and afar, reading the scene before entering it. She didn't have the street smarts Mom has and that I learned and inherited.

Maybe that's my fault, maybe I tried to protect her too much, but she should have had every alarm bell ringing that something was wrong and to not enter the trailer.

Damn it. Her petite frame hardly fills the doorway. She has Mom's long straight dirty-blonde hair that hangs to her waist. She never lets me trim it even though I offered an ungodly number of times, but she is stubborn. She has mom's blue eyes that sit doe-like on her, and they frame a sharpened nose and cupid lips. She is just a baby in this cruel world.

Barnette's man who was at his left takes one step back towards the door and grabs my sister by her arm, yanking her inside.

She yelps out in surprise, and I see her face contort into pain from his grip. She looks so tiny compared to him; there is no way he is under six feet tall, and he just manhandled her. I react before even thinking.

"Motherfucker!" I scream as I lunge across the room and punch this bald ass man on the side of his face.

He had to have seen it coming. My intentions were loud and clear, and yet he let me swing, and man did I swing! I put my full force into hitting his jaw, the only thing I am registering is the blood pounding in my ears. His bushy eyebrows go up in surprise, and if it wasn't for his lack of hair, they probably would have blended in with it. I breathe heavily as I stare at him with my right arm cradled to my side, the stiffness registering in my fingers.

His muscled arm reaches up and wipes at his lip where a small bit of blood is smeared from the punch I landed, and he stares at it as if impressed.

The man that was at Barnette's right laughs out loud, and I feel the presence of Barnette behind me. That alone makes my body react before my mind can control it. My body goes slightly rigid just as the sting of the punch to his hard ass jaw registers fully in my body and stinging hot flames lace up my arm. Andrea and my mother are crying loudly, begging him to spare me.

I keep my eyes on Mr. Cartoon. "Let. Her. Go." I enunciate it slowly so he can understand me, but I also don't want them to hear the tremble in my voice that I know is there. I'm going to break, and soon.

Mr. Cartoon looks up at Barnette behind me, who hasn't said a word, and hasn't killed me on the spot.

"Do as the lady said. Let her sister go."

My head swivels to look at him in shock. I wasn't expecting him to accommodate my request. I was ready to take another swing and go down trying.

Barnette looks down at me. "You have quite the fiery temper, and though I like my women to have a little fire in them, you need to learn to act more refined. We are not here to hurt your sister."

He wants me to be more ladylike. The man who runs a freaking mafia with drugs, guns, and money wants me to be a lady. I think the shock must show in my features, because he nods his head up and down as if to cement what he just said.

Andrea stumbles away as his man lets her go and I quickly get in front of her and put her behind my back. Her petite frame is flush against my own as she grabs onto me tightly from behind, and for the first time since those three have entered my home, I can feel the threat of tears try to overwhelm me.

This will probably be the last time I see my little Andrea, for who knows how long. I can feel her trembling wrack through my body. Taking a deep breath, I pat her arm with my right hand and use my left arm to hug her.

"You do not get to touch her—ever!" I don't care if they can kill me. I will die to protect her, and I always will.

My mom is silent in the dining room. I see her sitting there at the table with her Marlboro cigarette hanging from between her fingers as she glares at us, eyes hollow. The three men just stare down at me, and I feel like a small bug underneath a magnifying glass ready to be caught on fire.

Barnette explains, "Amelia, the agreement is you come with me and become my wife, and your sister is untouched. No one will be allowed to hurt her. She will have my full protection."

My hackles relax a bit at the understanding of the agreement; she will be kept safe.

"But..." There is always a damn *but*. "If you do not follow through on your part, then I will take her, and I will make her become my wife when she becomes of age. Do you understand what that means?"

I swallow hard, all the blood draining from my face. She wouldn't be able to get out of this life. She wouldn't be able to know what it's like to go to college, to have a normal relationship, to get a good job and make it on her own in a small three-bedroom home in a cute, little neighborhood.

She would have to have sex with him, a grown ass man.

Rage fills my veins again. No. Never.

"I agree to whatever stupid ass contract you and my mother made. As long as Andrea's safe," I seethe, meeting his eyes with mine.

Andrea sobs into my back as she realizes I am going to have to leave her. I don't want to leave her behind, I don't want to leave her alone with my mother, but it looks like I have to. Tears start to fill my eyes, but I refuse to let them fall.

"And making sure I am taken care of," my mother adds from her chair. I whip my head toward her in disgust. The person who put us in this position.

"I don't care what happens with her," I speak at Barnette and then turn to my mother, narrowing my eyes. "But I swear to God or whatever higher power up there who decided my life was fun to fuck with, Mother, if one strand of Andie's head is hurt or if you try to pull this shit you did to me with *her*—I will fucking kill you."

I have never thought about the death of my mother being at my own hands; I have wished a couple times for her death to happen of course, but I feel this in every bone of my body. I vibrate with the truth of my words.

If my little Andie gets hurt, I will kill her. I will kill her and live with the damn consequences.

Barnette claps slowly. The sound of it is so foreign and so unsuitable for this situation that I stare at him in open shock.

"This is such a beautiful family; I can feel how much love you have for one another." Sarcasm drips off his words, and I feel like a million little spiders are climbing up my spine.

His right-hand man looks grim, and if I'm not mistaken has a small amount of sadness in his features, but I must be seeing things because now his face matches the other guy, and both are unreadable.

"Come now, Amelia, let's get going. Being here is making me need a shower," Barnette drawls.

Shame blankets me like a hard coating on a pill. He steps towards me and pulls on my arm wrapped behind me over my sister, but I yank my shoulder back away from him.

"I am capable of following you out of here just fine. No need to manhandle me," I snap.

He lifts his hands up innocently and grins at me, the gesture mocking. I turn quickly and grab my little Andie by her shoulders, forcing her to look at me.

"You have to be strong, okay? I won't be here to help you. Do your homework, do the extracurricular activities, stay with Lacey, and call her if you need her. Do your studies so you can get a scholarship and get the fuck out of here! You hear me? You are smart; you've got this! You will have a better life!"

I am throwing the weight of the entire world on such tiny shoulders, but this has to be said. She needs to do this.

"Meli, please don't go! Don't leave me!" she sobs. Her blue eyes make me feel like I'm drowning in the ocean, and it hurts to breathe.

"I love you so much. I love you more than anything in this world. It's you and me against the world. Two obsidian pebbles in a sea of crystals." Our little saying that I created years ago.

"Two obsidian pebbles in a sea of crystals," she repeats back to me and hugs me tightly around my neck.

"Time to go—now!" Barnette barks behind me. That fucking bastard. My dislike for him is thick in my bones. I kiss Andrea on her forehead and give her a tight squeeze.

"You've got this. Keep out of sight, do what you've got to do, and watch everything," I whisper into her ear.

I get pulled by my arm again, and the fight I had in me deflates. I feel the heavy weight of the responsibility I have come crashing down on my chest, and I take small whisps of breath to keep myself from hyperventilating.

One man is in front of me and two behind me as we step out of the doorway to the trailer I grew up in and have been rooted down to all these years.

"Meli!" my sister yells as I continue walking. "Meli!" I hear my mom shushing her as she tries to calm her down, and there is absolutely nothing I can do.

I just agreed to a deal with the Devil, and I have no idea what is in store for me or what he wants from me.

CHAPTER 3

My New Reality

Amelia

I HATE it when dreams are of memories. How those memories slowly drench the freedom and colorful inspiration of false illusions, warping into some of my core nightmares.

I can see my mom and her best friend Cecilia dancing in the living room on the worn-down shaggy brown carpet. Mom is wearing a bright yellow crop top with a pair of her low-hanging booty shorts that fit her snugly, topped with her black combat boots. Cecilia wears a ruby-red spaghetti-strapped dress with a pair of faded black flip flops, and both have a cigarette in one hand paired with a glass of boxed wine in the other.

They are laughing and carefree as they dance to Pat Benatar and AC/DC living out the best of the 80's.

I like it when Mom is happy, her burgundy lips spread out in a genuine carefree smile. I sit there curled up on the couch watching them dance around each other as the music blares loudly.

Mom takes a look over at me and beckons for me to join them, and

I sheepishly smile out of pure embarrassment at the thought of joining them in their crazy dancing.

Mom rolls her eyes and goes to burn her cigarette out in the glass holder, placing her red solo cup down. She beelines straight for me and grabs both of my hands, easily yanking me off of the couch and onto their makeshift dance floor.

"Yeeeeesssss!" Cecilia yells over the music. "Let's see what moves you got, girl!"

I have never been one who could easily dance, but Mom starts swinging my arms back and forth while moving her hips, and I copy what she's doing. I feel the beat every time our hips twist and start to get the hang of it.

"Atta girl! You've got this!" Mom drunkenly laughs over the music as she starts spinning herself around.

All three of us start singing loudly once Joan Jet gets her turn on the station, and we all hit the beat to how we love rock n' roll. I haven't laughed this hard in such a long time; it feels so carefree. Being twelve shouldn't be as stressful as it is for me, but I live for these kinds of nights.

Suddenly, a sharp pain hits me in my lower belly that causes me to double over for a moment.

"You okay, honey bear?" Cecelia gets down onto her knees and looks up into my face.

She has always had a soft spot for me and insists on calling me 'honey bear' even though I am practically a teenager now. The pain turns into a cramp and starts to edge away. Tears rim my eyes, but it wasn't enough to cause them to spill over.

"She's fine, Cill!" Mom yells over the music as she goes back for her drink at the table.

"I don't know what that was, but it hurt," I reply to Cecilia, ignoring my mother. She looks at me with concern and peers at where my hands are over my lower stomach.

"It is probably just that time of the month is all. We all go through it. Maybe you should just lie down for a bit, okay?"

I nod in approval immediately as the achiness continues on. I know all about that time of the month; mine started early at eleven and harasses me every damn month. I should have started by now. I usually fall a few days after Mom has hers.

Maybe it's stress. At least, that's what the health teacher taught us in class last year.

It is so much fun being a 'young woman'.

I curl back up on the couch and watch as Mom and Cecilia continue dancing the night away, smiling as I drift off to sleep after some time passes.

I slowly start to rouse back to consciousness. Reality hits me like a ton of bricks, eager to smack me across my face.

Barnette had the actual nerve to put a blindfold around me when I got in the back seat of the shiny black Range Rover that was extremely out of place in my trailer park before drugging me.

I was terrified to climb in as I stared at the custom dark brown leather inside that smelled rich and new. I was still covered in blood, and my poor tousled messy bun hair was hanging on for dear life on the side of my head. I barely put my ass on the seat when he pulled that stupid thing out of his pocket.

I bet the neighbors were getting a load out of the drama. My life is now a fucking sitcom.

Barnette holds up the blue tie dangling it in front of me. "Are you serious?"

"Very much so," he had responded. No reaction in his facial features, no expression to his voice. What a sweet, loving husband to be.

His hand snaked out as he grabbed onto my chin like he had

done to my mother earlier. I could feel the crack in my exposed skin as he puckered my lips aggressively. For the first time since I met him, I felt fear for myself.

His voice was low and deadly as he warned, "You will listen and obey me. Thanks to you and your mother's stunt, my plans have been postponed for a while so you can heal, but don't make the mistake that I still have my own plans to fulfill here."

I glared back at him as my heart beat erratically against my chest. "What do you want out of me?"

That was the big question I wanted answered. The bright pink neon *why the fuck is this happening to me* question. He stared at me slowly up and down, taking in every inch of me as I shifted uncomfortably; I can still feel his gaze. Finally, he reached my eyes and leaned in slowly to my ear.

"To break you into being an obedient wife." My body had jerked at the response. I didn't know what to make of it.

He didn't give me much time to ponder on it, though, because his left-handed man who got in the back seat with me had grabbed my arms behind my back and slapped something hard and metal around my wrists as Barnette tied the blindfold around my eyes.

Then I felt a sharp sting in my arm and started bucking against the two men. I didn't stand much of a chance as the drug took effect, and soon in my already darkened vision, my mind fogged, and everything had disappeared.

I awoke to this pounding headache. Right now, my eyeballs feel like they have their own heartbeat as they try to escape out of my eye sockets.

I roll over as the nausea threatens its arrival up my dry throat. I try to peek through one eye, and everything spins off its axis.

What the hell did they drug me with? I groan as I attempt to get my bearings.

Fuck all three of them.

Fuck my mother.

Fuck this world who thinks my life is a damn joke!

The pain in my hands and face starts registering through. I peel open my eyes again to study my bruised and bloodied knuckles. I cannot believe I got into a physical fight with my mother.

Honestly, it was long overdue, and she had it coming. Still, though, it actually happened.

I groan again as I sit up slowly and gently rub my eyes. Finally, after everything stops spinning, I open my eyes and see where I am.

The room is as big as my living room was in the trailer. The walls are a rich, creamy sage with dark walnut-brown furniture. There's a dresser on the left wall with a flatscreen TV above it, an armoire on the wall in front of me, and an opening to a bathroom on the wall to my right. I look at the four-poster bed I am on and see the silky soft white comforter.

My entire body screams out in warning as it registers with me that there isn't any smeared blood on the comforter I am laying on.

I look down and see I am in a silky purple nightgown, my arms free of blood. My skin is clean. My clothes were changed.

Someone had the audacity to clean and change me. The feeling of vulnerability makes my chest feel heavy again, and I hate that feeling. My heartbeat begins to race, and my palms get sweaty.

Someone had the nerve to make me naked while I was unconscious, and that is not okay.

That is not justified.

I try to swallow down the fear and panic that wants to overwhelm me. Why? Why me?

I hear soft steps coming towards my closed door, and I yank on the sheets to cover my already exposed body.

I can hear the steps stop outside my door, and they pause for a moment. My own erratic breathing echoes in my ears as I wait for the doorknob to turn with every ounce of concentration I possess.

Knock. Knock.

What the fuck? My brows furrow. Did someone actually knock on the door?

Knock. Knock. Knock.

The fear disminshes as confusion overtakes me. "Ugh, yeah?" I don't know what else to say.

The door slowly opens, and even though the knocking threw me off track, I was still expecting Barnette to come in through the door, but instead it's his right-hand man. He closes the door behind him and steps slowly toward me.

I feel small in the bed with the way his height looms over me, but I straighten my spine and pull my shoulders back, so he doesn't know I am riddled with fear.

He stands there with his dark jeans, black button-up, and combat boots. Though it is an odd combination, he wears it as if he owns it, radiating confidence.

He comes all the way to my side of the mattress and leans against the dark brown post of the bed with his hands in his pockets. He seems comfortable, at ease, as if this is normal. I wonder if he was the one who changed my clothes, and my lip curls in disgust at the thought of it.

He smiles at me, causing the dimple in his left cheek to be pronounced in the scruff of his beard. "I like your fire," he murmurs deep from his chest.

I just stare at him. I don't know what he wants from me or what he expects out of me. Come to think of it, why is he here instead of Barnette? When the silence just echoes between us, he adjusts himself slightly against the post.

"I haven't seen anyone stand up to Derrick like that and live to tell the tale." He begins to laugh quietly.

I talk before I am able to stop myself.

"Mr. Cartoon's name is Derrick?" I retort, and his eyebrows shoot up almost to his hairline as pure astounded shock etches into his features.

"Mr.—who?" The dimple comes back as he begins to give a full belly laugh. I love genuine laughs, but I also don't like to be the butt of a joke, which right now is my life, so I just stare at him. "I have to tell him! He will never live that down. Mr. Cartoon?" He laughs again, and I roll my eyes.

"His bushy eyebrows were just floating on his face. Reminded me of some Mickey Mouse shit I used to watch growing up." I shrug my shoulders because I don't see why it's so comical. He sobers up as he watches my reaction.

"It is funny because he is the one Barnette sends to take care of business, so he doesn't have to bloody his own hands, and you just compared him to Mickey fucking Mouse."

Derrick is a hit man; I had punched a hit man in his face and didn't get killed. The shock weighs over me heavily.

"Why do you think he was so eager to drug you? That wasn't part of the plan, by the way, but a small girl did hit him in his face, and he had to show dominance." He winks at me.

This cannot be my life right now. I cannot be having this conversation about drugging, killing, and hitting. I must be having some seriously fucked-up dream where I can't wake up. One of those dreams where you feel like you have been asleep for years because it is so heavy and deep into your unconscious. This cannot be real.

His laughs eventually fade away, and I can feel his stare boring into me. I look back at him, matching his intense look with my own.

"This can't be real. I feel like I am in some deranged dream, and I just want to wake up. Why me?" I don't expect him to give me an answer, but I'm surprised when he takes a seat on the edge of the bed and sighs.

"Honestly, I don't know entirely, but I have a couple ideas just from observations. I just go with what the boss says." He shrugs his shoulders. "Barnette told us one day that he made a deal with Ramona." He shudders slightly, and he grimaces as he catches his reaction to my mother's name. "Sorry she's just someone I don't like to deal with at all, so when he mentioned her, I immediately saw the red flags and warning signs blaring to life. Not to speak too horribly of her, but she is a damn roach."

I don't know if that hurts or not. I feel like too many of my nerves are shot so that I cannot feel any more emotion than I already do.

He adds, "Again, not trying to kick a person while they're down. I get that's your mom—"

I interrupt him, "Doesn't matter. I grew up with her. I know how she is and how she does things."

He nods in acknowledgment and continues on.

"Well, anyways, any deal with her you have to do your homework on because everything has a double meaning with her, or a means to an end. I did my recon on you, watched you, learned you from afar—"

This is going to become a habit. I interrupt again.

"You've been fucking watching me? Stalking me?" I tremble at the thought, and it won't stop.

He shrugs. "Just the basics. I wasn't a peeping Tom, Amelia, I have boundaries." He looks at me pointedly as if I am an idiot who should know better. "I did my recon and saw what your life was about, which is a little sad and grim by the way, learned about the trouble your mother is actually in and how deep it goes so I knew what we were getting involved in."

She had a whole month to tell me about this yet she waited until the day it was going to happen to tell me. I fear the deep wound of betrayal is never going to heal.

He continues, "It is shitty that she waited until yesterday to tell you. That was very kind of her." The thick syrup of sarcasm drips from his words. Yes, she is full of kindness and selflessness, that one.

The heavy feeling of dread and confusion still chokes me tightly. "What does Barnette want with me? What is this trailer park trash going to do for the King of La Caìda?"

His gaze intensifies as if he is searching through my soul. His eyes darken, and his eyebrows wrinkle slightly in confusion as he peers at me.

"You have no idea the type of power you hold, do you? You have no idea the strength of being faithful and compassionate can bring to a table. The sacrifices you have made for the love you hold for your sister, the life you gave up protecting first your mom and then her, you hold loyalty to such a high standard that it makes a man want to earn it.

"I see why he was interested in you, and I get it. Your standards, your qualities you hold, are exactly what he needs at his side. Sadly, I don't think he is going to know how to handle you. You aren't a docile little lamb begging to be buttered; you are a fiery rocket ready to explode and show everyone what you are made of."

The feeling of dread evaporates slowly as he continues speaking.

"Trailer trash? I never once thought or saw that. You speak down enough to yourself, so the world won't hurt you because you already hurt yourself too deeply. I see a beautiful young woman whose life likes to kick her down, but she still has the balls to get up and throw a punch in a hitman's face to protect someone she loves."

Butterflies for some stupid reason erupt through my belly at the mention of the word *beautiful*. I roll my eyes at him and readjust myself as I try to get his words to stop affecting me to such a high degree.

"What do you get for throwing nice compliments to a girl while she's down?" I mutter. Not to mention, he is not even my husband-to-be.

"Now, I am no Romeo or prince charming. I definitely am more the big, bad wolf, but the thing about wolves is they are loyal, and they are territorial—two things we both have a strong foundation on. You are part of my pack now, and you are going to learn to hold your head up and grip onto that confidence you refuse to let yourself have. I also know you have nothing to be ashamed of."

My cheeks flare red at his deep grin, and then he winks at me! What the fuck? Does he mean...

"You didn't." Motherfucker, I swear, the nerve!

"No, I didn't clean you up or dress you. Your *fiancé* did that." I grip the sheet tighter to my chest. "Little sad your first reaction wasn't to take a swing on me. I'd like to feel your punch." He has the audacity to wink again!

I imagine all the ways I would like to make Barnette pay for getting to see me naked without asking. A sudden memory of my Aunt Cecelia informing me that the only way to take care of a man who did you wrong is to cook up some hot grits, trick him with hot food, then smack him with the pan as he leans in for a bite. It was aggressive then as it is now, but the image it gives brings me subtle happiness.

"Fuck you—" I pause as I realize I don't know this smug asshole's name. He raises his eyebrows at me, questioning why I stopped abruptly, then a moment later it dawns on him.

"Dean," he offers. "'*Fuck you, Dean'* I believe is what you were aiming for." I nearly groan. Too damn smug.

"Get out." If this was a cartoon, I would have smoke shooting out of my ears. "Get the fuck out now, *Dean*."

He grabs his chest as if I wounded his heart and makes a small pouty face. I point aggressively at the door.

"I said get *out*! I am sure Barnette wouldn't like you in here while I am in silky little nightgowns anyway!"

He walks casually to the door and turns before leaving. "Since when are you the one who cares what others think?" Dean says matter of factually.

As if he knows me. As if while he studied me all that time, he learned how I think and how I feel. I have never felt more exposed in my life than I do right now. I flip him my favorite finger, and he turns and laughs as he walks through the door closing it behind him.

I stare at the door for a few seconds longer than necessary and force myself to take a deep breath as I settle my nerves the best I can.

I feel both fatigued and anxious, and the constant battle between the two is taking its toll on my body.

I groan as I pull at my hair and feel the oiliness of it not being washed for a couple days. The slimy sensation causes me

attached bathroom. I stand against the wall opposite him and stare at him.

"Do you feel better after getting some rest?" he grumbles out. Does he fake his care for me? Is this supposed to be a show? I almost scoff at him.

"After being drugged and then violated while I was unconscious, yeah, I would say I'm just peachy." I shoot my best dagger eyes at him.

"You were not violated." Anger riddles his words at my accusation, and his calm demeanor finally breaks.

"Undressing me while I was not awake is not a violation in your little mafia handbook?" Maybe sarcasm is not the best form of communication I should be using right now, but I also cannot stop myself.

He rolls his eyes at me and pinches the bridge of his nose with his right hand. His exposed forearm shows ink I never noticed before peppering his skin. A part of a skull draws my attention, some words in what appear to be Spanish right along it, and swirls disappear to the other side of his arm.

"I was trying to be kind because you were filthy, and I didn't want you to wake up in that state." My mouth gapes open at his tone.

Barnette sees nothing wrong in the situation, and he is serious that he feels like there was no foul play. I stare at him in his short-sleeve button-up navy-blue shirt, his black slacks and suede shoes unscuffed and looking brand-new.

Barnette holds his hands in front of him as he leans against his knees and studies me right back.

I suddenly remember I am just in a towel and cross my arms over my chest.

"I'd appreciate going forward to just wake up bloody," I say stiffly, and he raises an eyebrow in surprise.

"You expect to find yourself in a situation where you have the chance to get bloody?" he asks incredulously.

"I fight my own battles for one, and second, if I am going to be hanging around you and your two goons, I expect my life isn't going to be one of walks in a garden with knights to defend my honor everywhere."

My hip juts out as the sassiness I have never been able to put into check sweeps through me.

"I am here to keep my sister safe, but don't think this will be a walk in the park for either of us." Clear that little standard up right away.

"You aren't a prisoner, you know." He splays his hands and gestures at the room. A big, clean, nice room.

"I am also not a docile little wife who is going to just lie on her back and cook, clean, and obey your every word." I didn't get to help make said contract, but I am allowed to negotiate. He cocks his chin at me, and I can see the muscles in his jaw tense.

"I wouldn't be happy with a docile little lamb, but I do expect you to not only lie on your back but bend over and take a fuck, too." I bristle at his words. "I have a maid and a cook. Just keep your shit together and yourself decent. As for obeying me,"—he gets up and in three strides stands before me—"I will get you trained to obey me, my little puppet."

My own jaw tenses at his crass assumption that I am the type of girl to obey.

"I am not a monster, and I am not going to keep holding your sister up and over your head to keep you in check, because I don't mind a little fire." He leans in close, making sure our eyes are locked and that he has my full attention. "But you will be a good little wife and listen to me, because you are now part of my world, and my world has chaos, blood, and greedy ass people.

"When I say duck, you duck. When I say run, you'd better run. And believe me, puppet, when I say let's fuck, we are going to fuck."

My stomach is completely in my ass, and I am not afraid to admit it. If his goal was to intimidate me, it worked. I swallow hard and try to take a small step back that won't catch his attention. I do not succeed.

"Good, I finally reached something inside of you. Now, get dressed and look half decent. You slept almost twenty-six hours, and I'm sure you are hungry. Dinner is in half an hour." With that, he turns and walks out the bedroom door.

In one whole sentence he managed to belittle me, admit to drugging me into a mini coma, and tell me what I am.

This is going to be an amazing marriage.

I offer the door my favorite little finger as he closes it shut behind him. A little déjà vu moment.

Ha! Make me obey. I may have to behave so my Andie is safe, but he'd best believe I am not going to make taking my choice away a walk in the damn park. I huff out a breath loudly.

Okay, play the part, I remind myself. *You must give a little to take a little.* Let's start with this dinner request.

I have no clue what he means by dress half-decent. He is wearing slacks for dinner, so I guess I have to wear something fancy, too. I look into the closet, and my mouth drops to the floor—maybe a little dramatic, but still it drops to the floor— and I will have to yank it closed with both of my hands.

His definition of half decent and mine are not exactly the same which is also to be expected. Fucking Barnette. Where am I supposed to wear this kind of attire to?

Floor-length gowns and coats with fur on them hang gently on their hangers. Which, by the way, is something I will never wear willingly. But where are the jeans? Where are the t-shirts?

I walk up the dark oak dresser and peer inside. I don't know why I am so anxious; it isn't like a snake is going to jump out and get me… or maybe there is. I have trust issues.

I shouldn't even be surprised by the amount of lingerie that is in here. Freaking Barnette. I roll my eyes at the thought of this man out there in stores imagining me in this lingerie. Ew. I open the next drawer and find slacks, so that's good. Okay, we are getting warmer to what I feel is half-decent in his eyes, so I quickly grab a pair and peek at the tag. Shouldn't be surprised to find they are my size.

I look back up again at what is hanging and behind the gowns I see some nice blouses, and some—holy shit—cashmere sweaters?

I am fancy now, I guess. I gently touch the fabric and am immediately drawn to how soft it is. It reminds me of Lacey's mom, and I yearn to feel a hug from that woman again as her peony perfume wafts around me.

A sad tug pulls at my chest at the comforting smell, but I shove it away. Now isn't the time. I had time to cry, and now I have to prepare for dinner. I grab the soft ocean-blue cashmere sweater and a soft plain black blouse hanging next to it and throw them on.

I walk up to the floor-length mirror and peer at myself. I look expensive, and I feel like these items don't belong to me.

I flashback to when Lacey and I played dress up in her mom's closet while she was running errands, and that panging sensation hits me again. Only this time, it isn't a little ten-year-old me wearing clothing like this, it's an adult me and these were bought *for* me.

I feel like an impostor, but maybe just maybe I can allow myself to enjoy it a tiny bit? Would there be shame in that?

I stare at the rows of shoes paraded around and grab a pair

of simple black flats before slipping them on. No way am I going to try on those death traps he has bought for me. I can only imagine eating shit the second I try to walk down the hallway. No one needs to witness anymore vulnerability from me.

I walk back into the bathroom and begrudgingly stare at the white vanity in the corner. I see the makeup, and I am intrigued by the makeup, but I have zero desire to put any on.

I wonder if no makeup can still have me looking "half-decent" for dinner. Fuck them, I am not wearing it.

Instead, I brush out my hair again, slap some product into it that should tame these curls, then I pray my hair stays semi-decent throughout this evening. The cut on my lip is bright red, and my eye is shadowed by a sick-looking bruise. There isn't much I can do about that, but what a reminder that on the last day of seeing my mom in God knows how long, we beat the crap out of each other. I sigh out in defeat; never a boring day for me.

I walk towards the door and take a shuddering breath. Once I leave this room, I will accept this next lifestyle that was thrown at me.

New clothes, new shoes, and a new place, but I still feel like the old me. I am putting way too much anticipation into turning this doorknob, and I know it. Still, the nerves are daunting.

I breathe out again, pull my shoulders back, and open the door as a thought pops into my head.

How the hell do I get to the dining room?

CHAPTER 4

Three Against the World

Dean

MARISOL HAS outdone herself again with the dinner she spent a good couple of hours making. I smelled the lasagna the second I walked into the house, and my stomach growled like a hungry trucker.

I look at the salad bowl, the plate of baked asparagus, the cheesy garlic bread, and the corn on the cob. I remember I looked forward to lasagna night at Barnette's house growing up and we would request to have this particular dinner at least once a month. Some things never change, and my mouth salivates in agreement.

"Do you think she will join us?" Barnette asks quietly from across the table. His plate is still empty, and he keeps glancing at the chair I am assuming he has set for Amelia.

"Did you ask her politely, or did you demand it?" I keep my tone casual so as not to raise his hackles.

He is in new territory when it comes to this girl, and it shows in his every action and response—or lack thereof.

Barnette sighs, showing his frustration, and my fingers itch to start loading up my plate.

Derrick walks in and sits across from me. He is sporting a small bruise around his lip where little miss broke some skin, and I can feel a grin stretch across my face.

"Don't," he snaps as he reaches over to start piling up his plate.

"Amelia isn't here yet!" Barnette chides him. Everyone gets to feel his nerves tonight.

"Look at my face. You think I want to wait for her?" Derrick gives him a pointed glare. "She is lucky to be your little wife to be or else—"

"Or else what, Mickey Mouse?"

We all swivel our heads towards the entrance to see Amelia standing there with pure fucking attitude radiating from her. I love it.

"What did you just call me?" Now it's Derrick's turn to gape like a fish, and I just howl out in laughter. I never dreamed she would call him that to his face!

"Sounds like she called you a cartoon character, Derrick," Barnette mummers from his place.

If it weren't for the fact that I knew him so well, I would say his voice was that low because he's trying to keep his laughter in control.

Amelia shrugs. "Don't take offense to it. You just remind me of Mickey Mouse when your bushy eyebrows shoot up into your non-existent hairline. It just connected together in my head, and now it's stuck."

She takes a seat at the place mat that was prepared for her. Honestly, she looks good, showered and with some nice clothes on her. But the marks on her face are still red from the heat of the shower and more pronounced than I'd like. What the hell kind of mother street fights her own kid?

"My name is Derrick," he states clearly while keeping his eyes trained on her. He is tense, and I can tell he is bothered.

So, I do the next best thing. I grab a slice of garlic bread and chuck it at him.

"Are you really going to let her get under your skin? Like, really?" I ask incredulously.

Barnette throws his hands over his face and groans. "This is not high school. Stop throwing food!" he grumbles loudly into his hands.

Derrick grabs the piece of bread I threw from the spot it landed on and takes a huge chunk out of it with his teeth. "Mmmmm, this is some good bread. Thank you, Dean." He winks at me, letting me know his mood is chilled out and he isn't angry by the toss.

This is what's nice about working with the men you've known for years; you can communicate without talking.

Derrick turns his attention to Amelia. "I'm not mad at you; I find you stupid and brave in the same breath."

She bristles slightly at his comment, but he continues.

"With that being said, I am not a damn cartoon character, and that is the only time you will get to land a punch, but since it was out of love for your sister, I will excuse it."

Her eyes are little slits staring at him. I don't know quite how to read her. I know women well, but she is still a surprising little spitfire.

"You didn't need to grab her like that." Her jaw is tense, and I can see how tight it is by the vein that is protruding along her left temple. I understand how defensive she is about her little sister. Hell, I feel the same way about mine.

The guys just stare at her in silence until Derrick breaks it.

"I am sorry for grabbing her like that. To be honest, I forget my strength at times and am used to handling men who are three times her size. I shouldn't have yanked her, but I did want her scared so she wouldn't cause a scene while we left."

It's my turn to have my mouth hanging open like a sucker fish. Who the hell is this man in front of me?

"You actually know the words 'I'm sorry'?" I ask in true surprise even if there is a layer of mockery to my tone. With that, I earn a chuckle out of Barnette while Derrick rolls his eyes at me.

"You guys are nothing like I expected," Amelia comments from her chair.

Her plate still lays empty and for some reason that enhances just how skinny she is. Like she survived on only scraps of food.

"You are more than welcome to fill up your plate. We were waiting on you," Barnette states, noticing the same thing I did.

"Are we supposed to be scary and boring while you live in a dungeon in our make-believe castle?" I ask, quirking my lips in amusement.

She wiggles in her seat uncomfortably while she leans in and starts scooping the tiniest serving of lasagna onto her plate. "Well, in a less dramatic way, yes."

That doesn't sit right with me. I side-eye Barnette, communicating that it's his fault she feels this way, and it earns me a scowl in return.

"You banter among each other like you're siblings. I always thought with the ranks it was just quiet, boring, and full of respect." Amelia shrugs.

"Ranks?" I ask, my forehead creasing.

"Well, you know,"—she points at Barnette—"big scary boring

boss,'—she points to me—"bodyguard who protects said boring boss and is willing to risk his life with nothing to lose,"—then she points to Derrick—"hitman who does all the dirty work."

She looks at all three of us, and we all stare right back at her. This girl is delusional if she thinks that is how any of this works.

"Is that how it's perceived from the streets?" Derrick asks. Of course he seems kind of smug; his description isn't all that bad compared to mine and Barnette's.

She takes a bite out of the lasagna before answering, and her eyes roll into the back of her head, causing my mouth to water immediately. I quickly load up my plate, already practically tasting it. Barnette stays stiff to my side and hasn't touched any of the food yet.

"I'm not boring," Barnette says flatly.

I look at him while I stuff a huge forkful of the lasagna into my mouth and grip a piece of bread to yank a chunk off.

"Wasn't trying to offend you," she responds, earning her a scoff from him.

"I didn't say I was offended." His brows are pinched in the middle while he stares at her. He is finding humor in this, huh?

Another moan escapes from her, and I look back to see she ate some of the bread.

"Delicious, yeah?" I remember trying it for the first time too and devouring a whole slice in three bites.

"This food is amazing!" A smile graces her face, and my heart does a little flip in my chest. Food also makes me very happy.

"You didn't get to eat much." It wasn't a question; it was a statement right from the horse's mouth. I give Barnette a sly scowl in between my bites of food.

"I gave my portions to Andie mostly and usually ate what was left over from the diner. Mom wasn't much of a Betty

Crocker mom, in case you couldn't tell. Usually, whatever money she scraped up went to her addiction, so

I did what I could to pay utilities and get the basics." She continues eating.

I don't think she understands just how sad the weight of the truth she just laid on all of us is. She doesn't understand how heavy it is, or maybe she has simply dissociated from it completely.

"Well, you won't have to worry about that here. There will always be food. They make sure the kitchen is always stocked. Food, snacks, pastries, you name it," Derrick states with some pity in his tone. If anyone of us here understands what it's like to be without food, it's him. He had the nickname scrappy in school because he was always caught digging through the trash cans for something edible.

"Do you all three live here?" she asks with a faraway expression on her face. I wonder what she's thinking about.

Barnette hesitates. "Well, I live in this main house, and I have a few other mother-in-law quarters here on the property for Derrick and Dean, but we all do live on this property." He finally takes his first bite of food after responding to her. After a few moments of silence, he continues. "I inherited this property from my father. It has been in the family for a few generations."

There we go, I appraise him silently. Nothing wrong in a little bit of communication.

"As for your earlier curiosity about ranks, I can assure you it isn't like that." He pointedly looks at me when offering that statement.

I blow out a heavy breath. "Technically, Amelia, we are pretty much on the same level when it comes down to it."

Her look of confusion bores into me, and I blow at the hair hanging over my forehead.

Splaying my hands, I continue, "Barnette and I started this thing together. This is both our baby. Fact of the matter is, he's got the pretty face and mind to deal with all the logistics of it, whereas my handsome face deals with more the backup and street-smart part."

I shrug my shoulders to show my indifference to it.

"I don't care about labels. I don't want to be known as the big, bad boss; I couldn't give two shits less, but I do get the respect I seek. Just, some people think I had to take the time to earn it when in reality I am just as big in this game as Barnette is."

Barnette and I look at each other, nodding about it.

We have spent so many evenings going back and forth about the whole situation. He never wanted the big title alone either. We both had the same plan going into this, just some things he can naturally understand more because of his father.

I am done getting pushed to be presented in the same limelight as him anyhow; I never wanted or needed it. You give respect, you get respect. It's as simple as that in my book, and I don't need a specific title for that.

"Respect is earned," Amelia comments softly as she peers down at her now empty plate.

I wonder how much of her life she was made to feel like she wasn't respected. Also, how many people does she actually respect?

She looks up at Barnette for a moment. A conversation seems to be happening between the two of them even though there is complete awkward silence, and to my surprise it is Barnette who looks away first.

"You should eat more. Add some meat to those bones."

Derrick thrusts his hand out in an effort to point to the food in front of us, and her flinch in response to his actions causes us all to stop.

She has been hit before. Derrick drops his hand down, and she shakes her head as if scolding herself while her jaw clenches.

"Are you saying I am too scrappy?" she snaps back. A defensive little thing she is.

"I did not say scr—" Derrick immediately jumps in to defend himself, and I know from the years of our friendship that word specifically wounds him deeper than she could have dreamed.

"He is merely stating you are very skinny, and though you had to starve these past few years, you do not at all have to starve here. Now, eat," Barnette retorts sharply, and I can see how rigid he is as he glances at Derrick who is as tense as a marble slab. We all know how hard it was for him growing up, everyone but her.

"You have no right to talk to me like that!" she growls right back at him. I sigh in defeat as I sit back in my chair. These two suck at communicating.

"Listen now, children, no one is trying to step on anybody's toes! How about let's call it and continue to eat so we can all—" I get interrupted by a loud creak as Amelia's chair scrapes back and she stands, clapping her hand onto the table and looking straight at Barnette.

"Respect is earned. Think about that as you sit there smug as an asshole with a top hat and stop talking down to me." Then she turns her fiery glare onto me, and my eyes open wide as I take the onslaught of her fury next. "I am not a child!" she seethes at me, and with that she walks out of the dining room, leaving us with the sting of her sassiness.

"Whelp, that went well!" I laugh with only a slight bit of uneasiness. Barnette lets out a long, tortured groan beside me.

"You've got your hands full with that one, dude." Derrick chuckles, but I can still see his tight grip around the utensil in his hand.

"She doesn't know," I defend her with a frown.

"I know. I'm not mad at her," he states evenly, visibly relaxing his grip. Barnette leans over and squeezes his shoulder.

"Never again." Barnette is solemn as he repeats his promise. He has made and kept that promise ever since we were kids. That day will forever be engraved into my mind.

Barnette and I were leaving school to head over to his house to shoot some hoops and scarf down hopefully a full pizza each.

We had only a few hours before he was going to go and take Cindy out, and I was going to have to be home on edge waiting for Dad to get back, praying he wasn't too drunk tonight and kept his hands to himself and off my mother. Barnette's house was the only escape I had anymore.

I heard a loud bang and glanced over to the side of the school where three large green trash bins sat. A kid was climbing into them, looking through them like a scavenging raccoon.

I squeezed my eyes to get a better look and realized it was Derrick, or as the school kids liked to call him 'scrappy'. I always thought it was a vicious rumor that was going around the school; I never believed there was truth to it.

"Is that who I think it is?" Barnette asked me in shock, squeezing his own eyes to get a clearer image of the guy.

"It is. I didn't believe it," I said quietly, unsure of how to proceed.

"He really digs for food, or do you think he lost a book?" I could hear the hesitance in his voice as his inner conflict warred between each other.

Should we help or leave him be and not embarrass him with attention?

Some laughter interrupted our thoughts and halted our steps. "Well, look at scrappy digging for some food!" I'd know that voice anywhere. Billy fucking Fibenson, the biggest ass hat that went to this school.

He and his goons went up to the dumpster laughing and chuckling at Derrick, and I could see him cowering and looking lost. Before I could ask Barnette about intervening, he was already marching right over to the group of them.

"Just leave me alone," Derrick begged, already sounding so defeated.

"What kind of nasty kid eats out of the dumpster? What, does your mama not love you?" They all laughed at the weak retort he gave.

I came up right behind a seething Barnette. Billy didn't even have time to register what was happening before Barnette threw a right hook and clocked him in the face. Billy dropped hard to the ground, and his goons sprinted into action.

"Who the fuck do you think you are?" one shouted, rounding on us.

"How about minding your own business?!" another yelled.

"You won't be able to take us all on!"

Adrenaline started pounding through my blood, I was always down for a little fight. Six against two wasn't bad odds. We might get a little scraped, but we could still come out on top.

"Big words for such a coward." Barnette's voice was lethal and low. Even I didn't fuck around with him when he got to this point.

"Let's see what you've got," I chimed in, cracking my knuckles with a smirk.

"Six against two? You guys are idiots!"

I heard a loud bang as Derrick's foot hit the side of the dumpster as he jumped out to join our ranks. He straightened his back and lifted up his fists. Huh, he was not used to fighting it seemed.

"Three against six," Barnette corrected.

I looked to see Billy still in a heap on the ground, pathetic really. The group exchanged wary looks with each other as they seemed to ponder what to do next. Run and leave their leader on the ground, or fight and join him on the ground.

I was wrong in what I thought they were going to do.

"Aaaaah!" one guy yelled as he ran straight for us, breaking the tense moment of silence.

You should never yell and give away your decision to hit. He learned that quickly as Barnette landed a matching blow to the side of his face, and I took the next guy who was already mid-swing even with being too far to connect with anything but air.

He missed me, understandably, and as his punch flew past me and pivoted his whole body, forcing his backside toward me, I dropped in a solid kick to the middle of his back, causing him to eat shit against the gravel with his face.

I knew Barnette was good on his own, so I peered over at Derrick to see him handling one of the kids just fine, impressed by the skills he had hiding underneath that calm demeanor of his. Maybe he did know how to fight, he just played them a little. We handled the six of them in no time, and all three of us had no wounds to show for it. Pity.

We all three stared down at the six of them laying there. Three were knocked completely out while the other three held their palms up in surrender. It wasn't a fair fight, but bully-like behavior had never been acceptable to me.

"Thank you, guys," Derrick said before going back to the side of the dumpster and grabbing his bookbag to take off.

Barnette and I stared at each other for a moment, a silent conversation passing between us.

"You like pizza?" I asked Derrick, causing him to halt mid-step. He

stared at me hard, and I could see his mind working at trying to connect why I'd offer.

"I don't need any handouts." He stood there trying to hold what pride he still possessed in his faded jeans and shirt with three holes littering it. He was dirty and starving; I could only imagine his home life. One thing we all had in common was we always wanted to escape our life at home.

"Not giving any. I like to hang out after school with my friends while we eat pizza and shoot some hoops. Offer still stands." Barnette shrugged his shoulders in indifference, but I knew he was hoping that Derrick's ego wouldn't stand in the way of a friendly invitation.

With that, Derrick nodded his head in confirmation with whatever discussion he had going on in his head and walked with us back to Barnette's house.

It's been the three of us ever since.

CHAPTER 5

Breakfast Of Champions

Amelia

"TAKE A PICTURE. IT WILL LAST LONGER," I snap at Barnette, who is sitting there in his casual business attire across the table from me.

Someone went through the trouble of making pancakes, eggs, toast, oatmeal, yogurt, and a nice assortment of fruit in a bowl. Do people really eat like this every day?

Barnette clears his throat, and I can almost swear I hear the faint sound of chuckling coming in from the kitchen.

But Barnette doesn't take his attention off of me, rather, instead he cracks his neck from side to side while keeping his eyes locked. I feel like prey does before they get eaten. I know it's coming, but I am just sitting here frozen.

"Is the breakfast not to your liking?" he asks, flicking his gaze down to my plate and then straight back up to my face.

I peer down at the eggs I was pushing around with my fork. They are coated in cheese and by far the most delicious eggs I've ever had.

"Nothing is wrong with the food. It's actually really good. I just got lost in my head a bit." I try to wheel in the defensiveness in my tone, but I struggle as I fear an idiotic sting of tears assault my eyes at the thought of all the mornings I had to go without food or sneak down to Lacey's in my pajamas while Mom was still knocked out cold from the night before.

I tighten my jaw, refusing to let one single tear form and trail down my cheek in front of *him*.

"Are you not a morning person?" His tone comes out a little harsher than before. Perhaps my attitude isn't to his liking.

Marisol, the keeper of the kitchen I discovered this morning as I came out of my room, comes bustling in with a pitcher of orange juice.

"I am whatever the hell I want to be. Why the sudden interest in fucking small talk?" I jab out.

Just as I finished my sentence, I felt a hard smack across the back of my head. My body freezes at the contact as I try to process who the hell just hit me.

"It will do you well not to speak to him in that tone or manner. There is no reason, absolutely no reason, for you to curse around the table, either. Mind your manners." Marisol's voice is low and unhurried.

Her dark brown hair with streaks of silver is pulled tightly back into a bun at the base of her neck, her hazel eyes in slits as they glare down upon me.

She has her hands on her hips, causing the apron to be pulled taut against the blue flowery dress she wears underneath it, making her figure become more pronounced. A slim but fit older woman.

"Marisol, it is okay." Barnette doesn't sound angry at all.

I pull my gaze away from Marisol to stare at him. I am

dumbfounded that he allowed his staff to even lay hands on me in such a manner.

He levels his gaze with me and has the damn audacity to shrug his shoulders and smirk! What the fuck!

My jaw tightens back up immediately, so hard I may crack a goddamn tooth. Fuck her and fuck him. I am not a little girl to just smack around anymore. I refuse to let anyone think they can lay a damn hand on me.

I turn my anger toward Marisol.

"Don't you ever lay a fucking hand on me again or so help me, I don't care if you are old, I will hit you back!" I match my tone to hers.

I shove my seat back and slam my fork down in a manner that may be completely childish, but I am seeing red and need to step away immediately.

"Excu—" she sputters just as Barnette pushes his chair away.

"You have no—" he joins, but I don't waste a moment before turning on my heels and stalking straight the fuck out of there.

I don't know where I'm going, and I don't even care. One thing I was taught growing up is you always respect your elders, but elders never once took into consideration how I felt about anything!

I can feel the threat of tears start to brim my eyelids again, and I don't want an audience for this.

I head straight for the French doors that show a humongous backyard on the other side and yank them open. The brisk air hits me, but it feels good against the heat I feel radiating off of me. I march straight out to the farthest tree I can find away from the site.

I need to be alone with my thoughts, I need to know I can

walk freely among this property when needed and take a moment to collect myself.

I reach a tree just as the burning sensation in my lungs starts to register through my thick fog of thoughts.

My mother slapping me across my face.

Her boyfriend hitting me when I told her to stop drinking.

Her one-night stand shoving me when I told them to quiet down when Andrea was asleep.

Mr. Carrington calling me trailer trash.

The teachers at school whispering how sorry they felt for me when I showed up to school in the same outfit for the third day in a row because we were out of laundry detergent, and I didn't know to use the washer.

I learned after that how to hand wash in the bathtub.

Fuck all of them!

Fuck them!

I slam myself down next to the tree as every emotion ringing through me creeps up my throat and bypasses my mouth to overflow my eyes. I stay hidden behind the safety of the tree, losing track of time.

Barnette

I sit back down at the table and lean my head into my palms. That woman stresses me the fuck out!

I can hear the soft steps as Marisol comes over to me and lays a hand on my tense shoulder. I don't move to shove it off, instead finding comfort in the tender touch. She has always been like a mother to me.

"I am sorry if I disrespected you in any way, but I am telling you right now that girl has a lot of manners she needs to learn," she says quietly.

I lift my heavy head to peer up at her small frame. Even with me sitting, I am almost eye to eye with her.

"You have nothing to apologize for, Marisol. We've just got to be a little more patient with her, is all. Chastising is fine, but don't lay another hand on her again." I keep my tone level so she knows I am not angry at her for laying hands on Amelia, but honestly it surprised me probably just as much as it surprised her.

It happened so fast I almost didn't process it at first, but then I found satisfaction in the way her jaw just hung open.

But I knew the second I shrugged my shoulder and gave a small smile to communicate my surprise as well that I fucked up because the hurt I saw flash in her eyes before her hot temper ran wild did not sit well with me.

Fuuuuuuuuuck.

"You have a soft spot for this one," she states as she studies me, pursing her lips in thought.

"She is my fiancée, Marisol; I should have some kind of soft spot for her. But her past wasn't kind. She isn't like the other girls I bring around here. She isn't here for money; she isn't a gold-digger, and she doesn't even want status. She was hurt and came from unfortunate circumstances. I just don't know how to talk to her." I sigh in both frustration and a small amount of anger. Why do I even care that she was hurt?

"See how you are talking to me?" She gives my shoulder a tight squeeze. She may be small, but she is surprisingly strong. "Just talk, boy. Stop putting your foot in your mouth and know that sometimes it is okay to open up to people. You don't always need a cold-hearted exterior regardless of your 'status'" She hand quotes the word and rolls her eyes.

"Marisol…" I warn. She may have a tender part of my heart, but she doesn't need to chastise me this morning too.

She tsks. "Uh oh. You have a feisty one on your hands, and her exterior may be the same if not stronger than yours. Don't misread her anger for pure rage because anger comes from hurt. Deep down, she is just a girl who is hurt."

My brows furrow together as I take in her words. My thoughts start to double over each other as I evaluate Amelia's actions, expressions, and moods while she's been here.

"Take from it what you will, but I am just an old lady who has been around the block. She has a cold, hard exterior that needs to be busted through, but that doesn't give her permission for her words and tone to be ugly either." She points her finger at me accusingly. "You may be my boss, but I raised your sorry butt, and no one gets to speak to you like that and be ungrateful for everything you have done."

I chuckle at her own show of sassiness, patting her arm gently. "Thank you for looking out for me."

She turns and starts to grab some of the dishes off the table to take back to the kitchen with her.

"No, I will get the boys to do it." I whistle out sharply to Dean and Derrick because I already know from the chuckles I heard earlier that those two nosy assholes are in the kitchen.

Dean comes through the door with a cat-like grin.

Anymore wider and his lips are going to run into his ears.

"Good morning, boss. Top of the day to you. How is it this fine morning?" he mocks in his brotherly tone.

I try to keep my own bristle of anger in check so as not to direct my anger to the wrong person.

"From all the chuckles I heard in the kitchen, I'm assuming you already know plenty about what is going on. Where's Derrick?" I retort flatly.

Dean plops himself down in the chair beside me and starts building up his plate like a teenage boy who hasn't eaten in two hours. Makes me flashback to when we were in high school, and he would come over and my dad would complain about him eating the whole fridge if we could digest it all. Dean's been my longest standing friend and one of my most loyal, which is both good and fucking annoying especially when he doesn't answer me immediately.

He plops half a pancake in his mouth before looking up at me and shrugging. "Said he had somewhere to be but that he would be back to eat some breakfast considering you were keeping it all for you two!"

I pinch the bridge of my nose, blowing out a frustrated breath.

"I told you two that you could join after fifteen minutes. I just wanted to see if I could have a decent conversation with her!" I grunt between clenched teeth.

"Yeah, and how did that go?" He smirks.

I pick up a sausage link from my plate and throw it at his face. Screw him. He knows exactly how it went with that little icy princess.

"That good, huh?" He laughs and grabs the sausage I threw at him from the table where it landed, shoving it in his mouth.

"Whatever. Mind your damn business for once." I stab a bit too harshly at my eggs as I scoop up a pile to shove into my mouth.

Everyone is always in my damn business, never an ounce of peace in this damn place.

Amelia

I stare off into the trees that seem to surround the property. Nature has always been intriguing and beautiful to me. The outskirts of the town have a bunch; it is a solid drive to get to it, and I have only been so far a couple times in my life.

How mundane, how repetitive my life was. Work at the restaurant, keep the house from completely falling apart, make sure Andrea is okay and has what she needs, clean up Mom and her vomit, and then wake up and do it all over again. My only escape was to Lacey's house or to the park across the bridge.

I loved those days I was able to escape over there with them or even myself, if I happened to have the day off.

Shit, I wonder if anyone called Wallace at the restaurant to let him know I wouldn't be going in anymore. He at least deserves notice for the number of times he let me take leftovers or orders that were done wrong home.

The wind sweeps through, ruffling the strands of my hair. My face feels tight and dry. I need to wash it; I know it must look puffy from all the crying I did.

I had rushed out of there so fast I didn't even realize I may need a jacket. I am in my dark jeans and short-sleeve t-shirt that hangs gently on my form. Nothing fancy, but the material speaks enough on its own that it wasn't cheap either. I don't want to be a dolled-up Barbie who listens and obeys every command.

Goosebumps break out across my skin at the thought, and I pick up on the sound of soft footsteps in the grass walking towards me. So much for being well hidden.

I don't turn to see who it is, probably Barnette to inform me to never speak to his staff like that again and how I need to keep quiet and listen. This man thinks he can control the strings to this puppet when I have no interest in being his puppet at all!

A form comes around the tree and sits beside me, yet I still stare straight forward, ready to be reprimanded and ready to defend myself.

I did not deserve to be hit upside the head regardless of how disrespectful I was being.

"I like it out here. It's quiet and one of the only ways I can actually think." I side-eye Derrick sitting beside me, much to my surprise.

He was the absolute last person I expected to meet me out here. He points a finger out towards the right side of the trees.

"If you go further down that way, you will run into the small farm we have here. There are goats, and chickens, oh!" He snaps his fingers, causing me to jump. "We also have a couple pigs. Oink, oink and all that."

I turn my attention to him, unsure of what he's trying to get at here by discussing this information.

"Is there a reason for you indulging me with this information?" My mind is so tired that I can't even evaluate what game he's playing here. He cocks his eyebrow at me.

He takes a slow deep breath and on his exhale finally speaks. "You know, not everyone is out to get you. You don't need to have such a sharp tongue when people are trying to talk to you."

Great, another person to chastise me, exactly what I need. He leans forward to capture my gaze again.

"But that is something that comes with time, and I get that. You have a very defensive nature about you, but again, I can only assume what you have gone through in life. It isn't my place to judge how you react to things."

Before I can bite my tongue, I snap, "Then why are you here doing just that?"

I can hear the venom in my voice, and my stomach sours against the anger I feel churning in me. I am automatically defensive.

"I don't mean to sound so hateful, I just… I just…" I don't even have a way to explain myself.

He shrugs. "Your defense mechanism. Your anger is your defense mechanism against what you've got going on in here." He pokes my forehead gently. "And in here." Again, he pokes me gently in the chest where my heart is.

His finger quickly retracts after the soft touch, but his words melt into me instead. I *am* defensive of myself. I am the only one looking out for me.

My breaths start to come out quicker as I attempt to take a deep breath and swallow down my emotions.

"I am the only one who has my back. And I still get put into situations I have no control over," I mutter, a grimace twisting my lips.

He nods his head in what appears to be understanding but doesn't say more. He looks off towards the right where he had pointed out where the farm is.

"I told you about the farm because I find spending some time with animals to be relaxing. Whenever I get overwhelmed or have something serious to mull over, I come out here and take a walk and usually end up there to feed the chickens or pet the goats. Goats are actually very peculiar creatures." He nudges my shoulder gently, as I think over what he just confided in me. He trusted me with something personal.

"So, your harsh, don't-give-a-shit exterior is just that? A façade?" Do we all hold an image over ourselves?

He raises a brow. "You do realize what kind of work I do, right? Should I be walking around all mushy and open-hearted? That is the type of shit that gets you killed here, darling, and I happen to like being alive."

Hmm, cute, he gave me a pet name too. I mull over that tidbit too; being soft-hearted here isn't safe.

"Can't seem to say the same about you, though," he adds, and that captures my attention.

"Excuse me?" It's my turn to cock a brow at him.

"Since we went to collect you... let's see, you were fist fighting your mom,"—he holds one finger up—"you punched me in the jaw, which by the way you are very lucky I am not holding a grudge against because I am impressed by your strength,"—second finger up—"and you continue to give sass to Barnette, Dean, and I which is either dumb or brave. haven't fully decided on your behalf yet, and four,"—his raises that fourth finger and puts it in my face—"you gave attitude to Marisol!"

The exaggerated gasp he gives right after is what makes my stomach turn slightly. "What's the big deal with Marisol?" I demand. Why is *she* such a big deal?

"A big deal? Girl, she practically raised Barnette. That lady is more of a mother to him than his own flesh and blood and the closest he has to family besides me and Dean, and you disrespected her this morning."

I side-eye him as I try to choose a leaf or tree to lock my gaze on. "Still doesn't give her any right to lay a hand on me," I mutter.

"That I agree with you on. She means it in a loving way, if that helps? She's smacked all of us around a bit." The endearment in his voice regarding her softens the anger I hold just a tad. I release the tension in my shoulders and roll them back.

"I do not appreciate anyone's hands on me that aren't welcomed." I pull my knees up to my chest, and I can feel his gaze on me as he tries to decipher what he can from the sentence.

He clears his throat. "Will it make you feel better if I tell you Barnette did instruct her not to lay another hand on you?"

I immediately scoff.

"I am serious, you little porcupine, he did tell her that she is to not put hands on you, but that she may chastise you," he adds, and I ponder that nugget of information.

"I am *not* a porcupine." Never before have I been compared to an animal.

He snorts. "Oh, darling, but you are. You are a grumpy little porcupine at that. But I get where you're coming from. Just try to remember that we aren't out to cause you harm. You have my word."

They need me alive and safe if I am to marry Barnette. It is hard to know whether his promise is coming out of dedication to Barnette or genuine concern for my well-being.

"Name calling isn't nice." I try to lighten the heaviness of the mood.

My thoughts make me feel like a prisoner. He sits himself back against the tree, gazing out at the trees. After a few minutes of silence, he clears his throat.

"Last night, I wasn't trying to be rude to you. I would never in my life call someone scrappy." I think I detect a hint of sadness in his tone and even with the prisoner predicament, it still does not sit right in my gut.

"I'm sorry. I know I am skinny; I just don't like it being pointed out," I confide honestly.

"Oh, I get it." His own soft words of confession, the echos of sadness still lingering.

"Is it a trigger word for you?" I try to make sense of where the hurt is coming from.

"I was bullied pretty much my whole childhood before those two came into my life." He scrunches his brows and clears his throat some more. "I got called scrappy and was horribly made fun of when I tried to find food out of the garbage."

My heart clenches tight at his sorrow filled confession. He was a starving kid at one time. Just like me.

"I didn't mean to trigger you." I mean it with everything inside of me.

"And I you." I know what he is referring to, and I can feel my cheeks redden from the embarrassment. I loathe that muscle memory flinch.

We sit in comfortable silence before glancing at each other with the agreement of a truce between the two of us and our shared tidbits of trauma.

At that moment, my stomach decides to give the most beastly-sounding gurgle I have ever heard in my life. We both just stare at my stomach for a moment as laughter begins to bubble inside of me. I can feel the heat in my cheeks from the embarrassment.

"I obviously didn't get much food in me before I stomped out of there," I sigh.

"Well, let's go get you some food then! Food is still at the table I hope, but it may be a little cold. You've only been out here for about forty-five minutes. That's if Dean left any food for us; he still eats like a teenager."

I roll my eyes, picturing a teenage Dean. These guys must have known each other for years.

"Food is food whether hot or cold. I can still eat it." With that, I get my butt off the grass and head back towards the house with Derrick in tow.

We walk back into the dining room and both Dean and Barnette cease talking at the table. Barnette looks at Derrick beside me with his eyebrows furrowed in question. Dean glances back and forth between us, then goes back to eating his food. I chuckle as I recall the comment about him leaving enough food for us. He isn't bothering to try and share at all.

"You know, for someone who apparently eats so much, you are awfully skinny," I remark.

His head snaps up as he looks at me, appearing surprised by my humor-filled comment. Derrick starts chuckling as he takes a seat beside me and starts filling up his plate.

I sit down as well when Derrick pauses before gulping down a bite of his pancakes. "For someone's belly who just yelled out like a trucker who hasn't eaten all day, I would have expected you to have been seated and already halfway through your plate by now."

I can feel my cheeks flush again at the remark, but I shrug my shoulders at my plate that was left there from before and dive into the cheesy eggs.

"Shut up," I throw out as my belly decides to rumble again loudly. Wincing, I scoop another bite and all three men start laughing. I choose to ignore all of them, but I cannot stop the smile that cracks over my lips as I try to get food down faster so my stomach will stop calling me out.

"So, she does smile," Barnette comments from across the table from me.

It's hard to read his expression; his face would seem expressionless if it wasn't for the intensity of his stare.

He is hiding his emotions. I wonder why.

"When I feel like it, I do." I give a small smile though, so they know I don't mean it in a snippy way.

Marisol comes into my room and takes a seat on the lounge chair in the corner of the bedroom, sitting tall and proud.

There is not one wrinkle in her entire outfit; her dress flows gracefully around her, fitting her like a glove but looking comfortable at the same time. Her gown is now a deep burgundy with matching flats, and her small little white apron casually wraps around her waist.

I like that they don't force her into those maid uniforms I've seen on TV. She has gotten to keep some authenticity to her, and a part of me is really happy for that.

Her face is set firm, even with the straightforwardness of her eyes, and no-nonsense poised mouth I know she has given this same expression thousands of times. Her wrinkles gently frame her eyes and lips showing her years here on this earth, years of perfecting this look.

My stomach is slightly unsettled, unsure of what is to come of this conversation. What is she expecting out of me?

I match her and sit gently at the end of my bed, bringing my right leg to curl up underneath me to be more casual and comfortable. Maybe if she sees me more relaxed, she may realize I am not looking for a fight. I don't have the energy to fight right now.

She still has not spoken, and I can feel tiny beads of sweat form on the back of my neck. I take a slow, deep inhale and let it out, and it takes every ounce of concentration I possess not to start wringing my hands together in anticipation.

Marisol takes her own breath. "You are a lost little soul, hm."

Not a question, but a statement, and definitely not the direction I thought this was going.

My brows furrow as I regard her.

"You act like a cat who had a pail of water dumped on it—on edge and not trusting." Now she is comparing me to a cat. Great, this is going well.

She moves forward slightly, the movement causing the involuntary flinch I loathe.

"You need to learn while you are here not to bite the hand that feeds you. From what I can tell, you came from a worse scenario than what is set up for you here, and you want to be angry and bitter—"

"You do realize this was not what I wanted, right?" I interrupt, the defensive hackles raised up and on edge.

Her index finger immediately raises up, indicating "one moment" from me. I feel like I am five years old again and being chastised.

"You were given a choice. From what I understood you had a choice, you may have not liked either option, but those are the cards you were dealt with."

Does she not realize how fucked up that is? Does she not see how I should not have had those two options to have to choose between! I feel like a porcelain doll with a bomb on the inside, ready to detonate and shatter into millions of pieces. I swallow down hard, and both my fists clench.

"Your mom put you in a predicament," Marisol finishes stating, then leans back, waiting for my answer.

"My mom has a way of getting into trouble. It follows her wherever she goes, and I usually have to pick up the slack." I can hear the bitterness in my tone.

Her gaze continues to bore into me. The sensation of a thousand ants crawling goes through my body.

"So, you seem to know that she is the reason I was given those two choices and how I obviously had to choose this," I snap. "But if you even consider my opinion, I don't want to marry Barnette. I don't want to marry anyone!" The last statement has my voice raised.

Anger sweeps through me at the thought of how this one thing that should be my choice as well is getting taken from me. Again and again things that should be my choice keep getting taken from me! I can feel the tears well up in my eyes.

"Your mom didn't do you right, and for that I am sorry." Her words cause my tears to stop in their tracks. Her eyes appear to have softened as they try to catch my own. "That being said, you need to take the opportunity presented to you and make the best of it, girl. Life gives choices, life changes paths—sometimes it may not be what we want, but it could be what we *need*.

"You are a good girl; I can tell that underneath all that anger it is actually fueled by pain. Embrace the pain to control the anger. Feel it, but mind your manners. We are not your punching bags here," she finishes.

How can her words seem so full of wisdom yet still make me feel like a tiny, tiny person next to her.

I wasn't trying to hurt anyone with my words. I wasn't trying to make anyone a punching bag. I do have the right to be angry, though.

"I should be able to decide who I marry," I state, sniffling slightly. I blink back the tears that hold to the bottom of my eyes with a steel grip. She does not deserve my tears.

"Barnette is not a bad guy. Believe it or not, he is a good boy with a big heart who has put humongous shoes on his feet to try and fit into." She sounds like a proud mother; a small smile graces the edge of her lips. "He will protect you and provide for you with everything inside of him—that I believe with my whole heart." She physically pats her chest where her heart lies underneath.

"You raised him," I say slowly.

"Why yes, I did have a part in his upbringing. He needed some guidance, and I provided it." She shrugs. "He is stubborn like a mule, though, and still has some of his father's ways in him, but I am telling you that there are worse options out there."

I mentally grind over her words, wondering what part of his father he has inside him to have caused her expression to slightly sour at the thought of it.

She rises up from the chair abruptly, the act of it causing me to do that unbearable flinch again. "I can tell you that you will never have to worry about him raising a hand to you, and if anyone other than me dares to lay a finger on you, he will intervene."

A sad expression flitters over her face, and I wonder if it is in reflection of her own past or at the curious thoughts of what caused my reaction.

"I don't mean to," I say weakly because I really wish I didn't have these knee-jerk reactions, and I hate the thought of her feeling bad for me.

"Of course you don't, honey." She walks slowly to the door but stops before grabbing the handle and turns to look back at me. "Just give him a chance. Take this as an opportunity. I can tell he really cares about you because I did in fact get a talking to for smacking your head and usually, he would never address my actions."

I reflectively touch the back of my head where she had smacked me. I am still holding a grudge about her actions during breakfast.

"That being said, manners are manners, girl, and I expect you to give him some," she adds, giving me a pointed look.

I bristle slightly at her words. I don't know how to take her.

"But going forward," she finishes, raising her chin, "I will not lay a hand on you again; I am sorry for that."

My mouth falls open at the apology. With those words, she departs my room, and I sit there in silence as my brain goes a mile a minute trying to reflect on everything that I've been through. This is the first apology I've ever been given by an adult who has hurt or wronged me.

CHAPTER 6

Not a Fucking Princess

Amelia

I STARE at the abundance of wedding magazines all over the coffee table before me. All week the guys have been in and out of the damn house, and I have been stuck here wandering the same floors, seeing the same walls, and doing the same routine.

They haven't invited me once, I have not gotten to hear from Andie, and I have none of my belongings with me. I am a prisoner.

When they are here, all they do is banter and coddle me to eat, along with making sure I am putting ointment and scar cream on my face where the last bit of lingering evidence from the fight with my mom starts to vanish away.

Anger stings all over my body in hot waves, and I try to control it with even breaths. Then, as I go to head towards lunch, *this* is what I see scattered all over the stupid coffee table.

I look at all the plastered-on greedy smiles on the pages in their overly-poufy white gowns and their dolled-up hair staying put using a whole bottle of hairspray, and I can feel every cell in me seethe.

I do not want to get married.

This is horseshit.

"So much anger for such a small person," Barnette chuckles from the door frame. The only smart thing he is doing is keeping to the perimeter of the room to stay away from me.

"Anger is the one emotion I seem to thrive in," I say bitterly while slapping down the magazine in my hand.

"Is it really such a horrible thing to marry me? I thought chicks dig planning their weddings." He stares hard at me as he tries to read every reaction I convey.

"Planning weddings is so fifth grade, and back then if I were to think or dream about my wedding, I would hope I would at least like the man I was marrying—maybe even *love*." I say the word a little too harshly even to my own ears, but the feelings are true, nonetheless.

"You don't think you can learn to like me?" His hand gestures to his whole body as if he's a walking prize.

"Tolerate at best." He chuckles at my response, and the sound irks me.

"You are such a spicy little thing. I guess I will have to learn to tolerate you at best, as well," he retorts.

"Says the man who took me against my will and is forcing me to marry him," I snap, and his gaze darkens.

His voice grows deep. "You came *willingly*."

"With my sister's safety hanging over my head," I remind him with a sneer.

"You really see me as a monster?"

"A monster who wears nice clothes, yes." I sit down and glare at him from the couch as he stands there in a soft long-sleeve olive-green button-up shirt and black slacks. Has he ever heard of jeans?

Barnette rolls his eyes. "Does my style bother you?"

"As much as your ego does." My lip curls slightly.

"What will it take to please you?" Is that a tad bit of desperation in his tone? No, that's impossible.

"How about, I don't know, getting to know your said fiancé? I am never opposed to a date. Instead of sitting here wondering who the hell am I marrying?" A smirk crosses his face. "So, you do want to get to know me." Ugh, twisting my words!

"Don't be smug. Or how about tell me what the hell am I getting myself into?" The true depth of those words sinks hard into my stomach.

His smug smile vanishes in an instant. "You don't need to be such a big part of this world."

"So, I am only *half* marrying you?"

He breathes out a frustrated breath and comes to sit next to me on the couch.

"You want to be a part of my world, Amelia?" I can feel the heat of his breath from how close he is. To show I am not intimidated, I do not move an inch and keep my ass still.

"I'm just saying that if I'm going to be made to be the mafia king's wife then should I not know what I am getting into?" I will not stay hidden here in these walls with no life. Too much of my life has already been taken from me.

"I like the ring of the mafia king's wife." Smug ass. "Are you finally going to acknowledge that you *are* my wife?"

I let out an exasperated gasp. I should not have used the term *king*; I should have known it would have gone straight to his damn head. "I am your fiancée, Barnette, not your wife."

"Yet." He wiggles his stupid eyebrows at me.

"You've been keeping me trapped here," I snap, and he seems to ponder over my words slowly.

"I am just keeping you safe, is all. Giving you time to adjust." It is hard to read the emotion on his face.

"You are treating me like a little princess who can't defend herself, Barnette. You think keeping me here isn't going to drive me up the freaking walls?" I can feel my voice start to become pitchy as emotion strangles my words.

"What do you want from me, Amelia? You are confusing as hell! You don't want to be here with me, but you want to be a part of what I do. You say you are here against your will, but I remember clearly the day you walked out of that door with us. And before you even start," he interrupts me as I begin to rebuttal against his little remark, "people get dealt things they don't want daily, and it is up to you to make the best of it rather than wallow in self-pity."

His chastising me bottoms out any sort of compassion I had towards him on anything and turns into pure, white-hot anger.

"I want *me* for once in my damn life! I want to be a part of what happens in my own life. I want my damn pictures and books I didn't get to bring with me, I want to talk to Andie! I miss her!" My voice cracks, but it doesn't stop my voice from rising. "Let me get a job or go back to my old job—"

"You don't need to work," he cuts me off. I can't even get a phone to contact her. How am I supposed to afford her a phone if I can't work?

"Okay, well how about bringing her here—" his ass interrupts me again.

"We cannot take a minor from her home. As much as I don't care about your mom's say, that is a whole legal matter we have to take into account," he states matter of factly. Laws have always been bent; I am sure he has bent plenty in his time, but because it is for me, he suddenly has a conscience?

"So, I have to just stay in this house while you guys do what, huh? Go sell drugs and guns, make people cry?" I feel the childish side of me coming out, but my rational side is busted.

Barnette snakes his hand up and grips my chin, yanking my face towards him. "You have no idea what we do outside of these walls. Nor the sacrifice and struggle we had to give to *earn* where we are."

I try to pull back from his hand, but he is gripping my chin too hard for me to move.

"Do you know what La Caìda even stands for?" he challenges.

I reflect on his name around town. King of La Caìda, but I never thought to look it up or even ask.

"No," I admit, deflating slightly.

"The fallen." His voice is low and throaty, causing a mix emotions to war through me. King of the fallen, that is what he stands for. "This world will take and take from you until you have nothing left. There is a basement to rock bottom contrary to beliefs it can always get worse, and I absolutely refuse to be there, but I acknowledge its existence. I can play the long game, I can make the trades, I can sell people their most guilty pleasures because someone is going to do it anyways."

My breaths come out hard as he continues to hold my face in his grip. "At least on my end, I can control what I do with the money. I support my city, I support my men, and I make sure those I love and care about do not want for anything."

I reflect on his words for a moment trying to understand how good and bad can cordially mix.

"So, because you help your family, you get a golden ticket to do whatever the hell you want?" I demand, but my tone holds no strength as I struggle with my thoughts.

"I also am the biggest supporter of our homeless shelters in town. I donate to the children's cancer society, and I single handedly helped start the organization to assist domestic violence victims escape their abusers using the connections I have through the greater part of the state.

"I am not a monster, though it is easier to paint me as one. Yes, I do fucked-up shit, but I also reach a lot more people in the position I am than if I was doing a basic ass nine-to-five job, Amelia."

I can't help the draw his words have on me, nor what being this close to each other is doing over my body. My eyes are in a trance, watching him talk, and it is taking everything I have not to believe his words. Does the good that comes from the bad justify the actions?

"So, you are saying you are a good guy who does bad things to be good." What a fucking circle that is!

"I'm saying I'm not as evil as they can come. So can you please just sit here and pick a damn dress so we can marry?" he sighs. And yet I am sitting here having to marry a man I hardly know, because he wills it.

"I don't want to be some damn Rapunzel stuck in the tower doing whatever her master says. I want to own some part of my own dignity, but instead I feel like a fucking walking impostor who doesn't belong anywhere and doesn't have a voice!"

The truth of the last statement hits me harder than I intended, and I can feel my eyes betray me as they fill with tears. But I will not give him the satisfaction of witnessing my pain.

I jump up and start to beeline for my room as he calls out for me from the couch.

CHAPTER 7

Keep Your Enemies Closer

Amelia

KNOCK. *Knock. Knock.*

I lie in bed and glare at the door, wishing with everything inside me that the person on the other end could feel it.

"Can I pleeeease come in, Amellliaaaa," Dean's voice singsongs from the hallway.

"Ugggggh," I groan as I roll myself out of bed and swing open the door. "What?" I demand.

Like earlier wasn't enough with these insufferable boys. They never give a girl any peace around here! Dean's happy smile falters completely when he sees me, and he has the audacity to look at me with big dark brown puppy eyes. Did I mention he's insufferable?

"Why are we still so cranky?" His puppy dog eyes continue searching my own.

"Didn't your mom ever teach you that you aren't supposed to ask girls dumb questions?" I snap. He touches his chest in a mock hurt.

"My mama taught me a lot of things, but no, Amelia, that wasn't one of them. Now, how about you let me inside and tell me what's going on in that pretty head of yours so we can continue on with tonight's agenda?" He shuffles past me and sits on the bench at the end of the bed. I watch as he makes himself comfortable, and I groan in defeat.

"Nothing. Is. Wrong," I state clearly through my teeth.

He gives me a 'you're full of shit' look, and it takes everything in me not to go over and smack it off his face. He would like it too much.

"Want to try that agaaaaain?" he singsongs. This man makes me want to strangle him. He is getting at the same level of frustration as Barnette—and that is saying something.

I grumble over back to the bed and lay myself down, yanking the comforter over my head. "You are all a pain in my ass," I mutter.

I hear him sigh and readjust himself. Peeking out from the comforter, I see he has positioned himself to lean onto the bed and look at me.

"Hey now, I swear I'll be gentle so that there won't be too much pain." He winks at me at his insinuation, and I grab the pillow beside me and chuck it at his face. He allows it to hit him with an *oof!*

Dean chuckles and places the pillow under his arms, making himself just a little too comfortable. He grins at me, but I can feel the change in him as he continues on, "Amelia, if it makes you feel any better, Barnette is already heading over to your old home to pick up some pictures and check on Andie."

That instantly lifts my mood. The weight of my stress momentarily vanishes at the news. Which surprises me; I trust Barnette enough to know he will make sure she is okay.

"I don't have many pictures to choose from or know where they are." I don't know what else to say.

My cheeks are still flushed from his flirtatious whims, and all the excess nerves I've been carrying feel like they are throwing a party in my stomach. I shrug my shoulders, and it dawns on me that he mentioned there was an agenda for tonight, pulling me away from my trail of thoughts on why Barnette didn't take me with him to see my sister.

"What are the plans for this evening?" I ask, narrowing my eyes slightly.

He scratches the back of his head. "Well, the original agenda was not to involve you, to be honest, but since you went all coo-coo bird out there and insisted you aren't to be a locked-up Rapunzel, Barnette feels inclined to bring you with us for a dinner meeting we had on the books tonight."

My eyebrows shot up in surprise. Especially about the fact that it was Barnette who made the decision to bring me.

"Derrick and I both don't think it's a good idea. It's not just a simple meeting whatsoever, but I also understand your side of it, too," Dean adds.

Aww, look at him being all sensitive. I sit myself up in bed as I mull over these supposed 'dangerous dinner plans'. Do I really want to do this?

"Is it like, dangerous as in guns and blood?" I ask, and Dean rolls his eyes at me.

"It is dangerous as in we will all be carrying and have extra eyes around the perimeter, but if everything goes smoothly then we'll simply be enjoying delicious steak and potatoes and walking out with all our limbs intact."

I purse my lips as I think about it for a moment.

"Aw, don't tell me now that you've got a foot in, you're going to chicken out," he playfully adds, but I can see the seriousness in his eyes. He does want me to chicken out.

Hmmm. I've never been one to back down from a fight. Why start now?

"Oh, I'm going!" I proclaim, swinging off the comforter and heading towards the closet just to prove how much I am really going.

I hear a soft sigh, so soft he was probably hoping I didn't detect it at all, and my stomach drops slightly. This must be dangerous, and that does scare me a little. I gulp down my nerves and stare into the assortment of clothing.

What the hell am I supposed to wear? A clearing of a throat behind me causes me to jump.

"Nervous?" Dean asks while he stands just a little bit too close. I can feel his warmth radiating off of him, and it causes the bundle of nerves in my stomach to go even more haywire.

Damn him, he knows what he's doing. I take a slow, steadying breath and take half a step away from him, even if his presence is comforting.

"This place is fancy, huh?" I know I don't even need to bother with asking, but I fear I'm going to have to wear one of those tall ass heels. I just pray I don't fall on my face. What if I need to run?

"It is nice. They have amazing steak, and I look forward to having a good-size ribeye tonight. You probably will order a little salad; those aren't too bad either." I can tell he is joking around with me, though I would rather be in silence as I ponder all these options. I can feel his chaotic energy behind me. "Definitely want to choose a dress and heels."

I look at the assortment of dresses with varying lengths, feeling overwhelmed about the choices. I have only seen this amount of clothing in one place when I would play dress-up in

Mrs. Carrington's closet with Lacey. It was always so much fun, and standing here now, I feel like I'm ten years old again.

My lack of jumping in and grabbing an item spurs

Dean into action, and he casually goes up to the left side of the closet and sifts through a couple pieces before he stops on a little black velvet dress with sheer long sleeves. It is short and has a scoop neckline, and even though it is plain, it is a statement all on its own.

Dean then turns and looks at all the shoes before grabbing a pair of strappy black going-to-twist-my-ankles-later heels and hands them to me with a small smile on his lips.

"You may not want to be Rapunzel stuck in the castle, Amelia, but you are a princess in this house, and it's okay to come in here and dress to impress. These are all yours, and no one can take that away from you. Own it."

I grab the items from him, and he gives me his signature wink before walking out of the closet, leaving me to stand there feeling like a complete impostor. His words made my heart beat faster even with the evidence that Barnette tattled on me to him.

I cannot help but wonder, though, would it be completely wrong for me to enjoy this just a little bit?

I stare at my reflection in the mirror after I finish putting myself together. I don't even recognize myself. Who is this woman staring back at me?

The makeup covers up the dark rings under my eyes gracefully, and the ringlets in my hair frame kindly around my face from the little up-due I pinned up. The red is bold and brave, the complete opposite of how I feel on the inside.

I am an impostor.

I do not belong here.

The little devil on my shoulder keeps whispering in my ear

reminding me of the little girl inside me that is enjoying playing dress-up.

My cheekbones are pronounced with the light pink blush I whipped on, and my dark eyeliner may be a little heavy and more seductive than classy. Never been one to do makeup, but with the amount of YouTube videos Lacey and I watched growing up, I must admit it didn't come out too bad.

I close my eyes for a moment, then stare back at myself in the mirror. Time to eat my own words. Let's do this, Amelia.

We pull up to a large red brick building that is surrounded by trees and twinkling lights. The lights illuminate the red hues of the brick, creating an illusion of the building being old and worn. The crisp black double doors with dark windows have sharp, clean gold letters that state 'Welcome to Balandgi's" on the doors.

A velvet red rope is blocking the entrance. We start walking towards the doors after the valet takes the keys from Dean, and as we near the rope a huge body-builder-type guy steps out from the shadows to unhook the rope from its clasp.

My quick intake of breath earns me a couple side-eye glances from the guys. The bouncer might as well have been a ninja with how well he was hidden.

His buzz cut gives me military vibes, and his dark, expressionless eyes sit sunken in on his stony face. His mouth stays set, with no hint of a smile. In fact, there is not an inch of him that appears to be welcoming at all. Aren't restaurants supposed to be welcoming?

Barnette steps closer to me and puts his hand on the small of my back, the warmth immediately accepted by the chill of my skin under the dress.

"Adam," Barnette states professionally with a small dip of his head.

"Sir." Adam nods back. "Welcome back, gentlemen." He draws his dead eyes to me. "Ma'am, enjoy your evening." His tone states the exact opposite of what he is saying. I feel his heavy gaze penetrate my back as we walk by that leaves me pondering if there was a threat underneath his tone. Maybe, I am simply over analyzing everything.

"Scared?" Barnette whispers into my ear, causing a jumble of goosebumps to pepper my skin.

"Cautious," I respond as honestly as I can. I am nervous and excited all at once, but I can't seem to shake the hostility of Adam's greeting us at the door.

We walk through the heavy black curtains that are hanging on the other side of the door, and it parts to the side to display a beautiful dining area. It reeks of class but in the most beautiful way.

Booths outline the wall in creamy black suede with rich chestnut dining tables. The middle holds a handful of tables in the same fashion, but with matching chairs and deep red cushioned seats. Candles light every table, and in the middle of the ceiling a huge crystal chandelier makes a beautiful statement piece. Layers and layers of crystals that twinkle all the hues of the flames flickering off of the candles.

Maybe only a good third of the restaurant is full, but with our entrance through the curtains I feel like a million sets of eyes are on me and I can feel my cheeks heat up from the attention and pressure to not fall on my face.

Barnette's hand is still on the small of my back as he leads me down the aisle to one of the larger booths in the back left-hand corner. Another focal point of the building because that booth sits smugly in the corner of the room where you can overlook the entire dining room without having to turn your head or back. I see why it is the chosen spot to eat.

My attention comes to rest on the hostess leading us through the aisle. She is in a beautiful red cocktail dress, her blonde hair pulled up in a messy bun at the nape of her neck that looks amazing on her, and she has long diamond dangle earrings hanging down her ears almost touching her neck. She walks confidently, and her heels click softly. I do my best to match my own clicks with hers to be in sync.

"Please have a seat." Her voice is soft and low, giving it a flirty vibe, and she has a seductive smile until her eyes land on Barnette's arm that is still extended where his hand lays on my back.

Her mouth straightens as she tracks it down, reminding me of a lioness observing its prey, and as she trails her gaze up my body to my face, I give her the sweetest smile I can muster up. I may not reek of class, I may not have diamonds hanging from my ears and confidence in my step, but Barnette's hand is on me and not her.

For the first time in my life, someone is staring at me with envy, and a small part of me enjoys how the tables have turned, even if it is at the expense of an innocent hostess.

I feel slightly bolder. Her nose immediately turns up at me as she sizes me up, her eyes narrowing slightly.

"Thank you," I reply as I start to sit down to scoot in for the men, matching my tone to hers.

Barnette follows me in as Dean and Derrick scoot in from the other side, both of them with a small smirk on their faces, but I ignore them.

I don't go looking for trouble, and I have never been the girl to compare herself to another woman; I am all for women supporting women, but I will also not be looked down on when I feel like a thousand dollars.

She slaps back on her sultry smile. "Your usual drinks?" She eyes each one of the guys as they all nod their agreement. Then she turns her attention to me. "Obviously, I don't have your order since you aren't a returning customer here. Would you like a few minutes to look over the menu? I can come back for your drink."

I am used to being singled out my entire life, so her little game doesn't give the punch to the gut like she intended to do.

This woman is reeking of jealousy, and it does not look good on her. Not one of the men speak as they observe our little chat, and I can feel the tension building beside me, but one thing I do want to be known for is fighting my own battles. I interrupt Barnette as he starts to speak.

I beam a smile at her. "Actually, I will have the same as my fiancé. Considering I will now be a returning customer along with them, it should be easy to remember."

I keep my chin up as I feel the fire burning in my stomach, and I pray with everything inside of me the fire feelings don't turn my face red. I have always stood up for myself when the time called for it, but deep down, confrontation makes me nervous and scares the hell out of me. I just hope it doesn't show on my face.

"Instead of the whiskey, though, please bring her a vodka cranberry," Barnette states to her, and I side-eye him to see that his expression is one of complete amusement as he turns his face to look at me, his eyebrow raised in question.

"Oh, come on, let her get some hair on her chest. She may like the whiskey!" Dean pops off on the other side of me as he starts chuckling.

I break eye contact with Barnette as I turn and smack Dean across the arm. The gesture breaks Derrick's composure, and he rolls his eyes at us.

"I bet I can handle my whiskey with a straight face, just

because I am a girl,"—I turn and give Barnette a playful glare—"does not mean I can't drink straight whiskey."

"Bring us four shots of gentlemen please, Stacy." Barnette holds my gaze as he speaks to her and does not break it as he lifts his hand to wave towards her, dismissing her entirely. "And I am sure you can handle telling the cook to make our usual order, plus one."

I don't even care to turn and watch her reaction to the whole situation, for in this moment I feel like a butterfly caught in a web; I am captivated by his stare. He dismissed that stunning woman who obviously has an interest in him to stare at me. Why does it feel like this is our most intimate moment since I found out we are getting married?

Derrick clears his throat, and I shake my head, breaking myself out of the spell. Barnette gives him an intimidating glare as his brows slowly crumble in the middle in question.

I look at the table and grab the cloth napkin that sits in front of me before placing it in my lap.

"I am going to be more impressed watching her try to eat the half of a cow that's about to be loaded up in front of her," Derrick remarks.

But as I look up at him to question what he means by half a cow, I see that his attention is purely on the front of the restaurant where we entered.

There stands three men all in similar attire. They have dark green or black button-up shirts, black slacks, and their hair is all slicked back. Two of the men stand more in front, and I am feeling Russian vibes off of them with how broody and muscular they are. I peer between the two men where the third guy stands, he is slightly smaller than the other two. His stance is wide and tense, and my eyes freeze once I look at his face.

He appears to be staring straight at me. Our eyes connect,

and I feel like I am trapped to my seat, as I feel tiny spiders of fear engulfing my insides. His sharp nose and pointed jaw cause his appearance to look anything but welcoming and rather unnerving.

I am starting to feel like this place is more trouble than it appears, so why did they end up agreeing to take me to this place?

"Don't pay Ivan and his men any attention. He enjoys causing a scene," Dean talks to me out of the side of his mouth, causing it to be slightly muffled, but the point comes across: ignore them. I feel a whirlwind of thoughts and emotions barreling through me, and I can still feel the heat of Ivan's gaze on me. I try to focus on anything to distract myself.

"Half a cow?" comes out my mouth like word vomit. I can hear the bit of anxiety I am feeling underneath my words. Barnette drapes an arm around my shoulders and pulls me into him.

"Hope you are hungry, fiancée." A little jab back at me for using the title at the waitress some minutes ago.

I can practically taste the change in atmosphere of the entire place as I glance slightly over to the three men and see them being seated across the way.

"Are you upset that I called you that in front of her?" I ask, even though I don't hear an ounce of anger or frustration in his words. I suddenly feel like a little schoolgirl on the playground, nervous that the boy I like doesn't like me back, and I cannot comprehend why.

"Never." Barnette sounds bold, and his answer comes out in a low grumble from his chest. I catch myself enjoying the way it sounds. Damn it, focus!

"Here are your shots." Stacy interrupts the moment thankfully as she places four shot glasses around the table.

"Let's see how well you match your words." Barnette doesn't glance at her once as he grabs a shot and looks at where mine was set to indicate for me to pick up my own as well.

I have tried whiskey before. It wasn't horrible, but I know for a fact I made a disgusted face after I tried to swallow it in two gulps. Why do I always have to smart off when I feel defensive? I take a quick inhale of breath.

Grabbing my shot glass, I look around at all three guys who are holding theirs up in unison in front of me, waiting for me to join them.

Fuck it.

I throw mine up there with theirs.

"To us three becoming four," Dean states, and I pray this crap doesn't go through my nose, embarrassing me in front of all of them.

Cheering, we all down the shot at once.

Liquid fire burns down my throat, into my chest, and curls into my stomach.

This shot is awful, and I regret ever saying anything about it. I do my best to keep my face stony like they do and not convey an ounce of emotion as I feel nausea churning with the burning sensation.

My throat tingles, and I can feel all three men staring at me. Fuckers.

"She is actually holding up better than I thought she would," Derrick states with a snicker.

"Look at her holding her shit together even though I can bet fifty bucks she is ready to chug down a chaser," Dean pops off beside me giving me a wink.

That wink did me in. It triggered the coughs that were tickling up my throat begging to be released. I cough out the burn, trying to keep the noise to a minimum as I basically suffocate myself in my arm.

"There it is!" Barnette laughs beside me, and I throw my right elbow into his side, rewarding my ears with the *'oof'* that comes out of him.

"Fuck all of you guys!" I rasp.

"Hey, I was on your side with this, Amelia," Derrick accuses me as he throws his hands up innocently.

"The rest of your drinks." Stacy's voice is monotone and sounds unamused by what she is witnessing between all of us. "Your food will be right up. Oh, and Barnette?" She speaks directly to him, and everyone sobers up quickly, me included, at the seriousness of her tone. "Ivan would like to meet with you when you have a chance."

With those departing words, she turns on her heels and makes her way back to wherever the hell she came from.

I watch as Barnette grabs his whiskey glass and raises it up to the three men across the way in a salute-like nature, nods his head, then takes a drink from his glass.

"Well at least they set aside their ego enough to ask first, eh?" Dean states as observes them for a moment before grabbing his own glass of whiskey.

"I don't like the way they came in," Derrick states. I try to analyze the way he says it and reflect back to how they walked in. The only thing that caught my attention was how they were positioned, how different it was from how these three go to places.

"I am assuming Ivan was the one in the middle." I keep my voice low in fear that they might somehow hear me.

"Yes," Derrick responds to me.

"May I ask a question about something I observed?" I wonder, biting my lip.

No one answers immediately, and I know that I am to be kept out of most of the politics of this said arrangement and how they do things, but my question is of an innocent nature.

"What did you observe?" Dean asks, and I know if anyone is going to tell me anything, it will be him.

"When they walked in, Ivan, who I am guessing is the leader of that trio, was in the back of the other two men. When you three go places, I notice Barnette is in the front while you two flank him. Does that mean anything?" I feel like it is an innocent enough question, and I look to Dean for an answer. I am pleasantly surprised when it is Barnette who clears his throat to speak.

"I will go down for my brothers and will always be willing to risk myself first. Whereas Ivan would rather his two trusted men go down first to give him time to escape." I can feel the truth of his words in my bones. Barnette is loyal to a fault, even at the risk of his own life.

"Ivan is a fucking coward we have to deal with for the sake of business," Dean mouths off beside me.

"Settle down. We are just here to give an ear to what he has come to say," Derrick mutters beside him. His hand rubs along his jaw in frustration. "I just don't like the feeling I'm getting.

"We can cancel and leave now," Barnette suggests, surprising me with how he will take Derrick's feelings as seriously as he is.

"No, no, let's play this out and see what happens." He shrugs.

"I will say that I don't like the way he stared at Amelia at all. He'd better know his place quickly," Dean states just as two waiters arrive at our table with our dinner.

I stare down at the plate in front of me with a humongous ribeye steak, a baked potato layered with cheese, chives, and sour cream, and a healthy serving of asparagus to complete it.

Holy shit, it *is* half a cow.

There is no way I am going to be able to eat all of this. I hear chuckles from the guys as they observe my eyes that feel like they are going to pop out of my head.

"You weren't joking when you said it was going to be a lot of meat." I look up to Derrick as my stomach starts to rumble at the delicious smell coming off our plates. "I am going to devour as much as I can for sure!" I chime as I dig in. I am so focused on stuffing my face that I don't even hear anyone walk up to the table.

"I've got a lot more meat to offer," a man whispers low into my ear, causing me to nearly choke on my food.

"In your dreams," I hiss back to him, even though nothing is going to change the fact that we have an audience.

"Dreams become reality all the time, *puppet*. You will be bent over in no time."

I can feel the flame in my cheeks and try to shove in another bite to hide my embarrassment that his words can cause such a reaction. Screw him for putting a blinding white light on me in public.

"This can wait until after we have eaten." Barnette's voice is strict and gives way to his irritation at having been interrupted.

I look up confused at his change of tone just to see Ivan standing there with his two men, all three of their faces looking stern and annoyed.

"As much as I enjoy watching you three stare at her eating as if it is anything fascinating to look at, I have matters I want to discuss, and waiting until you finish is not in the books for this evening," Ivan drawls.

I can feel the electricity in the air, the hair on the back of my neck standing upright, and I swallow down the bite in my mouth quickly. I take it by the way the three guys look pissed off that this was not the way they do things around here, which means something is not right. Shit.

"How about sit your ass back—" Dean starts as his hand snakes under the table onto my thigh and gives it a squeeze. Is he implying something? Should I be nervous?

"What is it that you want?" Barnette interrupts, looking at Ivan.

Ivan's head falls back as he starts to laugh obnoxiously. A scene is exactly what this man wants, and it looks like he's going to get it.

"Simple enough." Ivan looks between his two men before turning back and staring straight at me. "Her."

I feel a cold chill slip down my spine as all hell breaks loose.

CHAPTER 8

Round One

Amelia

A LOUD RINGING is making my ears feel like they're bleeding. I am laying face-down on the ground, and I just want this ringing to end!

I try to sit up to get some sense of my surroundings, but everything tilts to the side as my hazy vision starts to clear. A weird deep rumble gets louder as if the noise is coming straight for me, then like a bubble that's popped, all the noises barrel through as the ringing dies down.

Thump. Thump. Thump.

"Amelia, get up!" I can see dark brown boots running towards me, and I look up slowly to see they are attached to Dean.

He looks pissed off and panicked at the same time. But why? What's going on?

There are two more pops of gunfire, and I connect the dots on where the ringing is coming from. My blood feels like it is racing through my body, and everything is spinning out of control as I try to remember what the last thing that happened was before everything went black.

Dean leans down and grabs my arm. "Amelia! Get up! We've got to go."

I allow him to yank me onto my feet, feeling like my brain is detached from the rest of my body; I can't seem to move quicker. Weird black dots start to pepper my vision, and nausea begins to creep its way up my throat.

"Dean, grab her, Let's go!" I can hear Derrick in the background, and I swivel my neck to look for Barnette, but I don't see him. Where is he, is he hurt?

I look back to Dean and mumble, "What happened?"

Then everything turns black.

Dean

Amelia collapses in my arms, and I grip her body to my own. Poor little lady is in shock, and I guess the hard oak table smacking her in the face didn't help matters. Blood drips out of her nose and trickles over her chin, and in a fucked-up way looks a little hot with her ringlets surrounding her face.

I rush towards the back door and into the crisp cool air, carrying her with me.

"Is she okay?" Barnette hollers as he runs up beside me. His lip is bloodied up, but he looks to be in one piece other than that.

The back door kicks open, and a hot-tempered Derrick comes barreling for us. "What the fuck was that all about?" he sputters.

Barnette pulls Amelia out of my arms as I respond back with

the only truth I know. "I have no idea. Why in the fuck do they want her?"

I jump into the SUV as Derrick gets in the passenger side door. Barnette places Amelia in his lap as he straps them in. I waste no time getting us the hell out of here.

I look into the mirror, trying to read Barnette's face, unsure of what is going rapidly through his mind when a *bang* sound distracts me. I look at Derrick as he slams the side of his fist on the side of the door panel again, anger practically frothing at his mouth.

"Dude, you need to get yourself together!" I haven't seen him act like this in years.

"I knew something felt wrong, I knew it deep in my bones and yet I didn't say to leave. Now one of his men is down and Amelia is hurt, and we don't know why." I can hear the desperation in his voice as thick as his anger.

That is what we all want to know: Out of all these years of us working together side by side, why go straight for blood today? Transactions are the same, the amount we distribute, and profit hasn't changed dramatically; the only thing that is different is Barnette being engaged to Amelia.

I look back into the mirror and stare at her bloodied face. Barnette is using the cuff of his shirt to wipe what he can off, and she starts groaning from the feel of it.

What is wrong with Barnette getting engaged?

Then something simmers deep in my gut as I realize maybe it is *who* he is engaged to.

"I am telling you right now, whatever went down in there does not seem right. Do you really think jealousy was the main cause of this?" Derrick's frustrations continue, but at least he has stopped hitting the side of the door.

Barnette doesn't speak. I stare hard at him through the

rearview mirror, trying to read him, but his face is a steel mask. The whole evening has gone to shit, the stress on all of our shoulders.

Amelia starts to groan from her place in his lap. "What the fuck?" she grumbles as she touches delicately at her face.

Her poor nose took a hard hit from the table. I didn't know what else to do; when they pulled out the guns, I looked at Derrick and we both simultaneously grabbed the table and yanked it up as a barrier for her. I didn't mean to smack her nose let alone knock her out.

"Shh, you're okay. We're safe now," Barnette whispers to her, his voice soothing.

I stare back at him again in the rearview mirror. Seeing his soft side emerge has always been fascinating to me; he hardly lets it out, let alone lets himself feel it.

I can see her start to sit herself up when she realizes she is laying in his lap. The quickness of her movement causes her to make a gagging sound that I am all too familiar with. Nope, not in the car! I yank the car over and am out the door in a flash, barely putting the car in park.

I grab the back door just as a little miss flies out and vomits all over my damn shoes! I take a couple steps back in disgust.

"Oh fuck—" she groans between wretches. "Your shoes!" The vomit is chunky, and I just stare down at the state of my shoes in despair. "I'm sorry!"

She leans against the car as she tries to get hold of her breathing. I am not mad or grossed out, just unfortunate enough to be on the receiving end.

"You alright there, darling?" I grab some napkins from the middle console and offer them to her. Her skin is pale, but color is slowly returning to her cheeks and neck as embarrassment takes over her.

"I am so sorry about your shoes, Dean," she says meekly, her lips twisting in a grimace.

Barnette chuckles behind her, keeping close in case she slides over. "This isn't his first rodeo with vomit, Amelia. He is fine. How about you get back in here and we can head home. Are you feeling better?"

She nods her head as she carefully maneuvers around her mess and slides herself back into the vehicle. I make sure her gown is all the way in the car before gently grabbing her chin to look at me.

"I promise with everything in me that I am not upset, okay?" Her skin starts tinting red again as she does her best to nod her head in understanding.

I give Barnette a hard look; I still feel like something is off about the events of tonight, and he isn't saying anything. Maybe he really doesn't know anything, and the adrenaline is just causing my thoughts to race.

I take my shoes off on the side of the road before climbing behind the steering wheel.

With a sigh, I start the car and drive us home in my socks.

CHAPTER 9

Power and Control

Barnette

I JUST WANTED to come here for some peace of mind. I clench my knuckles tightly until the skin is pulled taut.

I need to find out what the hell is being said out there and who the hell else thinks they have enough balls to come and face off with us.

Maybe this goes a lot deeper than I first realized. Yes, I wanted to stir the pot. Yes, I wanted to climb the ladder, but I never once considered that Amelia could legit be put in harm's way.

Even though that woman drives me fucking mad, I don't want any harm coming to her.

No one has heard much here. A lot of the lower ends come to this place, and once you have a guy's testicles and dick in the right position—whether about to cum or with a gun barrel to it—they will squeal anything.

I was hoping to find out if what happened at Balandgi's was

due to jealousy of my frenemy or if they were sent by the tip top.

A soft series of knocks echo against the door, and I can hear it brush against the wooden floor as it opens and shuts. I already know who it is, and I don't even need to open my eyes. I stay positioned with my head laid back pointing towards the ceiling.

I just wanted to come tonight to implore about any intel and get my thoughts together. I did not come here for a booty call.

"Hi, Dakota, how are you doing these days?" I finally shift my head up to give her my full attention.

She stands there tall, proud, and confident in her white nearly see-through crop top which matches her white panties that hug around her as if they were painted on her.

Her long legs are extended by her blank canvas white platform heels that she wears without any hesitation and still continues to amaze me how gracefully she can wear them. Her curled dark brown hair in low pigtails hangs over her chest, framing around her breasts. The outfit is doing exactly what she intended for the look she wanted.

"Trying to appear pure and innocent with all the white today, hmm?" I swallow down the lust I feel building as I hungrily look over her.

It's been a while. Too damn long in my books.

She watches me drink her in and slinks over to me, placing her knees on either side of me as she perches on top of my lap. Fuccck. I lean back, giving her room to make herself comfortable.

Her lips curl into a smile. "I am pure and innocent, but the things I want to do to you aren't."

My dick grows hard underneath her, and I can't stop my

hips from thrusting up slowly against her. This girl has always known how to get me out of my head and edge me.

"Tell me why you've been gone so long. I've missed you." She pouts out her pink plump lips, and I resist the urge to not scowl at her neediness. Her job is just to please, not ask questions.

"Don't," I warn her once.

I came here to escape the very reason why I have been away for a while, and that is Amelia.

Amelia, who is supposed to be my wife, who's my damn fiancée, and I am here with a half-naked woman on top of me instead of her.

I feel a battle of my morals slamming against each other. Half of me knows Amelia wants nothing to do with me, nor do I see us fucking anytime soon in the future because I'm not going to force it. I would never force her.

The other half wants to wait until she is ready and remain faithful even if the feeling of Dakota on top of me is driving me wild.

"What's going on in that head of yours?" Dakota asks as she grinds down onto my cock, feeling how hard it is inside my pants. She leans in to put her mouth on my neck, and the battle inside of me decides to not be unfaithful. I gently stop her progress of leaning in and push her away from me.

"Dakota, I can't do this." I lift her leg up and off of me as I position her beside the spot I was residing on the couch. "Thanks, though."

I am unsure of exactly what to say. This is a job, though I am sure she can understand, but I also know in here they don't get much rejection which explains the confusion that is written all over her face.

I quicken my pace to get out of there and into my car before I change my mind.

What is wrong with a small release of satisfaction? I am wound up, and a quick cum could release a lot of this built-up tension.

I jump in my car and drive a bit too harshly out of the parking lot, the screeching of tires against the asphalt making me wince. But the sound alone brings some tranquility to my tense muscles.

If I didn't give a fuck about Amelia's feelings or her damn consent, I would go home, bend her over in that sweet little black dress she wore tonight, slide her black lacy panties I bought her over, and fuck her hard and relentlessly until every ounce of my cum fills her.

My dick strains hard against my slacks, so hard it is almost painful, and I grip the steering wheel until my knuckles turn white.

Fuck it.

I pull off of the main road and onto one of the side dirt roads that leads to who knows where and shove down my zipper.

Cursing, I yank my dick out and start stroking myself.

I imagine grabbing a fistful of her curly hair and gripping it at the base, demanding her neck to turn so she can look back at me.

I imagine her hooded hazel eyes locking with mine as she groans as I grind my dick deep inside of her, pulling out every sound I can out of her. Her groan turning into whimpers as I pick up the pace and thrust my dick in and out of her wet pussy.

Fuuuuck. The vein on the underside of my dick throbs as my balls grow heavy.

I think about her lips forming into an "O" as I pick up my speed.

God, what I would do to feel her pussy around my dick right now.

I sigh in frustration as I think about propping her ass up with both of my hands and pounding relentlessly until her whimpers turn into loud moans that echo off of the walls.

To hear her chant, "Yes, yes ,yes!"

I cum all over my hand, and it leaks down over my slacks, releasing myself at the thought of her.

Fuuuck.

She has already made me cum, and I haven't even gotten to fuck her yet.

CHAPTER 10

Round Two

Amelia

I STARE into the mirror at my poor bruised nose. How embarrassing that a table took me down. Embarrassment is one form of emotion I wish to never experience. That and humiliation.

I cannot help but chuckle out loud at myself as I try to imagine how I looked flopping to the ground after they yanked the table up. But my stomach turns aggressively as I realize the truth of what happened.

A very dangerous man, though cocky and loud, wanted me and lost one of his men in a shootout to try and get me.

Shivers ping pong aggressively through my body at the thought. Why did they want *me*?

What is so special about me?

I gently splotch some foundation over the plumb brown hues and sigh with ease as it covers it up nicely. Looks more like a shadow now more than anything.

The guys are giving me nothing to go on as to why the night

went down the way they did. I'm not sure if I should believe that they truly do not know what is happening, or whether they're hiding stuff from me, so I won't freak out? Honestly, I feel like I'm taking this whole ordeal rather well.

Maybe I should be more freaked out. Maybe.

Or maybe after all these years of living on edge and taking punches as they come, I've been desensitized to chaotic things, such as a man trying to kidnap me.

Oh wait, that has already happened.

The swish of my door opening against the carpet startles me out of my thoughts. Who the hell just walked in? I swivel my head to find in the middle of my room stands Barnette.

"Did you need something?" Even I can hear how harsh that sounded, and I flinch slightly at the abrupt anger.

"Well, hello to you, too. Your face doesn't look too bad." I almost roll my eyes. What a sweetheart.

"Wow, thanks, you know I was just staring at it in the mirror thinking it doesn't look like I was slammed in the face with a heavy oak table! The magic of makeup!" Sarcasm drips heavily, and I am not sure where my defensiveness is being driven from, but I cannot stop myself.

He sighs but doesn't respond immediately. We just stand there and stare at each other for a few moments.

Finally, I demand, "Do you need something, Barnette?"

"I didn't mean to hit you with the table, *Amelia*." The way he says my name causes butterflies to stupidly spin in my stomach.

"Have you found out anything on why they wanted me?" I just want the damn truth.

His hand grips the back of his neck as he exhales and takes a seat on the bench at the end of my bed. He sits straight up, and his face turns grim. This isn't good.

"No, Amelia, I don't." A strange hum rings through me at his answer. I don't know if I believe him.

"Shouldn't you be concerned with finding out *why* they want me?" This whole thing is insane.

"Of course I am! All of us are working to find out why, believe me when I say that, Amelia." He sounds sincere, and I feel guilty for not trusting him.

"None of it makes any sense at all. Why you want to be married to me, why they want me, why my whole life is just turned upside down. Like what the fuck!"

I don't mean for my frustrations to turn into a full-on spiral, but here it comes!

"Amelia, just calm down." Fuck-up number one.

"Excuse me?" I can feel my eyes widen and can sense how they are nearly bugging out of their sockets.

"Just take a chill pill for a moment and try to think rationally." Fuck-up number two.

"Barnette, I am thinking rationally, and I am eerily calm. Just because a woman is frustrated does NOT MEAN THEY ARE IRRATIONAL."

Damn him, he pushes every single damn button I've got. My voice is nearly in hysterics, and I gulp down a breath. I look at him with my eyes slanted hard, and his eyebrows are raised as if he is making a point.

"I don't want to argue with you." His comment catches me off guard.

"*Are* we arguing?" I respond, trying to keep my voice calm even though it's coming out clipped.

"It appears so, or else I wouldn't have made the comment." Smug asshole.

Again, a tense silence falls between us, and I take the

moment to simmer down my whirlwind of emotions, so his point is not made.

"I don't want to argue either, I just want to have answers," I finally sigh.

"That I can agree with you on. We all need answers. And I plan on getting them." He stands abruptly from the bench, causing me to startle.

"How do you plan on doing that?" Does he have a magic fortune ball at the ready?

He takes two strides towards me, causing me to quickly retreat my steps until my back hits the wall and he towers over me. His breaths come out rough as he leans over me.

"One would think you argue with me for just the fun of it," Barnette whispers to me as he completely invades my personal bubble. Tingles erupt everywhere as my inner devil sparks a curiosity about where this is going to lead. I don't want his head to get too large though and match his smug ego.

"I do enjoy showing you that I am not docile," I whisper back to him, my lips so close to his that if I were to just gently push up on my tiptoes, our mouths would clash.

"Is this our foreplay?" he mummers, and my brain fog clears up instantaneously. I shove at his chest.

"I am not fore-playing with you!" I holler at him, even though I know my body was responding to him. Damn this smug bastard.

He chuckles and rolls his eyes. "Okay, puppet, your body was not just pushing itself against me. We will just ignore that little tidbit of information," he states, all too pleased with himself.

I glare at him and physically shake the thoughts out of my head, swallowing down my retort. Let's get to the damn point.

"Barnette, how are *we* going to get answers?" I ask slowly, so as not to give away the shake in my voice.

"There is an event tonight that has a lot of people who I work beside and deal with that are attending, and I plan on going and finding out what information is out there." He shrugs his shoulders as if the answer is as easy as that, takes a step back, and starts to walk out the door. I can't read his expression.

"Do I get to go?" I blurt out without even thinking about if I truly want to attend an event where all these supposedly bad people are going to be at. Too late.

Barnette frowns. "Amelia, I'd rather you stay here and just know it is what's best."

"What is best? As if you know what is best for me, right?" I challenge.

He sighs as he stares into my eyes. "It is best if you stay here while I can find out what's going on."

He is going to lock me up again. I just know it.

"Absolutely not. I want to go." My stomach drops to my ass at my own words, but I would rather chop off my left arm than to be left stuck here alone and have no idea what's going on.

"Why can't you just be happy to be here and look through those damn magazines I got for you and pick out a damn wedding dress!" His frustration breaks through heavily. I can sense the anger building up in him, but don't worry dear fiancé, my rage has already been kindling.

"Because I am not a docile happy little lamb here, and I have no desire to plan a wedding right now and marry a man I don't know!"

"You want to get to know me? Yeah?" His breaths come out in puffs. "You want to know how this works? Last night wasn't glimpse enough for you to see how dangerous this can get? You just want to push and push and see more of it?"

I don't even hesitate. "Yes." I straighten my shoulders back and put as much strength into my posture as I can as I stare right back at him.

He just shakes his head with a scoff. "Fine. Get dressed in something nice." And with those sweet words, Barnette departs from the room and leaves me to figure out what the hell type of nice he wants.

He is frustrating to the point that I want to strangle the hell out of him. Just, you know, a small little squeeze that makes him choke. But nerves are going haywire in my stomach. What the hell did I just agree to? And how the hell does he even consider *this* foreplay?!

Not long after he closes the door and walks away, I stand there just staring at the abundance of clothing options I have in the closet.

Why the hell did I agree to do this? I am nervous as hell. A soft knock raps at my door.

Sigh.

Good, it better be him with more of an explanation, and he better keep to his own damn bubble!

I briskly walk over to open the door, ready to release some colorful words, when I am surprised by none other than Dean at my door.

I stand there dumbfounded, swallowing back my words.

"I take it I am not who you expected?" He chuckles.

"Well, no," I answer honestly, making a face.

"May I come in?" he asks, shoving his hands into the pocket of the hunter-green slacks he is wearing.

I take in his appearance for a moment, how the white dress shirt hugs his chest and tucks in cleanly to his slacks. His matching hunter-green jacket is unbuttoned and hanging open in a casual manner, but he still reeks of luxury.

"Want to take a picture?" he taunts, and I snap my gaze away from his dark brown dress shoes, narrowing my eyes at him in suspicion.

He stole my words from that morning. Isn't he smug? Asshole.

I roll my eyes at him. "Sure, come in. Now that I see how you're dressed, I take it I get to squeeze myself into one of those little dresses again." It's more of a statement than a question, and I already find my feet heading back to the closet to mull over what gown I'm going to choose.

"I am having this odd feeling that you don't like to dress up?" Dean replies casually.

I pop my head out of the closet and see that he made himself comfortable on the bench at the end of my bed. I automatically lift my lip into a snarl at him. Both at how comfortable he thinks he can be in my space and for the phrase 'dress up'.

"I am not used to wearing clothing like this. Also, your lovely sweetheart of a brother didn't give me details about where we were going and what to exactly wear. He is in his same stupid suit, so I didn't have much to go on."

I pop back into the closet and start shoving clothing aside to get a full view of them.

"Aaah, a woman after my own heart. You speak so fondly of my brother," he remarks with a chuckle.

I can hear soft, padded steps head towards the closet as I admire a baby pink sparkling dress that makes the little girl inside of me squeal like a princess. His voice comes from right behind me as he leans on the closet door frame. "Take my word, he isn't a bad guy. He is just a hell of a lot more serious than he sometimes needs to be."

I nod my agreeance. "Your guy's relationship with one another still is rather unique to me. I don't have much to go on really with—" I immediately stop myself from finishing that sentence.

Andrea and I's relationship is different because I had to raise her, nothing more or less. I continue chastising myself in my head and turn my attention back to the dresses, admiring the olive-green floor-length gown with the swoop neckline.

I change the direction of the subject and throw in a joke, "If you two grew up together then where did you learn how to charm and go with the flow, and he learned to be cold and distant?"

I yank on the next dress that is a navy-blue silky gown that has an extremely low dip in the neckline that makes me wonder how I could wear a damn bra in it. Or am I not supposed to wear a bra?

Dean clears his throat, causing my attention to go back to him. He stands there with his brows furrowed and his lips in a tight line.

"I know he's difficult at times and doesn't exactly have the best methods of communication," Dean says, and I roll my eyes at that understatement of the century, "but he means well and is more of a teddy bear than he lets on."

I scoff at the comparison. Barnette a teddy bear? Sure. His mouth turns into that smirk I have become accustomed to him wearing. "It is up to him to show that side a little more, but in the meantime…" He claps his hands together, causing me to jump back in surprise.

Dean raises his hands innocently, and a subtle look of concern pinches the space between his eyebrows. I wish I could control it better.

"My deepest apologies. I didn't mean to—"

"Forget about it. It's nothing. Continue with what you were

going to say, Dean," I sigh and peer back at the three dresses I just looked at.

"May I suggest the green perhaps?" His tone is still softened, which grates at my nerves, but I know it's coming from a good place, so I clear my throat and decide to ignore it.

I look at the green dress again and then roll my head his way, glowering at him. "Trying to get me to match you? Hell no."

I add a smile to my lips, so he knows I am harassing him, and it earns me a full little boy grin back.

"Well, why not? Don't you want to look as sharp and classy as me?" His eyebrows shoot up as he trails his palm down his suit, emphasizing his choice of attire, and I cannot help but chuckle at the goofball in front of me.

I shake my head at his opinion.

"Fine! Go with the blue. Final opinion, make sure to slap some heels with it and don't be afraid to dabble in the jewelry. We're going to one of our usual spots but it's nice and clean, and the food is delicious!" He pops his lips out and points his fingers in a gesture I would see Italians do on the TV.

I snort, glancing at the blue dress. "Yeah?"

"There's a genuine smile! I'll take it! Now, get ready and meet us in the foyer so we can go. Please don't be one of those girls who need three hours to get ready—I am starvvvvving!" he whines.

He has his hands in a prayer-like motion as if praying I am not one of those girls. Mr. Cartoon's comment about how Dean can eat them out of house resurfaces and causes a slight smirk to tilt my lips. Dean really is a giant kid with a never-ending appetite.

"Get out of here so I can change then! Or I will be sure to take a minimum of *two* hours!" I give him a pointed look.

He rolls his eyes as he turns to head out, knowing damn well I will not take that much time.

He begins to leave the room and I lose all ounce of self-control as my fear bubbles up and word vomits out of my mouth. "Dean, will I be safe tonight?"

Is it silly to ask? They protected me once already, but is it suicide for me to just jump right back out there?

He gives me a soft smile. "I think you will be fine. Tonight is an important night for everyone, and we should not be getting into any trouble." He releases a burdened sigh, hesitating for a moment. "But I mean, last night was supposed to go smoothly as well, so really it is a wild card tonight."

That doesn't settle my stomach at all.

He paints on a smile, nonetheless. "We've got your back Amelia." I can feel the truth in the words.

"I know you guys do, I just… I just needed to ask." I shrug my shoulders sheepishly. I won't admit my fear out loud, but I know he can read it in my body language.

"Oh, I almost forgot I got you a gift."

My heart flutters as he pulls out a black box from his pants pocket. Did Dean really buy me jewelry? He holds it out to me, and I just stare at it unsure how to respond.

"The box won't bite you," he teases.

I take it timidly out of his hand and open it. A gasp leaves my throat as I stare down at the beautiful necklace.

Dean grins, watching my reaction. "It's obsidian."

My heart pulses in my throat as I look at the wire-wrapped downward arrowhead obsidian necklace he just gifted me. Its edges are smooth, and it's polished to perfection. God, it is so beautiful.

"Thank you, Dean. I don't even know what to say, but thank

you." I stare at the even design of the wire and pull it out of the box.

It is a statement piece all on its own, and I decide right then I am wearing it tonight!

Dean gently grabs it from my hand and stands behind me, bringing it around my neck and making sure it clasps perfectly down between my breasts.

"Tonight, just keep sharp and listen to everything. You will not be out of any of our sights, okay?" Dean says.

A tender wave of relief washes over me at his words as I still stand there voiceless and dumbfounded by the gift. Dean leaves my room, and I look back at the dress I am holding in my hands.

I pull and tug at the decision on whether I should chicken out and not go or swallow down my fear and find out for myself why those men wanted me. I deserve to know; I deserve some damn answers.

I look at the necklace in my reflection, in awe of the beautiful stone. I will go and be brave, I decide.

That being said, if we are going somewhere as fancy as this dress, then I guess a little makeup won't hurt—and a quick shave of the legs!

Whoever invented heels either hates women or they only care about how much it can make a girl's ass pop and not have comfort at all. I slowly walk around the corner, and the hushed tones of conversation I was hearing on the way down the hallway immediately stop as they all stare at me.

All three guys' attention is on me, and I can't help but blush even though I feel like an ant underneath a microscope.

I'm going to catch on fire. The rush of blood reaches my ears, and I can feel my eyes widen in slight panic as I wait for someone to talk. I clear my throat in the most unladylike way thanks to my nerves making it hard to swallow.

I look at Barnette, who stands there tall and business-like in the same black slacks and button-up he had on earlier. He threw on a blue tie, though, and that blue! Huh, it looks awfully close to the shade of blue my dress is. I wonder if that's a coincidence…

"Well, we'd better get going or else Dean is going to starve to death." I do my best to bring humor to a quiet moment, and thankfully it earns me a couple chuckles.

"You look absolutely breathtaking," Dean whispers.

Barnette stares at me for a moment with an odd expression on his face. I can't ever seem to read the emotions he has.

"Yes, you clean up very nicely. We should get going." With that, Barnette comes up and extends his arm towards the door.

I'm not sure whether to be insulted by his comment or not. Why can't he just have said "yes, I agree" and move along with it?

Derrick walks up to me in a rather snug-fitting black suit himself and offers me his arm to hold onto. Leave it to the killer to help the girl in heels. I flash a quick glare at Barnette and gratefully grab Derrick's arm.

"You look rather handsome in a suit, Mickey Mouse," I remark, and that earns me a grin on his stone-set face and a shake of his head as we walk out and head towards the car.

Barnette stays quietly behind us, and I casually try to glance over my shoulder at him to see what the silence is all about. He is walking with a troubled expression as he stares at where Derrick and I's arms are linked.

I hope this doesn't cause any trouble for Derrick.

But I also cannot help but wonder if Barnette is the jealous type.

CHAPTER 11

Words Do Break Bones

Amelia

MY MOUTH IS STILL HANGING wide open like an opening to a cave waiting for a train to come through at any moment. Maybe a tad dramatic, but looking at this house I feel completely in awe of the size and beauty of it.

It's huge. Bigger than the guys' place, but I am not going to rub that tidbit of information in their faces.

"Take a picture, it will last longer," Dean mimics me from the side of the car where he is still holding the door open for me waiting to get out.

I flip him my favorite finger and take a second longer to gawk at what is in front of me.

I don't care if they think I am childish at the moment; I am not used to this life. I don't think I ever will be. Barnette steps into my vision and holds his arm out for me to grab, and I willingly do so.

I am intrigued and though I am nervous as all hell, I am also so excited to see the inside.

"Okay do we need to go over everything one more time, or do you feel confident about it?" Derrick whispers at my side, taking to my right almost perfectly in step.

"Stay in sight at all times, be with one of you at all times, don't say a word at all times, and try not to embarrass you at all times," I recite, earning a small glare from him.

"Don't sound like a spoiled brat. You twisted my words, Amelia. Just be incognito and stay with one of us at all times," he responds a little sharply.

"I am not a brat!" I bite out with a huff.

"This right here can pause until we get home," Barnette chastises us, and for a moment I feel like I'm eight years old again.

I slide Derrick one last sly side eye, then slap on the biggest fakest smile I can muster. We are here for answers and I, for one, am good at blending in and keeping my ears open, and that is exactly what I plan to do even before big head one and two started reciting rules.

My neck tenses up as the tightness in my jaw is exceeded from the strain of my nerves. There are a lot more people here than there were at the restaurant; it would be pure chaos if something were to happen here.

Fuck, was it smart to try to be involved at this level? Should I have just let the guys handle this?

We walk up to the grand double door entrance with its swirl of intricate designs from the metal, and I soak everything in like a kid in a candy store.

"Scared?" Barnette whispers into my ear, his voice sending a shudder through me.

"Cautious," I respond, and a chill of déjà vu threatens to overwhelm me. My attention snaps to Barnette's eyes, and I can feel mine widen as I realize just how dangerous it could be here.

"You are safe with me," he states calmly, and for some reason the strength of his tone washes over me like a protective shield. He squeezes my arm with his hand and as we enter the foyer, he puts on a small smile himself. "Let the night begin."

I have discovered that events like this are like a giant game of chess. Everything is strategic, and you are doing your best to mentally keep one step above everyone else. We've had small chats with so many different people by now that I cannot even keep up with who is who. I don't even recognize Barnette right now; he is being *nice* and *pleasant* to everyone, but he still holds the 'don't fuck with me' stance. He also knows everyone's names and I can tell you the second they introduce themselves it is in one ear and out the other.

My attention also keeps getting distracted. I cannot help but admire the dresses swishing around on the dance floor. Everyone looks so pretty and nice; smiles adorn their faces as they do their synchronized steps.

This is nothing like any of the 'parties' I had growing up. A small amount of sadness fills me as I think about home, but guilt quickly eradicates it. I should be living this new life to the fullest.

I glance back over my shoulder, trying to keep a balance of being polite to the group that Barnette is talking to while also yearning for the dance floor.

"Do you mind if I take the little miss for a dance?" Dean's voice breaks up the conversation, and I can't help the small smile that escapes my lips.

Barnette looks down at me and then zero ins on the dance floor as if sweeping for any bad thing that could happen. Once he deems it safe in his eyes, he finally nods his head, and I eagerly grab onto Dean's outreached hand before we scurry to the dance floor.

I halt almost immediately as my surroundings catch up to me. "I don't know how to dance," I admit.

Dean rolls his eyes. "Nobody knows how to actually dance, Amelia." He pulls me towards him and helps place my hands in the correct positions.

"Says the guy who is arranging me in what is supposed to be the correct form," I snip at him with a lowered voice. Excitement, fear, and nervousness are pounding through me, causing my stomach to be a jumbled, hot mess.

He snorts and replies, "Oh shush. This is just reading the room around us." I take small peeks around and see how he has me matched to the other females around us.

Okay, fair point. I will let him have it. He guides me into a swaying motion, and I quickly follow his lead.

"That is exactly how you do it, Amelia, good job." He offers me a wink, and I give him my best stink eye as I chastise him with my glare. He twirls me at that moment, and I cannot help the excited squeal that leaves me as I spin and for once in my life—I feel like a motherfucking princess.

We glide along the dance floor, starting to follow our own beat, and for a moment I don't care to find out why people are after me.

I forget that my life has been upside down and that I am only here because of the man—who I catch staring hard at me from across the room—deems it his will. I don't feel the heaviness of all the expectations placed on me, and I feel my lips turn into a genuine smile full of joy. Where's my damn crown?!

"You have a beautiful smile, Amelia," Dean comments with a matching smile of his own.

I don't dismiss the compliment, and I don't give him sass; I just accept the beauty of the moment and hope it never ends.

He twirls me again, and mid-twirl I am brushed up right

against another woman. I feel the coldness down my front before I even register that her drink toppled out of her hand and down the front of me onto the floor. Oh, shit!

"Oh my!" the woman gasps out in shock, a hand flying to her mouth.

I stare at her with her delicately painted red lips and long, shiny satin ruby red dress. It comes up around her neck in a swoop and along the collar of it hangs a bunch of very large, probably very real, rows of diamonds that I am sure are so expensive I am getting charged to look at them.

She snaps her fingers at me, and I shake my head to get out of the thought bubble I was in admiring her. "Are you okay? I cannot believe that happened." Now embarrassment floods through me.

"Oh no, don't be silly! Accidents happen!" My voice is a little too high even to my own ears. "I shouldn't have gotten so close. I am the one who should be apologizing," I stammer.

"Don't be silly, I never apologized." Her statement causes my brows to furrow as I try to gather everything that just happened in this short amount of time. She leans towards me and whispers low, "You know you should probably leave before everyone sees that big stain on the front of your dress. You don't want to be the talk of the future parties!"

Then she turns and just walks away.

Just like that. Goodbye.

Disbelief is still corded tight through me as I look up to Dean, and I can feel another presence come up on my right where she was just standing moments before.

"Let's get you to the bathroom to clean up." Barnette's voice registers in my ear, and I just nod my head in agreement as I follow them to the lady's room.

She really did not apologize for spilling her drink on me, and the realization of that bothers me deeply.

I keep my head down, so I don't have to personally witness any of the rubberneckers staring at the giant stain. We walk up right to an opening in the wall that has a hallway. It reminds me a lot of how restaurant bathrooms are, and I find it so odd that there are homes that have setups like this.

"I'll just be a minute," I assure the two of them as I continue walking down towards the bathroom.

My reflection greets me immediately in a giant mirror framed in gold accents. It spans so long that there are four different sinks that sit comfortably underneath it.

Why does anyone need a bathroom like this in their own home? How many people live here? Then I zero in on the front of my dress—oh, damn! I quickly grab a couple of paper towels and start patting the large glob, and much to my despair, it is not just wet but stained. I didn't even see what she was drinking and if it was colored.

I wonder if I can get this to a dry cleaner and then it won't be completely ruined, but to do that requires money. Shit, I don't have any, right?

I can see the lines form in my face as I glance up and look at what is on full display of my now ruined dress. We can just leave now, or maybe someone can take me home while the guys finish what they need to do? Yeah, let's go with that.

My bladder does a squeeze, and well, I figure I am already in here, so I might as well release it so I am not squirming on the way home.

Home.

I just called that place home.

I lift up my dress and bring it up and around my neck,

feeling ridiculous, but there is no way I am also going to get toilet water on this dress!

I hear female voices whispering among each other as they head down the hallway that leads into the restroom, their voices getting louder as they near. I do my best to shove out all the urine I can before they finally enter. Then I go to stand right when the girl starts to speak again.

"Did you see the look on her face when Marcella walked away?" one laughs, and more giggles join her.

I sit back down and peek through the bathroom stall to see three women standing there looking at themselves in the mirror.

All three are tall blondes. The one on the left has her hair in curls that cascade down her back, filling in the giant opening of her dress that clearly shows she is not wearing a bra. Her navy-blue sequined dress hugs her tight and shimmers all the way down to her black deathtrap heels.

The blonde in the middle has hers half up and half down, and her dress is a tight pastel pink satin statement that flows gracefully down to her silver pointed weapons on her feet. There is a slit on the right side that reaches almost all the way to her waist as she maneuvers herself in the mirror admiring herself.

Hell, if I looked like that, I would be admiring myself as well.

"Well, what did she expect to happen. A whore like her should not be at an event like this. What was Barnette thinking?" the one on the right speaks.

Her nasal tone full of disgust contradicts the beauty in the black ruffled gown she wears. It holds tight like a corset on the top, and around her waist are four full strands of diamonds that cinch together as black tulle ruffles feather down gently.

She looks stunning. If it weren't for the fact that she just called me a whore, I'd be in awe of her. I must have missed something.

"He seriously needs to consider what his lengthy attendance down at *The Office* is going to do to his name. Seriously, why does he need to spend that amount of time at a strip club when he can have any number of women at his beck and call?" the woman in the blue states.

So, my fiancé likes the strip club, eh? That's something I will have to think about later. One crisis at a time. Who the hell names a strip club *The Office* anyways? How fucking smooth is that!

"All I'm saying is she didn't need to look like she fit in among us either. I for one want the men to know I am full class and not just a walking piece of ass. She doesn't need to parade around like she belongs."

The sting of her words hurt deeply. This is like high school all over again. The false accusations and all the misunderstandings that gave me a bad image, but others soaked it in regardless.

Why can't I just be accepted for me? Why is this still something I have to fight for as a fucking adult?

The one in the pink starts cackling, and all the hair on my arms raises at the sound. "Well, if Marcella has it her way, she is probably out there slinging herself all over Barnette, and he will probably sneak away later to service her every need. That girl is so bad!"

She laughs like this other woman being bad is funny, yet when it is me who is walking around here minding her own damn business, I am a whore? I don't understand the double standards. I never understood them.

"She looked like she was ready to fuck Dean anyways. She is

probably fucking them both thinking her shit don't stink. Let Marcella have a piece of him. All I know is Dean is the one I'm eyeing, and I plan to have my way this time," the one in black makes her claim.

She adorns her lip with another even layer of burgundy. The color reminds me of my mother, and finally something other than betrayal and despair lines my insides; I feel my old friend anger. All I was doing was dancing with Dean. I did nothing, I insinuated nothing, yet these women are the ones talking about fucking them! How am I the negative one in the bunch?

"Whatever. Let her leave with the chauffeur looking like a sad little girl whose play time got messed up and we can make our moves. She doesn't belong here, and Marcella just put her in her place."

I don't belong in this world—I do know that. I already know with every fiber of my being that I don't belong in this world, but what I do know is that a little drink down my dress is the last thing that is going to take me down. Fuck them.

The women walk out of the bathroom, and I give it a couple of minutes before fixing my dress and flushing the toilet. I walk up to the sink and wash my hands slowly as I stare at my dress, and hair, and soft jewelry in the mirror. Taking a deep breath, I let it out slowly.

Those girls are as fake as the diamonds they wear around their necks, and I refuse to let them kill the little bit of joy that I got from tonight.

Even though being the brunt of such accusations still leaves me with a stabbing pain in my chest.

I just want to belong and be accepted.

I inhale a breath and force my eyes to harden. Not one person gets to see the tears of frustration trying to force their way out. I straighten my shoulders and slap on my best go-to-hell look.

I can hear chattering as I exit the bathroom, and I look over to see those three women talking to Barnette, Dean, and Derrick. They are all being friendly and cordial, but the second I come out the guy's eyes snap to me and check me over from head to toe.

The three girls turn, and the look of shock etches into their faces at the realization that I was in the bathroom the whole time.

I heard everything out of their snake mouths, and that brings a genuine smile to my face.

"Everything okay, puppet?" Barnette asks with an inquisitive expression. He tries to lock eyes with me, but there is no way he is going to get to see the deep truth set in my gaze.

"Pray tell, who did you bring along tonight, Barnette?" the woman in pastel pink questions.

I look quickly to Derrick and even though I still have the smile plastered to my face and the tears far from the surface. I see the small nod he gestures towards me as if he knows these women are fake.

"His fiancée," I state at the same time Barnette replies, "My fiancée," I take that moment to look up to him.

"Oh, I didn't realize you were looking for a wife!" the one in pink snips out, frowning slightly.

"You would think if you were dating word would have gotten around and everyone would know," the one in blue responds, shock embedded into her words.

I shrug my shoulders, ants itching along my skin and causing a fiery sensation to erupt through my belly.

I want to go; I need to go. The two are completely flustered, and it should bring me more happiness, it really should. I should be feeling smug and almighty, but their accusations play in my head.

I am not a winner here. Barnette walks up to me and pulls me to his side, his arm wrapping around my back as his hand rests on my hip, and he gives a squeeze.

I don't even have the energy to push him away or to think about his movement. I just want to go.

"Well, we're going to head out now. Let's go home, puppet," Barnette speaks to everyone but squeezes my hip again as he leads me to the left for the door. Derrick is already in the flank position.

"Oh, Dean! You don't have to go do you? Can I have a dance with you?" the one in black asks, almost sounding desperate as she reaches out and grabs Dean's arm as he goes to stand by Derrick.

Dean doesn't hesitate. "No," he brushes her off, and I am completely stumped. I have never seen him act so callous, so harsh before.

I quickly look to see the woman in black glaring at me, hurt clear in her eyes, but anger stated directly at me. She goes to stand in front of Dean, blocking his steps. Surprise lights up his face along with clear annoyance. I move out of Barnette's grasp and slip in between the two; Dean's words stop on the tip of his tongue.

I make myself as tall as I can as I look into her eyes. I surge every ounce of the bitch I am capable of being to the surface and lean closer to her to the point where it looks like I am about to kiss her.

"Don't you ever lay a hand on one of *my* men again or this *whore* is going to make sure your dress matches mine, but instead of a drink it will be your blood," I whisper my threat low, so other prying ears can't hear.

Her eyes get huge as her face pales, and I take the moment to give her a syrupy sweet smile and step back to pat Dean's arm gently.

"Let's go, men, I am tired." With that, I leave Queen Bitch with her mouth gaping open, and me and my three musketeer men walk out of the party with our heads held high.

The only thought keeping me stable is that I can cry when I lock myself into a steamy hot shower.

CHAPTER 12

Two Obsidian Pebbles in a Sea of Crystals

Amelia

Four Months after Andrea was born.

I HOLD the tiny bundle of this sweet little soul in my arms close to my chest. I dressed her in a soft pink pastel onesie with tiny little white bunnies all over it. It fit her snugly, and after feeding her a bottle she fell comfortably asleep in my arms.

She is so tiny when you look at her, but she is so big when you compare my arms to hers. It is a crazy concept to wrap my head around.

"Meli, what are you going to do?" Lacey asks me from where she sits beside me on my bed.

I look down at the burnt orange comforter she gave me a few months ago. It is so homey, and though it looks out of place here, it fits me. I see small little stains in a couple spots that have already formed from where Andrea has spit up a couple of times; she has been sleeping in the bed with me almost nightly because she hates the little cot mom got her.

I look up at my friend and peer into her concerned eyes.

Lacey has always gone above and beyond to be there for me. Even with all the hurdles of her father and expectations of the other kids, she and I kept our friendship strong.

"I am going to raise her as best I can." There really is no other way around this.

I can hear Mom still snoring from her room down the hall. She was up all night long arguing with some John she found, part of the reason why little missy is asleep in my arms because they gave zero fucks about keeping two kids up all night with their ruckus.

The fighting got so bad I had to push my dresser in front of the door in fear that he may try to barge in here and use me as leverage to push his way through my mom.

A never-ending cycle. A broken, dented, bruised-up damaged circle—and I am in the middle of it.

"She was supposed to be doing better! She was supposed to do this, too!" My friend's flustered voice peaks as she also tries to process the common betrayal of my mother's proposed words. "Is this why you haven't tried to call or message me?" Her hurt turns towards me, and I look away from her out of guilt.

"I wasn't trying to push you away, Lacey. That is the very last thing I want to do. I've just got to focus on her and me, is all."

My words aren't affecting her the way I was hoping they would, because the truth is that a very tiny part of me did try to push her away from this. From all this crazy that swarms around me like flies on shit.

Her life is so plush and easy; she doesn't have to fight for a damn thing in her life! I am not angry at her for it, I just am hurt that I was placed in this path and not one similar to hers.

"Liar. You always try to shove me away when you think I can't handle something." She cocks her head, the movement causing me to look back up at her. "I will always be by your side! No matter what happens, I will be here for you, you know this. So, stop pushing me away!"

Her fists clench and unclench, her tell-tale sign that she is frustrated beyond belief. Guilt is like a thick, heavy syrup coating my heart.

"I am sorry, Lacey; I swear I am not trying to do that. I just don't know what to do here! I just want the answers to how this is supposed to work. I want to know how to keep her safe; I don't want one bad thing to touch her sweet soul. How am I supposed to know why she is crying? Or how about when to start showing her how to crawl and walk?

"What if she gets sick and she needs medicine? Mom has her good days, but what if it falls on a bad day and she is completely zonked out and I won't know how to help Andrea?!"

Tears prickle the back of my eyes heavily, and I try my very best to blink back the threat of tears.

"Or teach her that there are bad people out there and to be always on guard because life is not fair! Life is mean and cruel!" My voice breaks as my rambling continues. "No one has your back; you can't even rely on Mom to keep clean long enough to make sure we have enough food in the house to last more than a couple days!"

The tears win as they drip down my cheeks and roll off my chin.

"I have your back, Amelia, always!" Lacey gets on her knees as she positions herself in front of me and Andrea, grabbing me gently by the shoulders. "I have yours, and I will have hers, too. I don't have all the answers for you; I don't even know those answers for myself. But I do know that you will not be alone. I will be there with you through all of this.

"If your mom is having a bad day and Andie needs something, tell me and I will try to ask my mom or try to get it for you. I may not have the answers, but you will not be alone in trying to figure it out."

Her friendship has always been my rock in this hard world. I don't know what I ever did to deserve a friend like her, a sister in someone who is not blood.

Tears track down her face, matching my own, because even though she has not gone through what I have, she feels the pain I have endured. Whenever I needed something or someone, she was there for me every time.

She adds, "You also have yourself concerned with things that we don't even need to face right now."

I know she's right. I look back down at Andrea as she sleeps so peacefully; she doesn't need to know the dangers of the world right now. She just needs to be able to grow and be healthy.

"I feel so bad that she was born on a path like mine, and not one like yours," I admit honestly. I'm not jealous of Lacey, and she knows that it isn't either of our fault who our parents are.

"You know what she has that you didn't, though?" Lacey asks me. I look at her and shake my head in response. "She has *you*."

My heart both crumbles and feels like it is being glued back together at once. A small laugh escapes me as tears rain down my face, and it turns into a sob. Lacey shuffles over to us and pulls us into a big embrace, her arms barely fitting around the two of us.

"She has two of us to go through this, Meli. You know the ins and I know the outs. I think between the two of us, she will have a better paved way than you did, and that counts," Lacey continues.

I chuckle through my sobs. I feel like a complete mess, as I relax my weight into her for a moment. I yearn for that moment of comfort.

I pull back away from her and inhale a deep breath to chill out my nerves. "I do know, Lace, that I want her to be real and authentic. I want her to know kindness and be kind. I want her to be filled with love and know how to give without needing to lower herself to get it."

I gently lay Andrea in front of me as she curls into her side, and I pat her back in soft, careful movements.

"I want her to know the truth of how harsh life is but not let it make her insides cold and dark. I don't know how to teach her all of that, but it's important to me that she does," I murmur.

I think about all of the people I have been surrounded by. How people look down on me, on where I live, how I dress, who my mother is, both adults and kids my age.

I swallow, adding, "I don't have much to offer her, but I will offer her my guidance and love." I will shield her from the pain those words and accusations people freely give me; she will not endure that if I can help it.

"You know money is not everything, right, Meli? Look at me and my parents; they have a lot of money, but they aren't happy people."

I reflect on Lacey's dad and how he has treated me. You would think as a man who has everything in life, he would be happy, but no. Mr. Carrington is a miserable soul and no amount of money or nice things will ever change that about him. Mrs. Carrington is no better; even with all her clothes, makeup, and jewelry she wears everywhere—she is a sad, miserable person married to a jackass of a man.

Her big crystal necklace pops into my head that she likes to wear to their fancy dinners. It is all so fake. Not the crystals, but their smiles and their lifestyle.

Lacey is right. Money isn't everything, and it can't buy happiness. It is an illusion I always lived by; I just never had it click until now.

"People are like fake crystals," I say slowly.

The look of confusion Lacey gives me causes me to chuckle.

I elaborate further, "So many people walk around here with fake smiles and think that because their outside looks pretty that their insides count for something. The only thing is, they were cut to look that way. Why live a fake life if there is no meaning to it? What's the point?" I ask her without asking. I know the answer already; there is no point.

"I want to be happy with who I am," she states, understanding where I'm going with my ramble.

"You know what has always fascinated me? Remember in science class last year when Mrs. Shenan showed us her rock collection she had in the back, all those geodes, pebbles, crystals, and the obsidian rocks?" I can see her mind reeling back as she recalls the class we shared last year.

"I do remember those. Oh! Remember that one rock that cut your finger when you grabbed it," she exclaims.

I smile at the memory, because that damn rock did cut my finger, and Mrs. Shenan was so upset that I had touched her rock without asking. I didn't mean to let my hands get carried away; I just was so drawn to it.

"That was the obsidian rock. Those things can be sharp. It was also beautiful, though. I was drawn to the natural black texture of it and how it was almost edgy-looking, and when she told me this was it in its natural form, I was surprised. This rock came out of the Earth ready to defend itself with its sharp edges. Then she showed me one that was altered by man and turned into a pebble. It was shiny and sleek, but it still held its edginess to it.

"It just felt strong, Lace, like even though the sides were softened, it held its core strength. I don't know, maybe I am putting too much into a damn rock, but…"

I move over to pull open my little nightstand drawer and pull out the two little pebbles that Mrs. Shenan had given me when I took such an interest in it. I show Lacey the pebbles, and she smiles at me as she takes one gently from me and observes it herself.

"It is beautiful," she murmurs, giving it back to me. A smile tugs at my lips.

Nodding, I add, "I'd rather be real and natural than something fake. And I wish the same for Andrea." I lean over Andie's little body and place the black pebbles on her tiny little chest, right where her heart should be, and I make a vow to that little girl. "Two obsidian pebbles in a sea of crystals," I whisper to her.

I can feel Lacey's arm squeeze my shoulder as she too looks down at little Andie. My eyes prick with tears as the promise I make surges through me.

This is one thing I can promise her: We will be real, and we will do this together.

CHAPTER 13

The Darkness a Monster Holds

Amelia

PEOPLE'S WORDS feel like sandpaper to the heart. I can't even be angry at anyone but myself as I lay here curled up in bed staring at the wall.

I am searing with rage at myself for even thinking I should feel joy, if only for a moment.

That feeling never gets to last long with me. Nothing positive ever does, it seems.

I have always been so careful, always waiting for the next shoe to drop, because as I already know from time and time again that shoe is going to be slammed down.

Whore.

Trailer trash.

Lost cause.

Waste of space.

The insults play on an endless loop in my mind.

I was never intended to feel pure joy. No matter how I look, apparently, I will never be worth more than a piece of chewed-up gum on the bottom of someone's shoe.

I looked and felt beautiful at that party, but I was nothing more than what they already thought of me. Useless.

Why should I care what those women thought? I can feel the rage kindle deep in my belly, stoking the flames of my despair. Why can't anyone treat me like a decent human being?

But shame washes over me, burning out the fire that had just kindled. Why is there always a war in my head?

It is completely exhausting.

I can hear a soft swish as my bedroom door opens, and I don't even bother to look to see who it is.

A soft mustard-looking fabric steps into my line of sight, and my eyes slowly trace up the material to see Marisol staring down at me, her hair in her classic tight bun.

"Mija." The genuine concern I can hear laced through her words pulls at my heart.

"Please, leave me alone," I request, even though I don't mean it. I don't want to be alone, but I also don't want to be hounded.

She frowns. "Mija, you need to eat. You have been in this room for two days, and you haven't eaten more than a few nibbles of food! Is my food not to your liking?" Her accent enunciates her words and makes her sound as if she were angry, but I know she is in here out of concern.

"Your food is delicious," I state robotically; I am too tired to try to explain and defend why I am not hungry.

"Is there something specific you want me to make?" She lowers herself down so she can feel my head, as if she is checking for a fever. "Are you feeling ill?"

I brush away her hand with all the strength I have.

"Maybe," I respond tightly. Maybe I am ill, maybe I just need to sleep for a few hours so I can feel better. "I should just sleep it off." I shrug.

"How about some soup?" she insists. Pushy little thing. I glance at her, peeling my eyes away from the wall to take in her stance. "You are going to waste away, Mija."

I cannot tell if she is genuinely worried for me, or if she is concerned about how I am going to look beside Barnette as I marry him.

Cannot have a skinny, pathetic wife to be standing beside the King of La Caìda. How embarrassing.

"I just want to sleep. I will be better in a couple days," I murmur and close my eyes. I lack the strength to hold them open, I lack the capability to slap on a smile today and fake it.

Worthless.

Unlovable.

Desperate for attention.

Disgusting.

Their words just play on a loop in my mind like a wicked little lullaby squeezing my brain to sleep. Hours pass by while I stay in the dark embrace of sleep.

"Amelia, wake up."

Drowsiness overwhelms me. I feel a small shove on my shoulder as whoever is trying to wake me attempts to shake me awake.

"Amelia." His voice becomes clearer. I peel open my eyes and look up to see Barnette standing there.

Where did Marisol go? She must have left when I fell asleep.

"What?" is all I'm able to get out. I just want to go back to sleep. I groan as he pulls the warm comforter off of me. "Hey!" I am able to shove out of my throat as my heavy arms search for the blanket he took from me.

"You need to get up and shower, Amelia. You've been in here for almost three days now!"

I wince. Has it already been that long?

"Marisol says you don't have a fever. Are you not feeling well anywhere else?" That can't possibly be genuine concern I see on his face, can it?

"I just want to go to sleep," I mumble. His mouth sets at my words.

"No, you have slept for three days. Get up," he demands. A small, tiny kernel of anger sets itself in my chest.

"Don't tell me what to do, Barnette. Leave me alone," I grit out as I sit up and grab onto the blanket he set at the end of the bed. He grabs onto it, too.

"You need to eat, shower, and get out of bed. We have dinner plans tonight. Wouldn't you like to come?" he challenges.

I probably stink, but I don't care.

"I don't want to go. Just leave me alone," I snap.

His eyes turn into slits as his own anger develops. "Eat." Pushy asshole!

"I will once Marisol brings me a plate," I state smugly, hoping that is enough of an answer to make him go away.

He swings his arm wide towards my dresser. "There are multiple plates and bowls already there waiting for you to eat, yet you are *not* eating them!" he hollers.

I glance at the dresser to see the evidence of what he is saying spread before me, making me grimace. I had no idea she kept bringing food; I didn't even know that the door kept opening and closing. That doesn't sit well in my stomach.

"Oh," is all I am able to reply, defeat heavy in my tone. The kernel of rage I had has been doused out.

"I need you to get up, eat, and shower. You don't have to go tonight, but it would be nice to see you out of the bed." He gestures towards my mattress, and I catch on slowly to his words. They are all so focused on me eating—it is annoying.

"Don't need the bride to be looking like a homeless wreck, yeah?" I mutter. There is no venom in my words like I intended, though; even my words are tired.

His shoulders bunch together at my comment.

"That has nothing to do with this. So help me, Amelia, get your ass up and eat!" he roars.

He is frustrated, I can see it in his stance, but I know the truth. I lay myself back down and curl into fetal position, not even bothering to fight for the comforter.

"Get up," he states again, but his anger doesn't fuel me. In fact, his anger drains me even more. The heat of it doesn't even burn me. "Amelia," I hear him say as I close my eyes, allowing the sweet sensation of sleep to pull me back down into its dark, unforgiving grasp.

My door slams against the wall, and my eyes snap open at the intrusion.

I look over warily to see Dean standing there with the look of pure irritation on his face. These fucking men never leave me alone.

The sandpaper behind my eyes burns, and I close my eyes again, trying to find relief.

"You are driving me crazy!" he growls. I peek an eye open and look at him.

"This is not about you. Go away," I huff. Why won't they just let me sleep?

"I thought you wanted to be a part of this. Why aren't you going with us tonight?" he asks pleadingly as he crouches by the side of my bed. "Amelia, did something happen that night in the bathroom?"

Huh, way to make some connections there, buddy.

"No," I lie, the falsehood sliding easily off my tongue. I don't want to bring him into the shambles of my mind. It's too twisted in here, too…

"Did those women do or say something to you?"

I shake my head, the movement causing me to wince at the soreness in my neck. No way do I need him to think I need him or anyone else to fight my battles for me; I just want time to process things.

His piercing eyes meet mine with utter seriousness. "Okay, then tell me how to help you, Amelia. Fuck! You need to get out of this bed."

I groan out with irritation. Can't a girl just get some peace around here?

"Why do you want me to go tonight?" I ask him, my voice raspy from sleep. He shrugs.

"I don't know. Maybe because I like your company? We all miss your lovely sense of humor."

I roll my eyes. This man and his dramatics, ugh.

"We've been working relentlessly on why you were targeted. Tonight, we all have a meeting with one of our regulars, and then afterwards Barnette is going to go to The Office and follow up on a couple loose threads."

Right, The Office. He came in here acting like he cared about me not eating, yet he is going to head over to the strip club after he gets his stomach filled up with dinner. Ugh, a fucking pig.

"Have fun." I am clearly annoyed; I can hear it in my tone of voice. I go to roll over, but he stops me by placing a hand on my shoulder.

"Please, Amelia, just small steps, okay? Maybe just a change and take yourself out to the garden get some sunshine?" he pleads.

I look at him, honestly believing his concern. He clearly missed an opportunity to say that I need some vitamin D, ending it with a signature wink. Do I really look that bad? Am I this pathetic?

"Okay Dean, I will try to get up." It is a small offer, but the fog starts to fade away from my mind, and I really don't want him to see me as this pathetic person who can't do basic functions of society.

He smiles at my offer. "Okay! That's great! Are you going to try to come with us tonight?" he beams.

"No," I say instantly, and his smile drops. He looks at my body still laying down in bed.

"Are you going to get up right now?" he asks.

I really don't have the energy for this. I shake my head, too tired to force myself up at this exact moment. He sighs in defeat.

"This is complete bullshit." Derrick's voice startles both of us from the doorway.

"Derrick!" Dean starts to chastise him, but Derrick walks straight into my room through my bathroom doorway, and I can hear him turn the faucets of the bathtub before the water starts running.

His grumpy steps lead him back to my bedroom.

"Get up." It's an order, not a request. My internal hackles want to rise; I can feel a small ember of annoyance as it tries to pull through the sludge of sleep.

"Derrick, you don't need to talk to her like that—" Dean gets silenced as Derrick's hand rises and cuts him off completely.

Shock starts weaving its way through me.

"Get up now." I can still hear the water running in the background, the only sound above the harsh static of the air as his anger pulsates through it.

"No," I say blankly. What part of not right now do they not understand? Derrick marches right over to me and strips me of my comforter. "Hey!" I shout hoarsely, my vocal cords strained from being unused.

"Bro, what are you doing?" Dean cuts in, clearly surprised by his friend's behavior.

Derrick ignores both of us as he leans over me, scoops my ass out of bed, and starts walking towards the bathroom with me cradled in his arms. What in the fuck!

"Put me down, you maniac!" I smack him hard in his chest, but nothing stops him as he takes me straight into the bathroom and then fucking drops me into the tub!

The water surrounds me completely, and I gasp up for air as the hot, steamy suds burns at my skin. I give him the biggest glare I can, and he grabs the soap off the edge and proceeds to squirt it all over me.

I sputter through the lather, "You son of a—"

"That's it, Derrick, get the fuck out!" Dean grabs him and shoves him out the door as I sit there fully clothed in the tub.

"She needs this!" he yells back at Dean.

They continue to scabble until I hear my bedroom door slam shut.

Muffled carpeted steps come across the floor, and I wait to see who will emerge after that scuffle. Dean steps into view, looking unsure of himself, and if I am not mistaken, a little scared.

I was just tossed into the tub by my friend Mickey Mouse. For some reason, that causes a ripple of bubbling laughter to come from my belly up through my chest and out my mouth. I am laughing so hard, and it confuses me as well as delights me to hear something other than nothing.

"So, we're laughing?" A deep set of confusion sets into his face, and I laugh even more at his reaction.

He finally joins in once he realizes it is safe to do so. I giggle until my sides hurt. Dean walks over and shuts the water off as I start hiccupping, the high of my amusement wearing off.

It feels almost foreign to *feel* something. Almost like I haven't laughed in years, but I know in my mind that it has not been that long.

I hate to admit it, but maybe Derrick was right; this was what I needed. A little pinch of water therapy. I smack at the bubbles surrounding me and sheepishly look up to Dean.

"I must have really stunk for him to get involved." I try to make a joke of it, but I know that the whole thing was not a joking matter.

"Listen, Amelia, you worried the hell out of all of us. I get you're settling, and a lot has happened over the last few days, but whatever that was, you cannot do that again." His words come out a little rough, but the sadness in his eyes tells me he's not mad at me.

"I'm sorry I worried you, Dean," I answer honestly. I never wanted to upset anyone; I just wanted to sleep. I wipe at the loose tears that break free from my tear ducts and let out a sigh.

"You are fine. Don't be sorry, just be okay."

He has no idea how difficult that small request is, how heavy it is on my already fragile mind, but I swallow down the pain of it and give him a small smile and nod my head anyway.

"Now, how about you get out of here so I can have a proper bath?" I suggest.

His eyes widen for a moment as I can see the different

emotions roll through his face. Finally, it lands on his usual cocky expression, and he gives me a half-grin.

"Sure, darling, enjoy your bath." He gives me a playful wink before leaving me to bathe alone.

The silence of the space surrounds me, and I fill the sound with small splashes of water as I slowly strip out of my soaking-wet clothing. I fill the loofah full of body wash and start scrubbing my body neck-down. I go through the motions of washing, shaving, and exfoliating until I can feel myself break through all the grime I have been sitting in for the last few days.

I finally pull myself out and wrap myself in the towel as I wipe the steam off of the mirror. Staring at my reflection, I can see the hollowness underneath my eyes. They don't even look hazel right now, just a deep murky brown. This right here is who Barnette wants to be married to.

My thoughts reflect back to Barnette as I try to worm my way into his head on what he thinks he wants. Then Dean's words register through my mind.

After dinner, he is headed to The Office, and if there was one useful bit of information I learned at that cocktail party, it was that The Office was actually the strip club he often frequented. That dickhead can't even remain faithful to the woman he is pushing to marry him.

I almost scoff. As if I am just an accessory to his arm, but I am no arm candy. No, sir. I stare back at myself in the mirror as I feel a kernel of purpose. I am more than just his arm candy.

I am me. I am whatever I want to be.

He may be able to walk around here and play or fuck whoever he wants, but I too can fuck whoever I want.

There were no rules in that contract from what I understand stating we had to be monogamous.

A wave of dizziness suddenly spins me off my axis, and I

grip the counter as I try to keep myself upright. Damn it, maybe I *should* eat.

I slowly walk over to the dresser and peer at the assortment of old and new food. I look to see what the freshest looking bit of food is, which is pancakes and cold eggs. It will work. I take a chunk out of the pancake and finish it in a couple of bites, grabbing the warm cup of orange juice and chugging the glass down. My stomach feels both relief and pain as it fills up.

Two rapt knocks on my door shake me from my little spell. The door opens, and I expect it to be Dean but am surprised to find Marisol coming in with a fresh set of sheets in her arms.

"Oh, Mija! It is so good to see you out of bed, dear." She gives me a quick smile before she makes quick work of my sheets and comforter.

I guess me standing in just my towel was not much of a surprise for her, but her Spanish nickname for me brings me deep comfort. I don't know why it does, but it brings a sense of ease to me.

"I can change my sheets." Embarrassment floods through me as I can only imagine how they must smell. I hold my towel tightly in my grip as I try to figure out what to do with myself.

"No need. You just get yourself dressed—try a summer dress, then go out to the garden," she suggests.

"A summer dress?" I question, raising a brow.

She stops her tackle against my bed and comes over to me. I feel awkward standing there with only a small piece of cloth between the two of us.

"My mama, God rest her soul." She makes the sign of the cross over her, and for some reason I just see her back straighten with purpose. "My mama always taught me that if I ever woke up feeling despair or deep, gutted sadness, or if I look into that mirror and don't feel confident, I should march into my wardrobe, place on a cute summer dress, do my hair, and then go do something I love.

"It is emboldening to make yourself feel better, but it's also important to bring in that feeling to the inside of you and lighten your soul."

In her sweet way, she just gave me advice on how to become confident. I smile at her as she gives me her motherly advice.

"You are a beautiful young woman, and I wish I could show you how true your beauty is. Even though your manners are a little rough around the edges, you do have a good soul."

She pats my chest gently where my heart is, right above the towel line. Surprisingly, I no longer feel embarrassed.

"I will find a summer dress," I tell her.

"Your soul was sick for a few days, but some sun will do you good." With that parting, she continues making my bed, and I take her advice, searching my closet for a summer dress.

By the time I emerge with a cute little white dress with baby blue flowers all over it, Marisol is out of the room, and I have a freshly clean and made bed.

I look longingly at the bed, wanting to crawl back between the sheets with everything inside of me, but I remind myself I need to go to the garden. I am going to go to the garden.

Time to drag myself out of my own personal mental hell.

CHAPTER 14

The Blood of My Enemies

Barnette

"YOU DID WHAT?" I stare dumbfounded at Derrick, who stands in front of me. Both he and Dean came barreling into my office to basically tattle on each other. Ugh.

Derrick shrugs. "She needed a little sober-me-up moment, so I just scooped her up out of bed and gently deposited her into the bathtub."

Dean nearly pulls his hair out of his head. "He threw her into the bathtub with scalding-hot water!"

I scratch my head as I try to imagine the whole scene that went down.

"It was lukewarm," Derricks states evenly.

"Both of you, knock it off!" Frustration riddles my bones. "Did you burn her?" I just want the facts.

"No." Okay, good.

"Did she cry?" I pray to whatever God he did not make her cry.

"Actually, she umm," Dean butts in. I look at him, almost

dreading what he has to say, "She actually laughed. Like full-on belly laughed."

"Oh really?" Derrick seems surprised but also too damn smug.

I, however, am in utter shock. Huh, that girl continues to surprise me.

"Why?" I ask, furrowing my brows.

Dean hesitates. "Well, I don't know. I didn't ask her why, Barnette, I just let her work through it."

I shrug and kind of chuckle at the thought of her fully clothed, laughing in the bathtub.

"Does she seem better?" I have been stressing about her for days, wishing and hoping she would snap out of whatever funk she was in.

"Well, I did not stick around, dude. I left once her laughing subsided and gave her time to have an actual bath." I could appreciate that; I just wish I knew more about her current state of mind.

"I am just impressed my plan actually worked," Derrick announces with a smirk.

"No, you are *lucky* that it worked!" I point out.

It could have gone completely sideways if she would have been pissed off by his actions. Honestly, to see her fire again is all I want.

I chuckle. "I am sure her little temper would have amused us all," I remark.

Dean laughs as if reading my mind. I roll my eyes at him.

"Okay, so any leads now that we can get all of our focus back on track?" Derrick jumps in, ready to get back to business.

I appreciate his solid need to keep track of work, especially when I've been wearing down the rug in the hall outside of Amelia's room with my pacing.

There was not a very proud moment when I almost went in there and scooped her up myself to place her in bed beside me to keep an eye on her. I was smart enough to talk myself out of the move.

I explain, "Sean wants me to meet up with him at The Office tonight, so I'm hoping that is the lead we needed."

Both men nod their heads in agreement.

"I also tried to follow up with Ivan and I still haven't heard back from him," I continue. "I am convinced he went off grid, which is actually the first smart thing he has done." He has sweet karma waiting for him the second I find out his reason why.

"Okay, okay, I am getting frustrated that we still have no grounds, but I guess we have to take small wins along with all of the chaos," Dean, always the one to look at the bright side of things, answers honestly.

"Derrick, how about you and I head out to Parkens and meet up with Pedro to see if they caught wind of anything?" I suggest.

I stack all the papers on my desk together and shove them into my drawer. Exhaustion washes over me, and I have to pinch the bridge of my nose to wake myself up.

"We will stop for some coffee on the way, dude. Tonight I am sure we will *all* get a good night's rest." Derrick heads out, probably heading to go get the keys and meet me out front.

I am full of relief to hear about the coffee; I have been drinking it like water lately. I just need more answers.

"You good, bro?" Dean checks in with me. He is the biggest little brother I've ever had.

I nod. "I will be; I just need more answers, and I'm looking forward to sleep tonight."

"Everything is going to be okay. You know that, right?" he asks me.

Somewhere deep in my gut, I know everything will be fine, but right now it's a bit too chaotic. I nod in agreement for his sake more than my own, hoping he doesn't push further.

"Well, I guess I'll keep this lovely place settled as you two do your research." He is the peacekeeper I need here right now.

I chuckle, "Yeah, I figured that if I left Derrick here, she may have a delayed response to his little stunt and shiv him while we were gone, so for his safety I am going to take him with me." I laugh as I picture her little temper going full-blown crazy on his ass.

I am still in utter shuck that he dumped her in the fucking tub! Dean laughs in agreement as he turns to exit my office.

"Have fun at the club tonight!" He hollers back to me. I growl in response.

"Fuck you, too!" I really don't enjoy that place as much as everyone thinks I do, but I am going to do what it takes to figure out what the hell is going on.

Okay, time to focus. Let's go find some answers.

<hr>

I stare at the man I have hanging from the rope and hook in the corner of the dark room. The shadows looming over him suck him into a deep, dark void which is what influenced this place's name in the first place.

People know they don't want to go down into the shadows with me, because there will be nothing but pain and misery if you don't answer my questions.

I expect answers today.

I take the knife with the curved blade and walk casually up to Dimitri, and his hooded eyes just trail along with my feet.

Surprisingly, even though he's already dripping blood onto the floor, he still has not shown an ounce of fear after he has been beaten and left here to hang for three hours to contemplate his next choice.

The fact of the matter is, Ivan is still in his stupid hiding hole, but Dimitri being out trying to scope out one of my warehouses tells me he's scared.

But he still has a goal of getting to Amelia.

And Amelia isn't theirs to have.

I bring the curved silver blade up to his exposed stomach, his long-sleeved silver shirt ruined and flapping open, drenched in blood and sweat. It is a pity really; it was a nice shirt.

Dimitri eyes the blade and then me. He starts to protest through the gag in his mouth, and it brings such sweet relief to my ears.

I usually stay back on these types of jobs and let Derrick handle it, but not today. This is personal.

"Have you had time to think about your cooperation?" I ask, smug and confident that he is about to spill all their secrets.

I expected him to give push back, of course. A lesser man would, but he held out long enough to show where his allegiance lies. Too bad for him, it's on the wrong side.

I push the blade in as I swipe across his bottom hip up to his rib, and he growls in pain from the knife cutting skin. He nods, and a moment later, I yank out the gag from his mouth. He breathes out long and heavily through the pain.

"Ivan wants Amelia to reach Mr. Al Shaer."

So, this *is* connected, I had a feeling this was the direction we were going.

I bring the blade to the other side of his hip and hover as I wait for him to continue.

"And… and… and he was going to take her and demand that he gives him a million dollars, or he was going to kill her," he blubbers out quickly, almost incoherently.

What an idiot. Ivan was going to kill her for a get-rich-quick scheme, not even thinking about the long-term consequences.

"You all are a bunch of fucking idiots!" I release some of the pent-up anger I had brewing like a storm inside of me. All of them make me sick, all of them piss me off, and all of them can fucking die. "How did you discover Amelia's relation?" I demand, fuming more by the second.

"By… by your connection," he stammers. I stop my hand from hovering over his skin again and stare hard at him. "We figured something had to give on you wanting to marry her. We dug around for some intel on her and discovered she was nothing and nobody, which gave Ivan a bunch of red flags."

So, this is on me? I caused the danger for her.

"You could not accept I simply wanted a wife?" I snap, my lip twisting in a sneer.

This makes Dimitri laugh, and it curls the insides of my stomach.

"Not with you, Barnette. We all know how fucking power-hungry you are! There's a reason for everything you do. What was going to make this any fucking different?" His smug smile enrages me.

I lash out with my fist before even thinking. He grins as he spits out blood.

"Aaah, sore spot for that one, huh? Tell me, Barnette, does she fuck like a good little whore?"

I lash out again as red takes over my vision. Fuck him, fuck Ivan, fuck how they talk about Amelia. The door behind me opens as Derrick comes striding in and pulls me off of him. It isn't until he bends down to retrieve the knife off of the ground that I realize I dropped it.

"Empty words from a sorry ass hanging by rope. He's a dead man talking." Derrick grounds me back from the anger that had control over me.

Amelia's life is in trouble because of me, and the guilt that comes with that realization almost knocks me on my ass. What the fuck am I doing?

"It seems like someone actually cares about that sorry excuse of a girl. I am sure her daddy issues make her a fun ride. Ivan was wanting to take her for a test drive before calling her daddy up—" The smug asshole doesn't get to finish his stupid ass rant before Derrick takes the knife and slams it into his gut.

Blood starts spurting out of Dimitri's mouth as shock keeps his eyes wide open. Those terrified eyes stare right at me.

"Enjoy hell. I will see you soon," Derrick whispers into his ear as the signs of life fades from his eyes and he completely slumps over.

"Empty words, you were saying?" I comment to Derrick, trying to play his words back to him.

He still holds onto Dimitri, and the handle of the knife is frozen in his hand. Finally, after a few moments of silence, he pulls away from the body, bringing the knife with him and wiping the blade of it on his pants to get the blood off.

"Some things are inexcusable." Thick emotion clogs through his words, and I know rape is an absolute zero tolerance trigger for him.

Me, too. He is lucky he was quicker to react than me, sneaky little bastard. I, however, would have made Dimitri's death much, much slower.

"Well, we know what Ivan's crew is up to then, so we have

some answers," I state, reflecting over the information I found out. It is out there now who her dad is, and this is going to blow up.

"You didn't want to enlighten us on your motives with her?" He directs the question at me with both curiosity and anger in his tone, but I know what lies underneath it—hurt.

"Look, I was going to let you in, I swear. Both you and Dean were going to know what the plans were once I started executing them. I just want us set for life and our families and our kids to be set for life. We deserve it, Derrick! We have earned it!"

The passion of my words barrels through me. That is all I have ever wanted was to make sure my brothers and I wanted for nothing, that we could watch out and protect those who needed it and stop those who were too greedy. Those who preyed on the weaker ones.

"What about Amelia? Does she even know about any of this? Does she know she has a father or that the reason why her life is about to be even more fucked up is because you exposed her life?"

I stand dumbfounded by his words. To be honest, from the get-go, I never considered her thoughts on this; I have been putting me first this whole time.

"Listen, I love you, brother. I do. But sometimes I wish you would realize that even though in the grand scheme of things you have our best interests at heart, and you mean well, your actions and words can also be selfish and damaging along the way. That's all I am saying. You should have trusted us, and you have to tell Amelia what's going on. Doesn't she deserve that?" Derrick challenges.

She does deserve it.

"Fuck, I know I've got to tell her. But how am I supposed to protect her from this if she doesn't even let me in? She doesn't trust me!" Frustrations flows heavily down to my fingertips, and I open and close my fists to try to relieve the pressure.

"Do you even care about her? Like, do you actually see yourself one day maybe letting her inside your inner walls and loving her?" he asks.

The harsh reality is she already punctured my steel wall I had in place to protect myself. It must be obvious; I thought it was.

"I do care about her. I care about her safety, her happiness—she frustrates me to no end over all her bitterness!" I try to keep my tone down as my voice vibrates off the empty walls of the small room.

Derrick sighs, "Okay then, talk with her. Explain to her what the hell is going on before things get worse and just be straight with us going forward, okay?" He straightens himself up as he demands my acceptance of this.

"Okay, okay, I will. I swear."

I don't break promises with my brothers, and this will be one I will take to the grave. We stand there staring at each other until Derrick's face finally fractures into a small grin.

"So, motherfucking Al Shaer huh?" He starts heading towards the door, and I follow.

"I still can't wrap my head how Ramona got her hooks into him." Why did he even look twice her way? "Well, I guess since we're going to the tippy fucking top, let's fucking do this, brother, chaos and all." I chuckle as we close the door behind us.

Yes, chaos and all, let the shitshow begin.

CHAPTER 15

Amelia

"WELL, don't you look all innocent and pleasant out here in the garden?" Dean's voice surprises from behind as I sit there feeling silly in my little summer dress out here on a blanket.

"I am both innocent and pleasant, thank you," I retort.

Somehow, Marisol was correct about needing some sun; I am feeling more and more like myself the longer I sit here.

I sip from my little dainty teacup filled with passion tea one of the maids was sent out to give me, and I feel the warmth bubble down to my belly. I feel so warm and cozy.

"You look beautiful," he responds, and I take a peek up at him, eyeing him suspiciously.

"What do you want?" I ask.

His goofy ass plops down next to me, and he takes my teacup out of my hand before gulping down an unforgiving amount.

"How dare you!" This butthole.

"What?" he chuckles. "Are you too above me to share some of your tea?"

"I am above no one," I answer with brute honesty.

He stares at me inquisitively but doesn't push the matter. We sit in comfortable silence next to each other, soaking up the late afternoon sun.

"You are worth much, much more than you will ever realize," he says softly.

"What do you want with me, Dean?" I just want to make sure this isn't all just another chess move. I can't handle being played even more.

"I want to protect you and keep you safe, Amelia."

I lean in close to him, so close I thought he would pull back, but he doesn't. My lips gently graze his as I reiterate my question.

"What do you *want* with *me*?"

Surprise filters through his eyes.

"There, um, well," he stutters, and it brings me great amusement, "there is a lot I want to do with you, Amelia."

I can hear the strain in his voice as the truth wins out against his petty cover answers.

"I want you to be happy and carefree. I also want you to myself as I kiss you and embrace you in my bed." Butterflies are flying through my belly, and finally I can feel excitement fill me. "Why do you ask?" he questions me.

"I feel like I have been a walking zombie for years, Dean, and I just want to *feel*," I respond. I want to feel everything. "I also know that all your flirtatious whims aren't without intention. I know you are attracted to me."

I feel a bit too cocky and remind myself to tone it down, even though it is a high I am riding. I love the way he's looking at me.

"You want me to make you feel alive?" he asks with a smug smirk on his lips.

I chuckle slightly as his ego inflates. "You make me laugh and smile, and you are kind to me when others are not. I have absolutely no fear when I am with you, and that brings me great comfort."

His smile turns soft as he eyes me.

"But yes, I want to feel alive again, Dean." I am playing a dangerous game, I know I am, but I feel no shame in it.

Dean sits silent for a bit as his mind seems to be running nonstop. He finally clears his throat. "Well, little miss, I've got some things I need to follow up on. How about you enjoy the sun some more, and we can catch up later?" he offers.

He is a good man. I give him a smile of acceptance and wave him goodbye as he jumps up and walks away. I will see him later. This high is contagious, and I yearn for more.

His words play in my mind. Do I want him to make me feel alive? I yearn to feel all the good feelings that come to mind with that implied question.

A small war rummages through my mind with the what ifs, and the devil on my shoulder wins.

Nerves fill me as I head up to Dean's apartment. My small white dress slightly caresses my thighs as I walk up to his door. Nerves are dancing everywhere in my stomach, and I want nothing more than for him to yank me inside of his home and hold true to his words from before.

Barnette is away shooting his shot or whatever at the damn strip club, so why can't I have my own fun while he is gone too?

I swallow hard and muster up all the bravado I can to gently knock on his front door. The dark stained wood feels hot under my skin, but I realize it is my own sinful intentions making me feel that way. The door gives way after a moment, and there he stands.

Dean's eyes widen slightly in surprise, and his mouth drops open as he scans me from head to toe.

Maybe he didn't see me fully over, or now he knows my intentions while I stand here at his door. I don't have much to offer, but he doesn't seem to notice.

He shakes his head slightly, causing the hair to go slightly over his eyes, the disheveled look causing me to tighten my thighs together. He wears no shirt, and a pair of dark gray sweatpants lay low on his hips. His muscles are defined and delicious, making me bite my lower lip, which draws his attention immediately.

I eye the wolf he has over his left pectoral; it looks to the side towards the right while trees and a storm surround it up into his shoulder and down half of his upper arm. It's beautiful work.

I gaze back into his eyes and can see his internal battle flicker through them, but I made it easy for him. I showed up at his front step.

I made the move; this next one is on him.

"Do that again," Dean whispers to me, his eyes trained onto my lips.

I smirk a little as I start to bite my lip again. Suddenly, I am yanked into his house and shoved up against the wall.

My dress slides up my thighs, exposing all of me to him. The only thing between us is his sweatpants, but he doesn't know that yet. I wrap my legs around him immediately as he grips my ass with the palm of his hands and his lips find me.

I drink him in, the way his lips curve against my own—the way his tongue dances with mine.

It feels hot and sexy while also dirty and all-consuming. He pushes up against me, and I can feel his hard-on push against me; it causes me to moan into his mouth.

Dean tries to pull his mouth away, but I grab his face to hold him steady, desperate for more.

"You already know Barnette is off at the club doing his thing. We both know the truth in that. I made sure no one followed me or witnessed me heading up this way. It's just you and me, Dean, please don't stop this." I breathe the words into his mouth in a rush, pleading for him not to turn me away.

Please don't send me off, please don't stop what was meant to happen all along. He hangs his head against mine and groans as he pushes his hips against me.

"Deaaaaaan," I moan, craving more friction.

His head snaps up at me, and I can see his resolve break. He pushes his hips against me once more, grinding his dick against me.

"Deaaaan," I moan again, anxious to feel more of him, *needing* more of him.

"Fuck me," he mutters out as the war in his eyes plays on full display in front of me. A moment later he slams his lips back against mine and carries me off into the bedroom.

His kisses are rough and hungry, as if I am the first drop of water from a walk in the desert. I greedily match him. A door is kicked open, and he drops me onto the bed.

My dress flares up around my waist, and his gaze latches onto my exposed, very naked, pussy. His hand goes through his hair, and he groans as he looks from my eyes to my pussy. I give him a smirk.

"You are going to be the death of me," he mutters.

I nod my head as he shoves and kicks off his pants, immediately climbing up and over me.

"I will die by your hand any day baby," he moans.

My heart melts at the sincerity of his tone and his mouth greedily devours mine again. Emotions sing through me, and it feels *good* to vibrate with life.

I let my hands roam over every square inch of him, the feel of his silky-smooth skin, the texture of his muscles.

He starts kissing my chin, then my neck. Sucking hard enough to leave a hickey. I grip his hair in my hand and give it a small tug. I feel his smile against my collar bone and use the moment to shove him over onto his back.

A small *"oof"* escapes him, and he looks at me with amusement in his eyes as I straddle him and start backing down on my knees until his dick is standing straight up right in front of me.

I didn't expect him to be as girthy as he is; I knew he was long by the feel of him against me, but he has both girth and length on his side.

I lick my lips at the challenge; I am not going to back down. I may choke, but my enthusiasm will make up for it. I spread out my knees, getting myself comfortable on top of him, and lean forward over him. I let a trail of spit leave my mouth and skim down the head of his penis and down the right side.

I lean forward and lick him from base to tip, then eagerly shove him into my mouth as far as I can go, earning a moan from him that almost makes me smile.

I push down until I feel my gag reflex wanting to introduce itself, then continue with the pace. I slide him in and out of my mouth, letting my hand gently cup and massage his balls as I get into a quicker rhythm. I hear another moan escape him, and the confidence boost that fills me with is delicious. I want to hear *more*.

I hollow out my cheeks, suctioning him, and Dean's hips buck up unexpectedly, causing me to choke as he hits the back of my throat.

I go to pull away when he suddenly grabs my hair in a tight fist and starts slamming his dick in my throat. I choke but don't let it stop me. Tears start pouring out of my eyes as thick saliva drips down my chin, and I hold onto his hips, allowing him to take full control of the moment and focus on not choking too hard.

I breathe through my nose, and he lets out another moan. The fire that ignites between my legs has me letting him go and slipping my fingers between my legs. He notices the movement, though, and pulls my face away from his dick.

Tears and saliva leave streaks on my face as a strand of spit goes from my lips to the head of his dick, thick with precum.

"I can cum at the sight of you right now," he groans, cursing under his breath.

I gently wipe the strand connecting us, and he leans into a sitting position, pulling me up and onto his lap. I feel him hot and slick against me as I balance my knees beside his waist.

I let myself lean into him, letting his dick slide against me. I want more of him, I want to feel him inside of me.

"Also, the sound of you choking on my dick? That's hot." I blush as he puts me on blast. I don't understand the glamour of the choke noise, but if he likes it then so be it.

He pushes me back, then leans in and licks around my nipples, drawing in my left one hard, causing me to yelp at the sudden sharp pain, then he releases and licks it again. He goes to my right nipple and does the same. Right as he draws in my nipple, his finger enters into me from behind.

I am soaked, and the sudden intrusion of his finger gives me some much-needed friction, causing me to mewl out immediately.

He continues fingering me and playing with my nipples, and I start gliding myself up and down as he puts in a second finger.

God, it feels so good to be kissed and sucked. His hand starts to trail up and around my neck, and he grips my throat tightly.

The sensation of losing my breath overtakes me, and I feel a slight wave of dizziness as he continues to pump his fingers in me and cut off my air. It is both frightening and arousing at the same time.

He eventually relaxes his grip, and I inhale a breath as small black dots pepper my sight, but I can feel the hot drip of my arousal soaking his hand.

I want to be choked again; I crave it. He pulls his fingers out, and I miss them instantaneously. He smirks at me as he shoves me onto my back and opens my legs up. He stares down at me hungrily, and I can feel the blush sweep over my cheeks, neck, and chest.

"I cannot wait to taste you." He lowers himself down to the end of the bed, grabs my hips, and yanks me where I align perfectly with his mouth.

Dean isn't gentle or soft about the way he starts to eat me out. His tongue spears me greedily as his thumb circles around my clit. My hips buck at the sensation he is causing from my clit; I never knew such a feeling existed.

I look down to see his eyes watching my reactions. My blush is already on full display. His mouth moves over my clit and flicks it gently with his tongue, causing my hips to grind into his face. He keeps flicking and licking it until suddenly, he suctions it hard into his mouth, making me cry out in pleasure.

He keeps up the motion of sucking and flicking, and my body starts moving with the sensation. Tingles spread from up into my stomach, and my legs begin to twitch. More moans escape me as I feel every nerve ending in my body shoot out with pure ecstasy, and then I feel the damn urge to pee. Fuck. Why now?

"Dean, wait," I gasp, trying to warn him. "Dean—" I push against his head as the sensation starts overtaking me.

Fuck! Then I feel the release. It feels so delicious. My entire body collapses from the impact of it.

"Holy shit, Amelia, you just squirted!" Shock laces his tone, and I look down to see drips coming off of the hairs on his chin. He pulls at his chin hair and grins up at me. "That is hot as fuck!" he growls out and climbs up my body.

"I don't understand what you mean by squirted." I don't know what he means by that, like maybe an orgasm?

"Not every woman can squirt. It is, I guess, like a type of orgasm where a lot of fluid comes out at once. All I know is that it's hot, and I'm glad you are enjoying yourself, but it is taking everything I have to not attack and fuck the living shit out of you."

His brows furrow as he becomes serious again, and the look of lust fills his eyes as he settles over me, using his knee to open my legs up even more.

This is finally going to happen! Fuck!

He aligns himself towards me, and I can see the muscles in his shoulders and arms go rigid as they try to keep himself still. Thoughts swarm his eyes, but the grin on his face tells me they aren't bad thoughts.

"On second thought, Amelia, I *am* going to fuck the shit out of you, and I mean every second of it."

Right as he states it, he leans back, grabs my thighs, flips me over to where I am suddenly on my stomach, lifts up my hips to where I am in doggy style, and slides into me without any hesitation.

I moan as I adjust to his sudden length. He grips my hips so tight there will be no way I won't have any bruises when he's finished.

He pounds into me over and over again, not relenting for a single moment. My moans come out incoherently as I cannot control anything I am trying to say or even how I sound. The sensation is intoxicating and overwhelming.

Every nerve in my body is electrified, and I feel hot and sexy. This build is happening in the pit of my stomach, and then I hear the most delicious sound come from behind me. Dean moans out as he leans forward and grips my neck, anchoring me as he pounds into me.

Between that sound and the sensation of losing my breath, my climax hits me so hard my arms give out and the top half of my body lays there as my legs convulse from the waves of pleasure that barrel through me.

My throaty moan rings out and not long after, he releases my neck as air rushes into my lungs. I hear Dean grunt and then slow down his pace as he finishes himself.

He starts to pull off slowly but smacks my ass hard enough to leave a handprint, and I yelp out in surprise, still trying to catch my breath.

"That's my girl," he chuckles as my body deflates completely, laying down beside me and pulling me to his warm, sweaty body. Both of us are breathing hard and rough.

A few minutes pass as we just enjoy each other's presence. It is Dean who finally breaks the silence.

"I want to have the whole weekend away to learn what you like." His fingers trail down my arm as he watches them intently, gently tracing my skin. "What makes your eyes close, what causes your breath to come out in pants…" His finger comes up around my other arm as he begins to face me again. "What makes you cum…" He gently trails my collar bone as he leans so close, I can feel his breath caress my lips. "What causes you to moan my name."

His fingers trail down between my breasts, and my body trembles at the thought of what he can do to make me moan his name.

My cheeks redden at how responsive my body is to his simple touches.

He is so cocky and confident in his words. He lays back as he grips me and pulls me flush against him. I can feel his warmth seep into me.

"I want to figure you out and become an expert in all things Amelia," he murmurs.

My thighs are wet, and my mind tries to come to terms with how excited I am feeling, at how much I already want him again.

He continues, "You don't like big shows, and you don't need diamonds or Gucci bags to win you over. You want safety and consistency—you want simple and beautiful. You are exquisite, but your taste doesn't match. You are exactly like obsidian."

My eyes that I didn't realize were closed as they listened to his words snap open, and I turn to look up at him.

He whispers, "I get it now—your fascination with obsidian. It seems so rough and sharp, but it is textured and strong. When polished, it is rich in beauty, more worthy than any man-made jewel beside it. A dark, gorgeous wonder that stands out."

He pushes the hair out of my face and grips the back of my neck as he leans into my ear.

"You feel like an outcast among the world, but you're the queen that stands out among the masses," Dean murmurs into my ear all slow and sexy.

My lower stomach tightens at the feel of him, and I feel another tremble take over my body. He chuckles as he leans back onto his side, positioning me along him and placing his arm behind his head to prop himself up.

Guilt filters through me as I greedily inhale his words and try to implant them into my mind. The way this man speaks to and about me awakens a piece of me that has always been dead.

I look at Dean as he lays there with his eyes closed, but a smile graces his lips.

Am I a horrible person for coming to him? Did I fuck up sleeping with Dean out of pure selfishness? We all have needs, we all have desires, and though I love how he talks about me and how he treats me, did I just use this sweet soul beside me?

CHAPTER 16

Secrets Burn with Curiosity

Dean

WE SIT on the couch opposite each other with our legs tangled up underneath the covers. Heart of Dixie or some chick show like that is playing on the screen and has Amelia's undivided attention.

I tried with every ounce of willpower to deny her when she showed up at my door, but I am only capable of so much restraint.

Still, how do I face Barnette when he comes back from his own moment of guilty pleasure and fun and admit to fucking his fiancée? Damn it.

This woman is anything but easy.

She tests every sense of control I have, and I have wanted her from the moment I locked eyes onto her.

Everything about her is so damn intriguing, and I am still pissed off that Barnette wasn't upfront and honest with the whole thing about her from the start. It would have been nice to have a little more time to gather more information about her and her circle before retrieving her.

I can see why he wants her to be his wife, but all I can think about is that genuine smile on her face after I twirled her, and I want nothing more than for her to be mine, too. A headache forms between my eyes at the stress of all this.

Her toes wiggle, causing me to bring my attention back to her. I didn't realize I was staring off into space.

"Everything okay, Dean?" she asks softly. I can see the concern filling her eyes; her brows are furrowed slightly as she stares at me, waiting for an answer.

"Do you..." I hesitate in asking this, but the only way to gain intel is by getting some intel. Still, I am at war with all of this and how there are so many holes in her life. "Do you know anything about your dad?"

Her eyebrows hitch together tightly, and her lips scrunch up in a slight scowl as the direction of the conversation.

"No, I don't know who he is. Mom says it was a drunken night and she can't remember much. It must be one of the dealers she brought through a few times." She shrugs her shoulders as if that isn't one of the most depressing statements in itself.

Her casual tone pisses me off, but I'm not mad at her but rather, her mother. That woman has some harsh karma coming her way, and it may be from me.

Taking a deep breath, I try another approach. "Do you and your sister have the same dad?"

At the mention of her sister, Amelia tenses up almost immediately. I can see her sharp steel mask she wears over her face when she doesn't want anyone to know what she is feeling snap into place.

"No. We don't." Cold and monotone. Why the sudden change in reaction to Andrea's dad?

"Don't like her dad?" Why the sudden stiff shoulder is what I really want to ask.

"No, I don't. And I don't talk about him either," she shuts down the subject. Okay then, noted. Now I need to investigate who the fuck he is, so I know why he bothers her so much.

I can feel rage start burning at the back of my neck at the thought of him hurting her when he was around, doing something to cause her so much pain that the mention of his mere existence pisses her off. I'm going to find that fucker.

"Don't go searching about him either. He is probably dead from an overdose in a ditch somewhere, so just leave it alone. He is not important. He is a nobody," Amelia insists.

I nod my head to please her, but that isn't stifling my next project. I will fill in the gaping holes in her folder, regardless of how much time it takes.

She props herself up and places herself in a sitting position on the couch. Her entire body is rigid, and her even gaze stares hard into my own.

"Do. Not. Look. Into. Him." She is cold and callous.

I try not to swallow too loudly, and my dick twitches at the excitement that her anger gives me.

I don't think she has ever looked this angry. Well, at least not directed at me. Who the hell is this guy and what did he do to make her react this way? My stomach bottoms out at the thought of it.

"Okay, okay, baby." I pull her back to me gently. Her body is shaking, and I feel like shit for bringing the topic up. "I am so sorry for whatever happened."

She doesn't respond to me, which is also not like her. I rub her back in gentle strokes, trying to soothe whatever turmoil is running through her mind. She sits up abruptly.

Amelia jumps up out of bed and starts looking around the floor. Her face is set in stone.

"Where are you going?" I ask, startled by her sudden outburst.

"I am leaving. You are fine." Her hand juts out, signaling for me to stop as I start to get off the bed. I freeze when I look at her face.

Her eyes look haunted. The only time I have seen that look is from the men who have experienced something life-altering, like the men from the Army, or Derrick after a particularly harsh mission. I feel sick.

She finishes slamming on her boots and heads to leave.

"Please stay. I really am sorry." I try to reach for her, while also respecting her request.

Why the hell did I have to ask? What the fuck is she so haunted by? She turns and looks at me, holding the door to the room in her palm and taking a ragged breath.

"It isn't you. Don't apologize, please. I just need to go. Okay?" she stammers.

I give her a slight nod and listen as she nearly runs through the living room and slams the front door behind her.

What the fuck just happened?

CHAPTER 17

Guilt Isn't Your Friend

Amelia

Two Days Later

I HAD AN ABSOLUTELY amazing time with Dean, but I cannot shake what I did. I cannot tell if my intentions were not pure.

What kind of person am I if I become like the people I loathe? I don't want to use people or hurt people.

Barnette hasn't been around for a couple days, and I wonder if I did something wrong. Of course I did something wrong! I fucking slept with Dean when I am supposed to be engaged to Barnette.

Yes, he may be doing shady shit, but that doesn't change who I am as a person, and I still have moral standards. Or maybe I shouldn't care at all. Maybe I should slap a smile on my face and tell him what I did.

Then there is the little fact he was asking about Andrea's dad, and I doubt me telling him to not look into him has deterred him.

"Everything okay with you?" Barnette asks me from across the breakfast table.

I push around at the eggs on my plate and try to shove past the nausea that is holding an iron grip on my belly. No, nothing is okay—none of this is okay. I can't think straight.

I reflect back to the last couple days, and I feel the thick regret coating my skin like oil.

I dressed up and soaked in the sun like Marisol suggested, but all it did was lead me to some off-the-wall choices. I glance shyly at Barnette, feeling the guilt eat away at me even though there is no reason I should feel it this thickly.

"I'm not hungry is all," is all I am able to honestly reply.

"Tell me what's on your mind," he demands.

Damn, has this man ever heard about asking kindly? My defensive hackles try to rise through the sludge, but I don't even have the energy to keep them standing.

I just want to go to sleep. I push away from the table and start to head back to my room.

I didn't even hear Barnette get up from the table. Next thing I know I am shoved up against the wall and Barnette has his hand wrapped around my throat.

"Why do you insist on making things so difficult?" he seethes. His eyes are dark and hooded as they stare down at me.

"I am not being difficult, Barnette," I respond, my voice monotone and lifeless.

You'd think I would be scared with him holding me like this, but a very stupid, defiant part of me actually likes seeing him come undone. I am not even trying.

"Why won't you just be a good little puppet and do what you are supposed to?" He looks between my eyes and tightens his grip slightly, causing my chin to rise up higher towards him.

I don't respond as I follow his gaze. What am I supposed to say to that? He knows I never been one to obey, but I am also at his mercy, especially now that I completely fucked up.

He licks his lips, and I zero in on the movement. His hot breaths warm my face, and my body reacts automatically to it. My hips tilt forward, brushing against him, and he takes one small step closer into my space, his body right up against mine.

He growls, "You play a dangerous game."

"A game isn't what I'm after." Guilt still seizes my insides, but now butterflies join in on the confusing mess.

"Then what are you after?" He focuses on my lips, waiting for my response.

The truth is I don't know what I'm after. Life here has not been what I expected; my whole entire life has never gone the way I imagined it would.

It was never an option to sit there and plan what I wanted; I never get a damn choice that is fair.

"Loss for words, puppet?" he taunts, narrowing his eyes.

"My name is Amelia. You would do good to learn it, asshat," I snap. My attitude is the only thing I can be in control of, and I let that little fire kindle into my temper.

He pushes his grip into my neck, straightening my head against the wall forcefully.

"Your wicked little temper is something I enjoy pulling out of you." My little fire gets doused with his cold words. He knows exactly what he is doing—taking my control away.

"Fuck you, Barnette," I say with venom.

"Please do." Lust fills his words as his nostrils flare.

"As if!" I respond as my words backfire on me.

"What did I say at the beginning, Amelia?" He reminds me of his words from a few weeks ago, and my stomach bottoms out thinking about it.

I try to take a slow deep breath as I keep my body still underneath the weight of his gaze. Barnette wants my obedience *and* my pussy.

"Well, you didn't give me a chance to duck before hitting me in the face with the table, nor did I get a chance to run out of there when I was knocked the hell out from said table that I could have ducked from. As for fucking, I haven't heard you say the words, Barnette."

A small smirk graces the sides of his lips, and it almost makes him look innocent- almost.

"What would you do if I say *let's fuck?*" he drawls.

I straighten my back against his hand, forcing him to move slightly with me.

"You said you wouldn't force me," I whisper as I balance my weight onto my left leg, bringing my right leg slowly up along his to his waist. He pushes into my pelvis immediately, and I can feel someone being just a little bit too happy to be between my legs.

"I don't see anyone being forced here." His jaw tightens as he tries to keep a leash on his control.

I bat my eyelashes at him, putting on as much angelic innocence as I can.

"I have no desire to be fucked by you," I state bluntly, but I can hear the lie in my tone.

If he were to pull my panties down right now, I would be soaking wet, and it pisses me off that he can have this type of power over me.

He gives my neck a squeeze, causing my breath to hitch.

"I think you're lying," he whispers. I roll my eyes, the only act of defiance I can give in this position. "I think you want me to pick you up and drag your ass to my room, where I bend you over my bed and fuck you until you are screaming my name."

He releases my neck, letting me take a gulp of breath, and I can feel the heat of him scorching hot between my legs.

"I think you aren't used to being denied, are you?" I laugh because the small flutter of shock passing through his eyes from me not just agreeing to screwing him makes it evident that he isn't.

I know, however, that he won't force me. He wants me to want him. He may be an uptight power-hungry asshole, but he isn't a rapist, and that brings me comfort.

"Here is the thing, Barnette, I don't screw the people I hate," I retort.

"Tsk, tsk, *hate* is such a strong word, puppet. Hate and love are very, very similar. They both cause the same amount of energy, and they both infiltrate the same core responses."

His other hand cups me between my legs, and I yelp at the unexpected touch.

"I can feel how warm you are. I bet if I were to slide my hand in between your panties, I would feel just how much you *hate* me." His smug smile makes me want to punch him in the face.

I drop my leg from his side and pull his hand away. I bring his hand up and fold his fingers in slowly, leaving his middle finger out. I keep my eyes locked with his as I pull his finger into my mouth and tentatively wrap my tongue around it, sucking it.

Barnette's jaw drops open, and I take the moment to enjoy the exhilaration of causing him to come undone. It's truly intoxicating.

Barnette loosens his hand around my neck even more as his finger pops out of my mouth, and I grip the button on the top of his slacks and unbutton him, causing his neck to shift down quickly. I barely get to see the shock and confusion registering through him, I am enjoying keeping him on his toes.

I unzip his zipper and quickly squeeze myself down the wall and onto my knees as I pull his dick out of his boxers.

Damn, he has length on his side, and a slight bit of intimidation registers through me, but I have never been one to back down from a challenge.

I lick my lips and pull his hard dick straight into my mouth and start sucking him off.

"Jesus—Amelia." Barnette's breath comes out in a pant, and it turns me on.

Screw him thinking he has all the control here; I have the control here.

"Finally putting that mouth of yours to good use," he groans, and I angrily grip my fingers into his thighs. He hisses at the pain of my nails digging in.

Fuck him. I quicken my pace, causing his words to falter. Good, just how I like him. I take him in deep and suction in my cheeks, sliding him in and out. His fingers grip the base of my hair as he tries to gain control of my pace, and I glance up at him and glare as he continues to fuck my mouth.

My drool spills down my chin as he matches my glare with his own. His cheeks are flushed, and his other hand tries to grip the wall, finding nothing to grab onto, and it brings me joy seeing his control come undone from me. That's right, Barnette, come undone.

I angle my neck up so I can keep my eyes on him while I take him as deep as I can, even gagging, but I don't give a fuck as I watch him come completely unraveled before me.

I grip his balls in one of my hands, giving them a squeeze as I quicken my pace, and his head falls against his arm on the wall as his hips start roughly shoving his dick down my throat. Tears start to stream down my face, mixing with my drool.

I use my hand to grip the base of him, rubbing up and down as my mouth slobbers the tip of his dick.

"Fuck!" Barnette hisses just as I use my hands to keep his pace up.

His dick swells in my mouth, announcing his release, and he groans as ripples of hot semen spill into the back of my throat.

I don't release him; I continue swallowing while he is in my mouth, and he squirms under my hold. Where is my fucking crown? Because the king just lost a bit of his control by me. I push him out of my mouth and wipe the remaining spit off my lips and chin, standing to face him.

"Look at that. Seems my mouth does have more than one use," I mouth off at him, sassiness in full swing. "Be a good boy and go get cleaned up. Oh, and Barnette, next time I want to play chess, we play."

With that, I turn on my heels and walk straight into my room, leaving him speechless in the dining room. Two can play this power trip game of control and I will let him think about how much power he just gave me over him.

I shut my bedroom door behind me as my emotions become a tornado between feeling powerful, aroused, confused, and betrayed.

This damn battle of feelings at war inside of me and I wish it would all just settle down!

I feel duped, like the small amount of time of feeling happy and content was an illusion meant to come down and shatter me completely.

I am barely holding on to this world as it is; I cannot handle anything more out of my control, and yet here I am diving head-first into more shit.

The door opens just before I make it to my bed. "Amelia?" Dean's voice penetrates the black cloud that has already started wrapping itself around me like an old familiar blanket.

"What do you want, Dean?" I am already exhausted from what just went down. I don't want to talk; I don't want to face this.

"Are you mad at me? Did I upset you in some way?" he begs for an answer, trying to come up beside me. He gets in between me and the bed, and I huff out in response. Why do they always interfere with me taking in the comfort of the bed?

"I'm not mad at you." *I am mad at myself,* I chide internally, avoiding his eyes as I look away from him.

"Then what is it? Do you regret what happened?" His voice drops into a whisper in fear someone will walk by and hear him.

"No. I just..." I pull away from him as he tries to push a strand of hair behind my ear. I am much too aware of the dried-up drool down my neck. "Dean, no, I just don't think it was a smart idea, and I am so, so sorry that I did that. I crossed a boundary I should have respected."

He watches as I start to pace back and forth. It feels like I am a bottle left open and upside down, draining everything inside of me at quick speed.

"I don't regret it. I don't regret you, but I am to marry your best friend, and even though this whole thing is completely out of my control, I don't want to cause issues between the two of you," I add.

That is the truth. I don't want to break up their friendship, though I don't even know if Barnette would care if I did sleep with Dean if it stays in the past.

"Listen, just slow down and breathe, okay?" Dean steps in my way again, and it takes all my energy to stop myself in my tracks so I don't run into him. "This does not need to happen again, okay? I will respect that, and I will respect you, but I don't regret it, and I feel with my whole damn damaged heart that you and I have a spark that is undeniable."

Just rip my heart out of my chest and stomp all over it, why don't you?

"What about Barnette?" I can't help the whimper that comes out with my words. A whimper much to my dismay at the fear of not only upsetting Barnette but also losing him.

Dean sighs heavily, "Truthfully, I don't want to hurt him either. It isn't like you're just someone he brought home, and we can share—" he slips. My eyes bulge out.

"Oh, so you guys share girls?" I gasp, interrupting him. He raises his hands innocently.

"Now, hold on, there is nothing wrong with that. Don't be on your high horse and try to judge me or him, missy," Dean states.

Why do I suddenly feel dirty? I shouldn't for them sharing girls; I am the one who slept with the best friend, and that should make me feel shameful. Then I blew Barnette. God...

"You are right in that he wants to marry me, which still hasn't enlightened me on *why* he does." So many unanswered questions, they are drowning me and submerging me in misery.

Dean sighs, "Sweetheart, all I am trying to say is I don't think it is that big of a deal. I can talk with him—"

"No! No, he cannot know because what if he kicks me to the curb and goes for Andrea?" I sputter.

Shit! I didn't even think about those consequences. What the hell am I doing? What the hell was I thinking? Just one big giant piece of selfish shit. How could I do this to her?

"He would never. He wants nothing to do with her—" Dean jumps to defend Barnette.

"Just stop, Dean, please. Just please, I am begging you, please don't tell him. Let's keep this between us and just go back to normal." What if I lose that connection with him? God, why am I so fucking stupid?

He deflates. "Okay, I won't say a word, I swear, Amelia."

Tears well up heavily in my eyes, and I fear I am going to lose complete control if he doesn't get the hell out of my room.

"Please leave," I whisper. Thankfully, it doesn't come out mean or full of bitter hate, it comes out broken. Exactly how I feel.

Broken.

Damaged.

"Just hold on," Dean starts to beg. His eyes are big and rounded, reminding me of a puppy dog begging for attention.

All I know is how to hurt people.

"No, just go, Dean, please. I need to just get my head together. Please." I try to hold back the tears, but they start trailing down my face in a steady race on either side, and my insides shudder as they start to crumble.

He looks at me as if I've dropped the world's saddest news on his shoulders. They droop down as he leaves my room slowly. So slowly, as if hoping I would stop him.

But I grip my sides as I head for the bed, trying to keep all my pieces together. Trying to keep myself from breaking completely.

I just hurt people.

I just put myself in positions that break me.

I am my own monster.

CHAPTER 18

Who's Your Daddy?

Dean

"I DON'T LIKE this for her. She is just lying in there staring off at the wall. It isn't okay!" I look at Barnette and try to get him to understand the severity of the situation.

Depression is real, and depression kills. That last episode was not a one-and-done; this is something she is legitimately struggling with.

"I am not taking it lightly, Dean, I just…" he sighs heavily and grips the bridge of his nose between his thumb and index finger. "I don't know how to handle it. Also, it's a bit shitty she is this depressed over being in our world. What is so wrong with marrying me? I am the king, I am the boss, I—"

I interrupt him quickly before he continues on his better than thou rant. He should know it's more than that by now.

I try to calm my voice down. "She doesn't give two shits about status, Barnette; she is not that type of girl. Not to mention she didn't exactly willingly go into this decision." I try to bring up that second part softly so as not to irritate him further. It doesn't work.

"She *had* a choice. Nothing was forced." His hand strikes through the air as if his words are final.

I scoff. "So what? You or your sister, that is your option. You get taken or she does. You see how protective she is of her little sister. Hell, she fucking punched Mick—" I quickly stop at the reference of the new nickname she created in my mind for my partner. "Ahem, Derrick in the face when he touched her.

"Do you really think she is going to give her up to three strange men that showed up in an hour's notice of her finding out her mom sold her out? Like, think about it, man." I just want him to understand and think more outside of his sharp-edged square box.

Barnette starts pacing back and forth as he typically does when he is deep in thought.

"I wasn't going to really take the little girl. She was never an option for me," he mumbles more to himself than to me.

I deflate at his admission. Even though I know he isn't a complete dickhead, sometimes his actions do surprise me, even with me blindly defending him.

"Maybe that is something she would like to hear, you know, a little bit of communication. Besides, think about this from her perspective, not just yours, bro," I scold him.

He glares at me for a moment before continuing his pacing, and I take a seat on the black bar stool against the counter in the kitchen.

It is only 8 a.m. and my stomach is rumbling, smelling all assortment of breakfast sitting there waiting to be eaten, but seeing the state Amelia was in after the maid said she refused to eat, none of us felt right to dig in until we came up with some kind of game plan.

Finally, Barnette blows out a breath. "I guess I can go in and talk with her. I don't know what to say, but it's ridiculous for her to be cowering away in the dark again. I am not going to drop her into a bathtub full of water; she's got power in her blood, and she needs to use it. I know for a fact she knows how to engage it!"

My eyes shoot to him, immediately confused and focused by the comment. "What do you mean by that? Power in her blood?"

Her mom sure as hell doesn't hold any kind of title other than 'deadbeat mom of the year'.

He shrugs me off, and it only serves to enrage me.

"No, I need you to clarify. If I need to know something about her—hell, I am protecting her too, you know? I need all the information."

I need to know anything and everything about her. This is more than just them. Yes, she pushed me away, but I know she is just confused and feeling powerless. Nobody here enjoys that feeling.

Barnette goes back to pacing as he thinks about it. Back and forth. Back and forth. Finally, after a couple of minutes of me glaring at his head, he stops and confronts me.

"Her father is who I am talking about," he grits out.

No one knows who her dad is; I saw nobody show up in the month I was watching her, and no one has mentioned a father. I assumed he was another low-life. Her birth certificate was left blank in the father's margin.

"Does Martin A. Shuar ring a bell to you?" Barnette drawls, cocking his head.

I can feel my eyes open slightly as I stare at him. No fucking way. How did Ramona end up putting hooks into him?

"Exactly," Barnette responds to my lack of speech.

Everything just clicked together.

This whole crazy fucking plan of his makes sense know.

"You're marrying her for connections to him. That is why she is so important," I breathe, hardly able to believe it myself.

Barnette nods in response and then turns on his heels, grabs a plate of pancakes from the counter, and goes to walk away.

"Does Derrick know?" I demand. How could he keep us in the dark about this?

Barnette turns to look at me with regret marring his features. "Yes, he found out a couple of nights ago." That stings a little.

I was just kept in the dark on information that could also mean my life or death.

Barnette gives me an apologetic look, then turns and heads towards Amelia's room.

This wasn't about pussy or some strange infatuation with Amelia at all; it was to be connected to the biggest arms dealer known in the US and Russia.

This just became extremely dangerous.

***

Barnette

I slide into the side of my candy apple Lambo with a crisp black interior.

I usually like to take this baby out for joy rides when I want to have the top down and feel the wind flying by me, blaring Linkin Park down Route 158, but today it is to be used on a slightly secret mission.

I don't need the guys involved in this one, and I am not

going to show up to another female with all three of us to intimidate her.

I want her to come on her own. I hope to whatever God is out there that she does.

I may just throw her into the car and drive off if she doesn't want to.

I don't think I am going to have to force her, though.

Damn it! I slam my hands into the steering wheel. Since when do I fucking care so much? I should just let Amelia lay there in her damn spiral.

It is not this awful to marry me. I know she craves control just like I do, so what the hell happened between yesterday's events and this morning? What sucked out her energy and power she held, leaving me with my dick hanging out of my pants?

I had never felt so drawn to a woman than I did in that moment. Then for her to not even acknowledge my existence when I brought her pancakes and just roll over to go back to sleep had everything in me wanting to yank her out of bed and shake the hell out of her.

I have done nothing to her for her to hate me so much.

I stop at the incoming red light and watch as a group of small girls play Double Dutch on the sidewalk.

Such sweet innocence. They have no idea right now how fucked up the world truly is. They aren't damaged like the rest of us yet.

Damaged.

Am I damaged goods to her? I wonder if I have too many scars, too many secrets wrapped up in my head.

Can she sense all that lies beneath, and it bothers her?

My stomach drops as a thought intrudes into my mind. Does

she consider herself damaged? What if this isn't about me, and this is all just her? Her own battles, her own trauma?

I am sure growing up with a mother like hers caused a lot of heartache and bullshit in her life.

My knuckles turn white as I grip the steering wheel. What kind of fucked up shit did she go through growing up with Ramona?

I need to talk to her.

The tires squeal as I pump the gas too quickly, trying to reach my destination at the small local hospital that is only a couple minutes down from the trailer park where Amelia lived in.

During Dean's research time on her, we have discovered she has a very close and personal friend, and I know deep in my gut that she is the one that Amelia needs to see right now.

I reflect back on the shock on Dean's face when he discovered who her father actually was. I am pretty sure that my face was an exact replica of what he expressed when I first found out, too. How the hell Ramona ever got that man's attention, let alone banged him, truly amazes me. Ramona is a fucking roach, but Martin is a legend and a motherfucking king.

I want to be a true king too, and fighting fair will never get you to that point.

He thought by paying off Ramona that half-ass check would keep his little secret hidden away forever, but I do my homework on the men I look into, and I dug in deep into his background.

The perfect little secret just waiting to be found, and how the hell have I been the one to have found it first is beyond me.

Or maybe the others were taken care of first? Shit.

I pull into the tiny parking lot outside of the hospital. People's heads are turning as they take in my sports car. I know it is a bit flashy, a bit much for this side of town, but it's my baby, and I want to drive her every chance I get.

I pinch the bridge of my nose as I stare at the double glass doors straight ahead. Dean has been telling me to try harder with Amelia and to be more understanding.

It isn't that I don't want to be there for her or treat her right, it's that I simply do not know how to.

Dad taught me that your woman is your object to do what you please with, and she should do as she is told. Mom was obedient and followed the rules. For some reason, though, it never set right with me. I like Amelia's feistiness and determination. I want that part of her back.

Yes, I want her to be obedient, but not at the expense of what makes her... her.

I feel like there is a constant war inside of me when it comes to her, and it drives me fucking mad! It is similar to the way I felt like a tug of war with my father and Marisol on how to treat a woman and what makes a man a man.

Marisol was never terrified of my father. She always stayed respectfully quiet, but after Mom died, she took it upon herself to try to teach me her ways. Or as she liked to put it, "the correct way". I still roll my eyes at how that woman holds her head so high. She felt it was up to her to raise me to be kind and observant, to listen and not lust.

I've never had an issue with lusting after a woman, but there was a time period where I didn't care what my actions did to the few girls that I did give my attention to—even if they were at the same time.

One of the girls showed up to my house one day in high school, and I remember just standing there watching her cry about how I broke her trust, and Marisol overheard the whole conversation between the two of us. Well, it was more so her cries and me agreeing and saying, "Well, it was fun while it lasted," before seeing her out.

Marisol had come out from around the corner so fast and whacked me on the back of the head so hard I saw stars. That isn't something that just happens in cartoons.

That day she sat me down and explained to me that women have many layers to them. That regardless of how they portray themselves to be and say they don't care, all those underlying layers contradict it. They feel, they care, they love with everything they have, and they just want to be loved and cared for back.

I remember that faraway look she had in her eyes as she stared out the kitchen window trying to get me to see her way, how she looked inspired and sad all at the same time.

She had stated, "Give a woman a place to call her own, and she will make it a home. Give a woman loyalty and time, and she will give you her whole heart. Give a woman respect, and you will have a powerful ally. Do not ever estimate what a woman is willing to give, because a woman has the power to break apart her body to give life for her child, and she will break apart her heart and mind for a man whether worthy or not. Don't be unworthy, don't ever show a woman how unworthy you can be. Always be worthy. Always.

"Because a woman can bounce back from the madness a man can bring upon her. She can find herself, and she will never allow herself to be broken down again, whereas a man who gets broken down gets lost in the madness and very rarely do they come out of it. Women are powerful. It is up to you to have them be a friend or foe, and by the looks of the road you are taking, why, you remind me of your father, and if you've noticed, he was a lonely bastard even when your mom was alive."

Her words made me uncomfortable. Her blunt statement about my mom stung my heart. It made me reflect back on how unhappy my mother was, the way she always looked sad until one day she didn't.

There was a period of time right before her death where she held her head up high, she always looked her finest, and she had a smile on her face—except when my father was in the room. When he entered the picture, she had an expression of indifference but still carried herself with grace and dignity.

I later found out she was having an affair, but I couldn't even be mad at her for it. My dad still held his sour expression and angry outlook until the day he died.

Maybe he did in fact get lost in the madness.

A powerful ally is what I want out of Amelia. A loyal companion can come later, and she can learn to love me eventually.

I just hope this Lacey can help me help Amelia.

CHAPTER 19

Kindle the Fire

Amelia

I WAKE up and stare up at the ceiling. The feeling of heaviness overloads every bone in my body. I try to roll over and find I hardly have the strength to even do that.

Is it possible to feel like even your blood is heavier? A fog clouds my mind, and it dawns on me that I have felt this way before, like I am lost at sea and am never going to know my direction home.

I feel hopeless. I feel, and I hate this word as much as I hate the feeling, depressed. We are down that road again.

I finish rolling over to my side and pull my knees up to my chest underneath the blanket, desperately wishing I had my fuzzy one from back home.

Home. A deep sting stabs me quickly in my chest—a physical ache.

Did that place *ever* feel like home? Did Mom ever make it feel like that was my safe place, my security blanket, my escape from the world?

Home is nothing like they portray in movies or in the books. I tried to escape into books and did find solace in them once upon a time, but then coming back to reality hit me harder and harder and I had to let it go because my reality growing up was so depressing.

Then Andrea came into this world, and I threw my whole life into raising her, protecting her, and guiding her into doing something more and better than me. To not rely on a mom who chose drugs and alcohol over their own daughter. Addiction is cruel and not just for the abuser.

I remember when Andie was first born, though Mom did stay clean for a little bit. I was actually impressed with the way she was able to quit and get it together to get things for her and do things with her like feed her, change her, having to bathe her.

I was freshly thirteen and had no idea how to care for a baby, but I did learn a lot in those first few months while Mom kept it together.

She taught me the basics, and I picked it up quickly. From there, however, she went back downhill—it just took one person to stop by the front step and shake a little baggy with a wink for some action, and she plummeted down into her never-ending spiral.

I will never forget that day of Mom standing there in her faded red long-sleeve shirt and black leggings. Christmas was a week away, and we were all in some kind of festive color and had a small tree in the corner of the living room to celebrate the exciting holiday. The red and green bulbs we found at the Goodwill down the street adorned it, and I was so excited to have found a little long-sleeve green dress with ruffles on the bottom of it to put on Andrea. Mom actually smiled when we got it.

The look of defeat will always haunt me while she stared at that man. I saw how her whole entire body froze while her eyes locked onto that little baggy. That look of her self-control collapsing as she glanced back at us told me everything I already knew was going to happen.

I was to raise Andrea mostly alone. Merry Christmas, Amelia, time to figure it out.

The crushing weight of the memory abandons me back into the room.

I feel like I am floating in a sea of dark, murky molasses. I am hardly moving, but I can feel the small amount of movement floating by me.

I know there is motion. I can sense it, but I cannot move with it. I am stuck. My lungs don't want to take in a full breath.

Blood doesn't want to flow to my limbs. My thoughts even feel slow. Is it weird that I can acknowledge everything that is happening to me? This tepid paralysis is corrupting my brain. It's a slow death of the mind.

Knock. Knock. Knock.

I glance slowly at the door, and I cannot even muster up the energy to answer. *Go away*, my voice echoes through my mind. *Leave me alone.*

Bang. Bang. Bang.

The door wobbles under the impact of the fist banging on the door on the other side.

"Oh! Move out of the way, I don't need to fucking knock!" I hear a small feminine voice on the other side, and surprise lightens me as it echoes through the door.

"Wait—" Now there is the masculine voice I expect. The door barges open and in walks the last person I expected.

"You look like shit," my best friend states as she stares at me curled up in bed.

Her blonde hair wisps around her sharp, flushed cheeks. I can see the sadness in her green eyes that contradict the anger in the way her lips are pinched.

She immediately turns and looks at Barnette, who is also standing in the doorway. He stares at me with his casual mask of indifference, but in his eyes, I can see the slightly pinched corners of concern that frame them.

"What the hell did you do to her?!" she yells.

Shock overcomes his entire features as she starts smacking on his chest and arm. He doesn't even move to block her as his aloof expression stares down at the tiny frame of my best friend.

I can't help myself; I start to laugh out loud. Laughter fills the room as she shoves him out the door with all her strength, stopping momentarily to stare at me. Then right before she slams the door in his face, I see Barnette have a small smile on his lips.

I would have thought I made it up, it happened so quickly. The door is already closed and locked as Lacey runs to me, and I let the moment pass.

"Lacey, I missed your damn face." Tears start to spill over as I hug my longtime friend. My ride or die because she has been through it all with me. The murky waters I felt around me have started to melt down my limbs. Her hug feels like the first breath of fresh air I have had in weeks. Tears fall harder down my cheeks as I squeeze her tighter while my strength comes back to me.

"Girl, you have no idea how scared I was when Andrea told me your mom sold you. I looked everywhere I could for you. She wasn't sure who it was too, and your mom wasn't giving me anything to go on except that 'you were fine and taken care of' and 'how grateful you should be'. I almost decked her right then and there! Then I was going to get the police involved—" She pauses, seeing the horrified look on my face.

My heart feels like it stops in my chest. Lacey can see the instant fear in my eyes and quickly shakes her head.

"No, no, no, I didn't involve them. I didn't say shit. I know how everything with Andrea is; you would probably kill me if she got taken. Girl, I wouldn't do that to you, you know that."

She hugs me tightly, and a couple of her tears that were threatening to spill over slowly trickle down her own face. I can feel them splatter on the back of my shoulder.

If anyone understood that whole situation, it was her.

I love her so much.

"But seriously,"—she pulls away from me—"you look like shit. I haven't seen you look like this in years." Her mama bear tone is in full force as she takes my face in her hands. "When Barnette came to me at work, I—"

"Wait, Barnette tracked you down?" Another strong emotion rocks through me, everything enhanced after being numb for so long: shock.

Her eyes soften. "He tracked me down at work and girl, for some 'tough, scary man'"—she air quotes with her fingers—"he looked downright lost when he asked if I could help you get better."

She crawls into bed beside me and snuggles into the blankets, an old routine for the two of us.

"I think he actually likes you," she remarks, and I roll my eyes immediately at her misguided observation. She chuckles at me. "I'm serious!"

"We are in a complex agreement; it is a contract and nothing more," I confess.

She gives me a knowing look, and I shuffle to my side to face her.

"I'm serious!" I mimic her words back to her. "He just doesn't want me looking bad is all. Our wedding is coming up. You cannot have a damsel in distress, mentally ill wife when you are the big bad wolf," I mutter out.

She smacks my arm, rather hard, if I may add. "Don't talk about my friend like that." Her tone is serious as she tries to capture my attention with her eyes.

Then her next words strike a low blow that hits me hard in my stomach.

"Andie wouldn't want you to talk like that about yourself." Tears immediately strangle my eyesight.

"I miss her so much," I sob.

"She's okay. I check on her every day, I promise!" Lacey swears, trying to reassure me.

I know the truth of her words deep in my bones.

"Your mom is even being good right now. I can tell she isn't as drunk as she usually is, and after I gave her a tongue lashing that would make the devil proud, she promised that she only brings men home while Andrea is at school."

I gaze up hard at the ceiling, inhaling sharply.

Lacey adds, "I told her that if anything ever happened to her that happened to—" I raise my hand to cut her off.

"Thank you. You have no idea how sick it makes me feel not being there for her. But I know she learned her lesson with me, so even though I am terrified of that scenario, I also am aware she doesn't want to repeat history."

My hands start trembling as my nerves go into overdrive about the topic.

"Plus, I would kill her. I think she knows I am capable of it now. What more do I have to lose? I already don't get to see Andie. This lifestyle isn't safe for her."

"Is it safe for you?" Genuine concern laces through her words.

"Was my world ever safe for me?" I fire back with intense anger, but not at her just this life.

"I would rather see you angry than depressed, Meli. Keep that anger kindling. Let it power you up and motivate you to get out of this situation."

I feel the fire of it in my veins.

It feels good to feel something other than the void of nothing. I sigh as I relish the sensation of it as I think about her words.

Keep the fire burning.

CHAPTER 20

We're Under Attack

Barnette

HEARING Amelia's laughter through the door helps relieve the tension out of my shoulders. It is so good to hear her fucking laugh again.

"Seems a bit obsessive the way you're standing outside of her door, boss." I look up to see Derrick leaning up against the wall observing me.

I roll my eyes at him. Though I should feel annoyed by the intrusion of privacy, I cannot help but feel relief.

He admits, "But it's good to hear something. I was a little concerned about her."

"Well, if anyone can help her out of whatever is going through her mind, maybe it's her." I shrug.

I start to walk down the hall towards him and head for my office.

"As for me, I have business to return to. Any word back about what is going on with our latest shipment?" I inquire, glancing back at Derrick, who falls into step with me as I expected.

I can always rely on him to get straight to business with me. Besides, I need the distraction or else I am going to be stuck standing outside Amelia's door all damn day.

He answers, "A lot of ruckus, to be honest. Someone keeps intervening with our supply, and then the shop down in Berkeley got ambushed even though—"

"When the fuck did Berkely get ambushed and why the hell am I only hearing about it now?" My mind starts going a mile a minute trying to think back through any threats that have been made towards the supply and any reason why the shop was attacked. Who the hell is trying to sabotage my work, and why now?

Some of the blood drains from his face. "Sorry, boss, it was yesterday. Dean and I knew you were stressed about everything going on here, so we handled it, and we are digging into it thoroughly, we swear."

I rub a frustrated hand down my face as I take in his words, walking into my office and taking a seat at my desk before I acknowledge Derrick again.

"Not telling me what is going on with my operations is a problem. I need to know everything regardless of what is happening here!" I slam my fist down on my desk out of frustration.

"Barnette, I get the frustration, and be mad all you want, we just wanted to have your back, okay? It was nothing personal." He enunciates it slowly.

"Where the fuck is Dean?" I demand. The wheels in my mind are spinning as I turn on my computer to check the footage from the shop.

"Dean is down at the shop dealing with everything and checking it over."

"How many men did we lose?" The dreaded fear of that question's answer sours my stomach.

"We lost eight men." Derrick's face is somber as he relays the information I requested.

"Fuck!" I slap at whatever is at my desk, causing two picture frames to go flying into the nearest wall. Who the fuck is killing my men?

"Dean is going to figure it out. I am just glad he wasn't one of them. He has been going back and forth between Berkley and Parkens the last week."

Dread fills me as I feel the vomit layer thickly at the base of my throat. If I had lost him, it would have felt like losing a blood brother. I look up to Derrick, who stands rigidly, ready to go into action the second I give the command. His words dawn on me as it registers through my anger.

"Why has he been spending so much time between those places?" I try to reflect back to the last time I saw him stay at his own house here, but we have all been so busy with our own shit that I cannot remember. I know why Derrick is at Parkens, but not Dean.

"He is working on something. Won't give me much to go on other than it is just a personal side quest, but says it's important. Has been going back and forth between the two spots as well as going into town. I don't know what he is working on specifically, I just figured when he thought it was time to let me in, he would."

Derrick shrugs his shoulders indifferently at his words. That is how we work. We have complete trust in one another and know we can rely on each other to lean on later.

At the thought of possibly losing him, though... I need to know what has his attention.

"But I did have Sam print up a copy of the file he has put together and bring it to me for safe keeping. With all the unexpected attacks, I figured if by some small chance it does deal with Amelia, then we should have backup just in case. I didn't read it, though, I swear. I have no idea what is in this file." Derrick leans over, handing me the manilla file he was keeping tight in his hand.

I didn't even notice he was carrying anything, which just shows how out of my mind I am. Jesus, I need to get my head in the game.

"I will say, though..." Derrick leans back and places his hands on the chair in front of my desk. He grips it tightly before he speaks the rest of what is on his mind. "I feel deep in my gut that what he is working on does have to do with Amelia."

His gaze catches mine again, and I can tell he is searching my expression. I know those two are closer than her and me, I know he cares about her too. He does have a protectiveness about her that I have recognized since he started getting intel on her. It doesn't surprise me that he is still digging, but why does it bother Derrick?

"Are you thinking I should feel concerned?" I furrow my brows as I regard him.

I am not sure what he is trying to read in my expression. I can't even focus on the file right now, and I place it on top of my desk, instead putting my full attention on him.

"I don't know how you should feel, bro, but as a friend to both of you, I am just saying that Amelia has both of your hearts. And while yours is business over romance, I am not sure that Dean's is purely business."

I mull over his words and his observations. Anger doesn't fill me at all, not an ounce of it. Amelia is an intriguing spitfire that makes you want to get burned; it wouldn't surprise me if Dean would be interested in her in that way. The mistake however, is believing that my interest in her is just business, because it isn't.

"I will talk with Dean next time I see him," I close the conversation down. "Right now, we need to figure out who the fuck keeps messing with our operations."

Derrick nods in understanding, and I jump up to head out the door with him.

Dean

Eight men's families I have to contact and explain what happened. Ruthless, unnecessary destruction is the true definition of this, but greed is the final monster that runs this whole show.

I sigh out loudly as I rake my sore hands through my hair. My hands have been clenched in tight fists since I received the news this morning. Fuck!

"Dean, I can go and deal with the families. Seriously, you don't have to do any of it," Pedro's voice breaks through the tornado of thoughts and emotions I have tearing at my mind.

I look up and see Pedro in his typical soft blue button-up shirt, black khakis, and hiking boots. For some reason, his weird ass shoes bring me a small bit of comfort, some familiarity regardless of how little a detail it is. His salt and pepper hair is disheveled from being a part of the breach debrief this morning; a few frustrated scratches already dried up dot his face.

"No, Pedro, I appreciate it, but you know how I feel about

this." My shoulders weigh down from the burden, physically dropping my shoulders down as I lift my head up to meet his gaze head-on. "This is my job. I can do it."

Pedro nods in understanding. He may disagree, but he is a man of respect. He is one of the few I would rely on to be at my back when shit goes down.

My original plan was to come down here and take the folder I have been working relentlessly on off the computer and present it to Barnette. I searched for answers, and I finally received something worth bringing to attention. I can still feel the desperation run deep in my veins when I ran to check the computer hard drive to find it completely wiped out—all that fucking information gone!

I can feel the anger burn as it laces with the despair, and it becomes acidic throughout my whole body as it starts to bubble to the top.

Who the fuck is attacking us and why? At least now I know who Ramona screwed around with and who Andie's sperm donor is. Just need to dig more into that lead. What I do know for sure, deep in my unsettled gut, is that this has everything to do with Amelia.

CHAPTER 21

Death's Last Kiss

Amelia

DANGER. Greed. Humiliation. Isolation.

The weight of those words, the irrational heaviness of how those emotions affect me mentally and physically, has brought destruction upon my life.

What is wrong with me?

What was wrong?

I feel the ache in my bones and even the soft caresses of my blood that is flowing through my body aches at the touch.

Too long I have felt like I had to go and go, don't stop or else everything will fall apart. Make sure Mom was alive, make sure the doors were locked, go to school and ignore the kids, get good grades, make sure Andie has food and clothing, make sure I make it to work on time, pick up every available shift during the day, save every penny I can, and most importantly do not let anyone in.

Go, go, and go.

There is no off button on this fucking merry-go-round.

I am so tired.

Everything hurts.

Even the weight of my eyelids feels like a ton of bricks ready to submerge my eyes into my brain.

After Lacey left, I felt a relief in me I haven't felt in a long time. She let me know she was checking in every day with Andrea, and she let me know that Barnette admitted to her that he has no intentions of bringing Andie into his lifestyle.

Seeing her out the door was bittersweet, and I had a moment to think that maybe, just maybe, everything was going to be okay.

Then on my walk to the kitchen, I passed by Barnette's office. I peeked in out of pure curiosity to see how his man cave was set up. It's all dull tan tones on the wall, helping the dark walnut furniture pop out at least. His desk is huge and has three screens sitting on top of it. Who needs that many? Honestly, though, it's fitting for him.

I glance at two broken picture frames that lay haphazardly on the ground. Someone was angry and took it out on innocent pictures.

I walk towards the pictures to see who they are of when something catches my eye. A single file sits on the top of his desk, and damn it if curiosity didn't kill the cat.

A tug in my chest makes my fingers itch with curiosity. Will it hurt to just peek inside of it? Just a little peek?

I walk slowly inside, maybe being a little too suspicious. Coming around the desk, I gently lift the file open, just a small amount, and am careful not to move it a single milliliter. My breath hitches as a picture of the face I least expected stares right back up to me.

No, no, it can't be. My stomach twists as if a knife had been jammed in, and an audible sob escapes me.

Beside the picture in typed little black letters it states: Matthew Lauona.

It's Andie's father's picture who stares into my soul. I slam the file shut, not caring if it's moved at all, and rush out of there.

What is going to happen to me?

I feel scared and sick to my stomach. They pushed and pushed and now they know.

I will never get to escape what happened. I thought if nothing was said, if I told Dean to please not look, they would respect it. The betrayal of their digging lines my insides.

When will this feeling go away?

Why do they need to know? How much did they find out? Does Mom know they got his information too?

There are so many questions, so many.

Why does this world have to be so cruel? One of my biggest kept secrets is about to be forced out into the light. I am tired of it; I am tired of carrying this impossible weight.

A wicked little voice whispers into my ears, caressing the side of my face gently as I move my face in to try to listen through to the muffled sound.

"Just leave the world behind."

"What will change with your last breath?"

"It would be easier if you didn't have to fake it."

I can feel the truth of those statements as it settles over me like a warm knit blanket. Nothing would change.

It would be easier if I didn't have to plaster on a smile, if I did not have to force myself out of bed, and if people didn't have to push themselves to feel concerned for me.

It would be easier if I didn't have to face any of it.

I look at the untouched plates on my nightstand beside the

bed. Barnette and Dean have been nonstop trying to bring me snacks.

Even Marisol graced me with her presence and chided me yesterday morning that if I don't eat something, I am going to turn into dust for the wind to sweep away, that she is planning the wedding to be in three weeks, and I need to be ready.

I didn't even blink at the news. I never got to have a say in my life. Why should I be surprised when it gets planned for me anyways?

I have no rights to how my story is written.

How much I wish I was dust right now.

They want me to be healthy for the wedding. I am nothing more than a tool they are trying to utilize.

I don't want to be a bride. I don't want to lose one more piece of me. I don't want one more thing taken from me even if it is my last name.

They've already dug too deep into everything with Andrea, and they are going to discover a cold hard truth, one that I have given my life up to protect, one that will lead to another secret that I am deeply ashamed of and that I wish was buried six feet down.

Why can't he just leave the secrets be?

I will just bury the secrets with me. If there is no me, there is no more digging.

I don't think this life was meant for me. Maybe I was just born in the wrong time, or whatever this God is that apparently decides where we go accidentally put me in this life. He chose a man for me that doesn't care about me and only wants me for business.

Dean is kind, but in reality, a man isn't enough to keep me thinking this world is going to get better. I am probably just an easy target.

I'm available. I am there. I. Am. Here.

With Andrea, I did everything I knew how to make sure she had a foot up in the world.

I just pray with everything inside of me that it was enough. That the guidance I gave her, the love I poured into her, the kindness I tried to teach her to see even when all I saw was darkness is enough to get her out into the world.

It is a terrifying world. Full of pain and betrayal. False beliefs and heartache. There is violence and blood. Who can you really trust?

And I was placed here.

I walk back and forth, pulling at my hair as I grip the sides of my head.

I can physically feel these thoughts seeping into every pore of me like a thick layer of tar. This isn't me. This sadness isn't healthy for anyone to be around.

I feel like an infection just ready to take the world out, ready to affect others who try to get near me.

Though the thought can be comforting, it is also terrifying.

I don't even know why I keep trying.

Who am I to think that things are going to change? I am supposed to plan this wedding, I am supposed to pretend I am happy, but I am lying to myself that I deserve to be out of that life and play dress-up in this one.

What if the truth causes them to look at me with the same disgust that I feel?

No matter what path I take, there is danger every which way I turn.

No matter what I decide, I still end up hurt somehow.

It is time for all of this to end.

The gears that have been moving slowly in my mind finally come to a stop. Everything stops moving.

A sensation of peace washes over me at the thought. It is really as simple as that. I am the one who has to put an end to all of this; I deserve to be out of this.

I am more than a business transaction.

I am more than a victim to men who hold power over me.

Andi will be fine without me. She has gotten this far. Besides, I was never what she needed. She deserves more than what I ever had to offer, what I was capable of offering.

For the first time in a long time, I have come to peace with a decision. I am ready to be done with this world.

I slowly make my way to the bathroom. My steps are steady and sure. This will be my last night. I might as well enjoy some of the moments before I die.

I look at that beautiful bathtub and run some hot water. I have been wanting to use this tub to its fullest since I first laid eyes on it, so I might as well get to enjoy it. I pour some lavender bubble bath in and scoop in some Epsom salt from the glass container on the small table on the side of the tub.

I slowly move to the medicine cabinet over the counter and open it to see the Tylenol, ibuprofen, Advil, Benadryl, and cough medicine lined up smoothly next to each other.

Everything I would need if I didn't feel good, and boy does my mind feel ill.

A thick paste of sickness has coated my mind for so long, I am ready to be done with it. I take a few pills from each bottle and swallow it with a gulp from the tap water in the sink.

No hesitation, no second-guessing. I just feel peace.

I slowly slide my clothes off in the mirror, taking in how I look. The unseen scars that I carry all over.

How does nobody else see all the pain this body has endured? How can I give a reasonable explanation to how I feel if there are no wounds on the outside of my body to show? Why does it take visible proof for someone to believe the pain someone has endured?

I can see where all the unwanted touches and hits have been, and I can feel the heavy burden in my chest of all the painful words that have been thrown at me time after time.

I turn back towards the bathtub and shut it off. I slide myself in slowly, enjoying the sensation of the bubbles against my skin and how sweet the aroma around me is. It feels amazing to simply lay here. I rest my head back against the ledge and look up at the ceiling as if the answers to all my questions may be there waiting for me.

I don't know how much time I spend like that, but I notice myself start to drift away, or maybe I am drifting back from wherever my mind had wandered off to. I pull myself slowly out of the bath, and dizziness causes me to tilt almost completely out of the tub headfirst. Shit.

I take my time drying off, always keeping part of me against the counter. I brush out my hair and gently take the coconut oil lotion and apply it to my arms, chest, and stomach.

I grab more pills from the bottles and swallow them again, then take a chug out of the cough syrup bottle as if it were whiskey. The taste of it causes me to almost choke on it; they should really make better-tasting medicine.

A laugh escapes me at that thought.

What would it matter even if they did make it taste better?

The results of tonight will be the same.

Something is definitely wrong with me. Another chuckle escapes my lips.

I bend over to put lotion onto my legs and quickly decide against it. Could it be possible to feel like you are drowning without any water?

I just want to go to sleep. Yes, I think that would be for the best.

I clean up the counter and put everything away. There is no reason to leave a mess. I walk slowly to the bed and climb in.

Everything feels like it's in slow motion, almost to the point where I don't feel like I am moving at all. Every move at this point is deliberate.

I pull the soft blanket up over me and all the way to my chin.

I am so tired.

I am so, so...

CHAPTER 22

When Misery Tries to Win

Dean

I STAND THERE at the side of Amelia's hospital bed. She has a tube down her throat and IVs in both her arms.

I am not even processing what the doctor is telling Barnette, nor what Lacey is mumbling from the other side of the bed as she holds onto her tiny hand.

When Marisol came out yelling and screaming from Amelia's room this morning, all of us panicked. I can't get the image of Amelia laying there lifeless out of my mind. She was covered in vomit and urine as her body had started to shut down from all those pills she had taken.

The fact there weren't empty bottles scattered everywhere is what hits me in the gut. She took the time to put everything away while slowly dying.

What was so seriously fucked up is that this was the decision she went with.

"Is there any stress going on in her life?" The doctor's questions filter through my thoughts.

"Yeah! Her not seeing her little sister is a big stressor," comes Lacey's snapping reply. "You couldn't even get them a damn phone to communicate?"

Honestly, I didn't even think about that. I look at Barnette, seeing he appears just as dumbfounded as I do. A phone would have been easy and harmless.

"Is Amelia unsafe?" I can tell the doctor is uncomfortable asking the question to Barnette, but the way he looks already so broken staring at her small body in that bed, it is obvious to everyone in the room that this affects him too.

"She is safe with me. She is safe with us," he grits through his teeth, trying to keep his emotions under control.

"Is she going to have any lasting effects from this?" I finally gain the courage to ask.

The doctor hesitates. "To be honest, her lab work and everything is coming back manageable. Whatever is out of normal range we can fix, but we won't know how her brain was affected until she is extubated and awake. Only time will tell on that."

I swallow the hard ball of emotion in my throat and pull the chair up beside Amelia's bed and sit down. I knew she was struggling; I just didn't know it was to this point.

Did I push her? Did me looking into her past push her over the edge? I wonder if she discovered that I found out who Andrea's dad was somehow.

"What happened?" Lacey directs her question at me, and I try to keep my own tears in check.

I swallow. "I think I pushed her; I asked her some questions, and she got defensive. I wanted to know why. She told me to leave it alone, but if it jeopardizes us in anyway, if its information our enemy could use against us, I need to know."

She stares at me accusingly, her eyes in slits cutting me like a sharp ass knife.

"What information was she willing to die for? What broke my friend so bad she thought this was the answer?!" Lacey's voice rises into a yell, and I cannot blame her.

I can feel a presence come up behind my back, and I already know it's Barnette as he, too, wants to know what happened.

"I was asking if her and Andrea had the same dad. She got defensive and said no and gave me nothing to go on regarding it. Her dad is dangerous, and I need to make sure that Andrea's dad isn't a threat too."

Lacey becomes pale white and rigid as she stares at me.

"When did you ask her?" Barnette asks from behind me as he tries to gather a timeline.

"About four days ago." Right after we had our rendezvous…

"When she started to spiral again." He connects the dots.

"Andrea's dad is nothing to be concerned about, and all we know is he is a deadbeat piece of shit that is a nobody and should rot in hell for all eternity." The venom in Lacey's voice stills us all. I make a small side note to never get on her bad side.

I pause before continuing, "He is an obvious deadbeat because nothing was coming up after all my research. Even asking around, that whole time frame was a blur to so many people. Most of them state they didn't even know or see Ramona being pregnant at all. It was all so under wraps, it just seems suspicious. Then I got a lead on who it could be, but I haven't got to go into depth with it."

Lacey doesn't move her accusing eyes off of me for a long moment. I can tell she is deciding something in her mind; a small war is happening in that brain of hers.

"Lacey, if there is anything you can tell us…" Barnette pleads. The sound is foreign coming from him.

"It isn't up to me, guys. Don't you see that is the whole damn point? Ask Amelia, talk to Amelia! This isn't my information to share. Have you guys even stopped for a moment to ask about her past, or about what she went through? Huh!" she sputters.

I feel like a twelve-year-old boy learning to talk to females again. So, basically an idiot.

Barnette doesn't say shit after that as he reflects on his own thoughts. I look at Amelia's still form; the only movement is the breathing machine forcing small movements in her chest as it rises and falls in a systematic rhythm.

Lacey glares at the three of us. "Her life was not easy at all. She never got a choice in anything. She never had a say in what happened. She took care of Ramona, and then she took care of Ramona and Andrea. It has never been to just take care of herself until you three goons took her away from the only thing she knew."

"I never wanted this to happen to her. You have my word on that," Barnette admits beside me, voice low. None of us wanted this to happen.

"I told you she needed help," I accuse him, a small bit of my desperate anger slipping through.

"I couldn't predict she would jump to this!" he defends himself, throwing his hand up in the air.

"Alright, that's enough. There's no need to attack each other because we are tired and wired up," Derrick reprimands from the door. He turns to Amelia's friend. "Lacey, how about I take you home so you can get some rest, and I will deal with these two?"

She grips on tightly to Amelia. "I don't want to leave her!" she panics.

Derrick frowns. "I need you to go check on Andrea and be with her and Romona. They already called Ramona, so I can only imagine what she is saying in front of her."

Oh shit, I didn't even consider that roach.

"Oh, fuck, okay, I will check on her. Shit!" Lacey jumps up and slings her bag around her shoulders. "Listen," she pauses and turns towards us, "if you want her to be happy, Andrea needs to be in the picture—period. I know you all think it's unsafe, but how unsafe is it for her to be with Ramona without her? And before you dig further, talk to Amelia about it. Please just think about it."

Moving in a teenager to the bachelor pad? Now that would be interesting. But with Amelia being sought after, I don't think bringing her little sister into our home would be safe.

Then again, she has no safety outside of our home either. Even with one of our men occasionally poking around making sure everything is alright.

Barnette grips my shoulder as they finish leaving the room and closing the glass door behind them. I pat his hand out of comfort more for me than him, but he shifts his grip and yanks me up out of my seat to face him.

"What the fuck, man?!" I throw my shoulder back to force him to release.

Barnette's face seems emotionless except for the way his eyebrows scrunch together, but I can't tell if its confusion, anger, sadness—I don't fucking know.

Then it occurs to me.

He *knows*.

"What happened between the two of you?" he demands. Oh, what a loaded question.

"We needed to know all the details, Barnette—" His hand raises up to stop me.

"Is something going on between the two of you?" The anger that laces those words cause me to hesitate, and that hesitation gave him his answer. His eyes narrow dangerously.

"Listen, this is business for you, Barnette. I care about her. I have legitimate feelings for her!" I try to keep my voice down, but damn it who is he to question me? "Besides, you were still meeting up with Dakota—"

Barnette's eyebrows shoot up to his hairline.

"I'm stopping you right there because no, the fuck I was not seeing her. I stopped that almost immediately after bringing Amelia into my home."

Well, fuck.

He adds bitterly, "I didn't screw around at all. I was hoping that Amelia would come around to me."

Now I feel a mix of guilt and anger.

"First of all, you didn't communicate with us or with her that you cared more about her than just a business deal—a deal, mind you, that she didn't want a full part of. Second, how was I not supposed to fall for her? She is fucking feisty, tempered, and sweet all rolled up into one. She is the whole fucking package deal, and it is not my fault it took you longer than me to figure that shit out!"

Barnette's eyes turn into slits the second before he punches me square in the jaw. The pain registers through my skull, making me wince.

"Did you fuck her?" he asks through clenched teeth.

"Not to kiss and tell, but yes, Barnette, I did!" I smirk at him as he swings again, and I allow him to land the hit. I can feel the blood dribble down my chin from where he busted my lip open.

"She is mine." His body shakes from the anger that is radiating through him.

"She is her own damn person. She came to me; she came to my door! I treat her with kindness and respect while you are over here bossing her around!"

He hesitates as my words register through his mind.

"She went to you?" He almost sounds defeated, and I lose my smugness.

I sigh, wiping the blood from my face. "Yes, Barnette, she did. She needed to control something. You haven't tried with her."

He looks over at Amelia and walks slowly up to her. I stay put where I am standing, not wanting to interfere with whatever thoughts are going through his mind.

"I knew she cared about you. I saw the smile on her face when you two were dancing." His voice sounds far away, as if he is reflecting over every moment between the two of us since we brought her home. "I haven't made her smile like that." Damn it.

"Barnette, what did I tell you before? Communicate with the damn woman. Talk with her and tell her what you have going on in that fucked-up head of yours. It would do us all some good if you kept us all in the loop," I state with a hint of joking. Then I stare down at Amelia too. "I care about her a lot. I want nothing to happen to her, I want to protect her—hell, I want to love her. And I love you too, bro. I didn't mean for it to get this far, but it did."

Barnette doesn't respond to me for a couple of minutes while he sits there holding her hand. He strokes her hair out of her face gently, exposing a whole different side that people rarely get to see from him.

"I have real feelings for this girl. I don't know how to explain how she lights something up in me even with her defiance," he murmurs. "I don't want to give her up."

I blow out a deep breath. Neither do I.

"Listen, we have shared women before—"

"She isn't the same," he snaps.

"Okay, okay. Well, maybe we shouldn't have to make her choose. Why can't she just have both of our love?"

The word *love* causes his body to go rigid as he swings his head towards me.

"You love her?" he whispers. I really fucking do.

"Do you?" I challenge back.

Barnette stands up again and faces me. I can tell he is fighting with something internally while trying to keep in control so as not to get us kicked out. How we are still here after two sucker punches to the face is beyond me.

"She is to be *my* wife," he states, emotion warring him down.

"She can be married to you, that's fine, but I also want to have a relationship with her. We both care about her, we both want to protect her, and we both love her. Why can't we both be with her?" I demand.

I have to swallow down my nerves as I stand toe to toe with my favorite person in the world.

We have never been at such high odds before, and I don't want to lose my friendship with him at all, but my heart deserves some happiness too. Barnette's hand runs through his hair as he looks at her then back at me.

"How about we do something we haven't don't since Amelia has come into our life." My ears perk up, anxious to hear his next words. "How about we ask her what she wants when she wakes up?" Now *that* is impressive. My little Barnette is growing up.

"That would be the smartest thing we have done in a long time," I chuckle.

He murmurs, "She will come out of this, Dean. She is a fighter; she is too damn stubborn to just die on us like that. Amelia just had a moment of weakness, but she will be okay."

I look down at our little fighter in her bed, and my heart swells. "Yes, she will be fine. She will be okay."

How lost and lonely did she have to feel to get herself to this point? Guilt racks through me as a wave of dizziness overwhelms me. Barnette grabs my shoulder to steady me.

"Maybe you should get some rest. I would say I'm sorry for hitting you, but I don't regret it." He chuckles honestly, and I shrug him off.

"What's fair is fair. Just glad we got to a neutral territory is all." Whatever she wants and decides, I will respect full heartedly.

Barnette nods. "I'm going to stay here with her. How about you get some rest and tomorrow start fresh on looking into who broke into our system so we can see who is behind this? They are going to pay for killing our men. Blood for blood."

I feel the heaviness back on my shoulders weighing me down at the thought of those deaths and those poor families. We all need justice.

"Alright, just text me if anything changes or happens. Okay? I will stop by later tomorrow with an update, then we need to discuss Andrea—"

Barnette raises his hand to stop my direction of conversation.

"Tomorrow," he states, and I nod in agreement.

I walk over to Amelia and lean over to bring her hand to my lips. I hope with everything inside of me that she makes it through this okay.

Please don't die, Amelia.

CHAPTER 23

Hello, Consequences

Amelia

THE HARSHNESS of the bright white lights attacks my eyes. Sandpaper is the only way I can describe this sensation I feel. I roll my neck and look down at my body that is underneath the crisp white and cream linens that are tucked in around me. I am tucked in like a porcelain doll.

I don't want to be a damn doll.

I slowly lift my right arm, followed by my left arm. The blood flowing is almost painful as blood rushes around to my unused limbs. How long have I been out?

My gaze shifts around the room, but nobody is here. I am alone.

Good.

An unused tray sits on the faded light brown bedside table beside me; I try to stretch my neck to see what is in it, but I can't catch a glimpse.

I shove the blankets off of me as my stomach rumbles loud

and obnoxiously. I slowly sit myself up and am accompanied by a wave of dizziness.

Nausea claws its way up my throat. I grip onto the bed rail tightly and try to gain my balance. Maybe I just need food?

I reach out and move the cover off the plate of food, and the onslaught of scents hits my nose before I can even register what I am looking at. Tears immediately fill my eyes as saliva coats my mouth—oh fuck! I jump up and bulldoze my way into the bathroom.

I barely make it to the toilet before I wretch up pure stomach acid from the lack of food in my gut. There is nothing there. My throat burns from the intrusion.

Damn, this is fucking gross. I pull away from the toilet as the smell of bleach starts to fill my senses and turn towards the sink. I let the water run and warm up as a small bit of longing for the sensation of warm water makes me yearn for a shower. Realistically, though, I probably cannot stand much longer.

I rinse my mouth and bring the warm water over my face; I can feel a slight upturn on my lip as I run my hands over my mouth. I look up into the mirror as tiny droplets fall from my chin and suddenly, the night flashes through my mind.

The way my body started slowing, my blood and pulse lulling their movements. The only peace it brought was it muddling up my racing mind, the thoughts that hounded and hounded me, taking all of my peace.

Those thoughts slowed, those feelings halted in their tracks. How peaceful greeting death was. The heaviness of how I felt takes my breath away.

The feeling of immediate regret weighs heavily on my shoulders. A war within myself.

How can there be two different parts of me in this one single body? I stare hard at myself in the mirror, looking at my cracked lips that are still slightly swollen from the abrasion of the tube they must have needed to put in.

My eyes are slightly sunken in from the lack of food and the heaviness of all my body had endured during those hours.

What was I thinking? How could I have followed through with that?

What about Andrea?

Tightness immediately envelops my heart, a deep painful tingling bursts through my chest, and I can feel the wetness on my cheeks from my tears before I even see them.

I try to bring that peace I need so desperately in my heart. I just need my little Andie in my arms.

I wince as a pounding onslaught hits the side of my head, the memory of the night I met Andrea seeping to the surface.

A secret I buried that wants to be set free.

Pop.

What the hell was that?

My legs become soaked, and I feel like I am peeing all over myself. What the hell is happening?

My stomach tightens, and the sensation causes my heart to start racing. I throw the blanket off of me and roll myself off the bed.

My stomach is huge. Everything has been so sore, but Mom said that was to be expected. Mom said that the uncomfortable feeling is normal. I try to stand up when my stomach starts having the biggest cramp I have ever felt in my life.

"MOM!" I yell out in full panic. I am still peeing myself, and I cannot get it to stop. Why am I peeing everywhere? Why is it still coming out?

The cramp is so strong I double over onto the bed, and black spots cover my room.

"MOOOOOOM!" I scream through the pain. Why isn't she coming? What is happening to me?

The pain finally releases, and I am able to waddle out my bedroom door. I go left into the bathroom to get myself on the toilet.

I am not gushing anymore, but it has not fully stopped. I yank my pajama pants down and sit on the toilet. I look down and my stomach immediately turns sour at the sight of reddish liquid on my legs and floor.

Why am I bleeding? Where is the blood coming from?

Another cramp rampages through my body, and I yell out from the pain. Tears run down my face, and I hold onto the counter with all the strength I have.

Make it stop! Make it stop, it hurts!

"By golly, what is all that yell—" My mom finally appears in the doorway to the bathroom, but her words stop short.

Her gray shirt is wrinkled and hanging off one shoulder, her blue pajama bottoms are slightly raised up her legs, and her face is so pale she reminds me of a ghost. She looks scared out of her mind, and that causes my fear to escalate completely.

My breathing comes out in my gasps as I try to wrap my head around what is happening.

"Mom, what is—I don't know what is wrong," I say in between pants. My body starts shaking uncontrollably, and another huge cramp tightens my stomach. "Aaaah!" Sobs tear through me, and it spurs my mother into action.

Mom runs up and gets on her knees in front of me. She places both her hands on my face and holds my head firm to stare right back at hers.

She reassures me, "It is going to be okay. We got this, okay? We got this. Honey, the baby is coming, that is all. You are in labor."

Labor? I have seen women on TV go into labor. Mom told me a couple weeks ago that it could be any day now; I just didn't think it was going to be today. I didn't want it to be today. I am not ready; I don't want to have a baby!

"I can't stop peeing, Mom!" I sob. I cannot get my body to stop.

Everything hurts so bad, and this awful feeling is happening down there—I feel like something is trying to rip me open! She has the audacity to chuckle at me.

"Oh no, honey, no, it isn't pee. That is your fluid that was around the baby. Your water broke. That means the baby is going to be coming any time now. Any time!" Her words seem to have made a light bulb switch in her mind because she stands up suddenly and opens up the bottom cabinet to start grabbing towels. "Let's get you in the tub, okay? Let's get you in the tub so that way we don't make a big mess, come on."

She grabs my arms and uses all her strength to lift me up. My legs almost buckle underneath me.

"It hurts!" I grip on tightly to her as another cramp tightens my belly and I sob again.

Bang, bang, bang!

Someone's at the front door.

Mom stops and looks at me, and I can see the fear rattling through her. Who could it be? Is it the cops?

Bang, bang, bang!

"You stay right here, honey, I will be right back, okay? Try to stay quiet."

I slam back down on the toilet as she rushes through the door to see who is here. I can hear the door sweep open against the carpet and hushed whispers following right after.

A cramp takes over, and the pain is so much stronger than before. How could they get stronger? Why are they stronger? What is happening? A loud cry escapes my lips. I can't be quiet; I cannot stop crying.

"Move!" I hear. I recognize the voice immediately.

Before I can even process the sound of someone's feet on the carpet, Lacey's body takes up the entry of the doorway.

"You didn't need to be so pushy, Lace!" Mom grumbles from behind her.

Lacey's face is pale as she takes in the probable horror scene in front of her. I become overwhelmed again as pain overtakes my entire body. My stomach, back, and private area are shred apart, and my legs start shaking uncontrollably.

The sound of my cries echo off the walls of the tiny bathroom, and it spurs Lacey into action. She runs to me and starts rubbing my back.

"Shhh, it's okay, it's okay," she soothes with a tremor in her voice. "She is going to be okay right?" her shrill voice yells at my mom, breaking the soft tone she had just a moment before.

"Oh, Lace, she will be fine. She is having a baby. We knew of this, it's okay." But I can hear the worry in her tone and the stress layered underneath it.

Can I die? Right now, I do want to die to make this pain stop! This pain is unbearable! Tears drip off of my chin as it trembles and shakes my teeth.

Lacy looks down at me in concern. "We need to take her to a hospital!" she yells as I grip onto her from the wave of pain that starts crashing through me. "There's so much blood—I keep slipping!"

Her feet are unsteady beneath her, but she does not loosen her grip on me. I look at Mom pleading with her through my eyes.

I watch as Mom takes in everything around her. Her gaze starts at the floor, then trails to the tub, pauses at Lacey, then she locks eyes with me. The look that overcomes her face is an expression I have never seen on her before. She has this... look of regret. The sadness in her eyes bores into mine just as another wave of pain starts and my cries break her out of her trance.

"No, no, hospital. Don't need them to take the baby or Amelia into the system. They will be separated."

That word alone spurs so much fear into my mind, I immediately start shaking my head no, no, no uncontrollably. I cannot go into the system. I have heard horror stories.

This life I have learned to manage. I understand my mom, but the system is unknown and broken. No way!

"Shhh, Shhh it's okay, Mel. You aren't going anywhere. I won't lose you, it's okay," Lacey tries to whisper into my ears, reassuring me. I can feel her shift her head back towards my mom as she holds mine tightly to her chest. "What do we do?" She seems so tiny asking in such a desperate voice.

I think she is just as broken at the thought that I lack control of this situation and we need to ask my mother for help. How do we do this?

Mom claps her hands together, causing us both to jerk at the sudden intrusion of sound.

"Okay, here's the plan—we got to get her into the tub, alright? I'm going to get a couple towels down for her, just keep holding onto her."

Mom's voice fades as she runs to the dryer next to the kitchen. She starts talking on her way back, and the shakiness leaves her voice as she continues announcing the game plan.

"She will lay in the tub, and the towels will help keep her upright, and it will keep the mess in mostly one spot. I need to see if there's a head down there so we need to get those pants all the way off, honey, so we can see when the baby is coming."

She struts in and lays down a couple of towels. Lacey starts removing my pants from around my ankles with her left hand as she keeps her right hand on my shoulder.

"A baby is coming out of me." I don't know what else to say. I don't know how to process this. Why? Why is this happening to me?

Mom stands to my right and points to my left side at Lacey. I don't know how they are communicating. Everything is like a fog with a faraway echo. Are they talking? I get lifted off the toilet, and I have the cruelest sensation that my insides are going to fall out. My head spins as I try to move through the heaviness in my legs to get them to move; I feel like I can't walk at all.

"Come on, honey, shuffle them feet, baby, shuffle." Mom's voice breaks through the fog barrier, and the softness of her tone is so sincere and so soft.

A tone I don't hear from her very often, but it makes my heart ache, so I shove my face into her and cry.

"Mommy. Mommy, it hurts," I sob into her chest.

"I've got you, baby. I've got you, it's okay." She pats my hair the best she can and hugs me tightly to her. The comfort of her hug was all I needed at that moment. "Come on, let's get you in this tub before the next contraction hits you."

Contraction—that's right. I read about that when Lacy and I were looking up about pregnancy and babies. Contractions help the baby come out.

I feel like all that reading didn't prepare me for the actual pain I was going to be having, but everything I read comes flooding back to me.

"Lace, baby, go in the kitchen and grab the orange medicine bottle I have in there. There is only one orange one; you cannot miss it," Mom orders, and Lacey rushes out of the bathroom while Mom takes another towel and uses her feet to clean up the floor.

"Mommy, I am so scared," I admit as I hold onto the sides of the tub. My teeth start to clench from the pain.

Sweat pours down my face and back; everything feels wet, slimy, and gross all over. Mom's whole body slumps in defeat before she kneels down and looks at me.

This is also a look I have never seen her do. She reaches out her hand and cups my cheek gently.

"I am so, so sorry you are hurting baby. I am so—" Her voice cracks, and she clears her throat. "I am so sorry you are in this mess. If

I knew—" Again, she chokes up, "if I knew that anyone would have hurt you like that, I would have hurt them first."

She looks so sad and sincere; her expression causes my whole heart to shatter.

The sober her always has more feelings; the sober mom always cares more for me. Why can't she always be sober?

Lacey rushes in with the little orange bottle and a glass of water. My mouth immediately becomes parched at the sight of it. Water, I need water! Mom pulls out a pill and grabs the water to hand to me.

I don't question it; I just take it and chug the whole glass as if it may be my last for months.

"Okay, Meli, you've got this. We are going to be okay." She kneels next to my mom and wipes the hair off of my sweaty face. "Do you need anything, more water? Food?" Her big eyes search me up and down as if the answer to her worries are there.

"No food right now, honey. I don't want her to vomit and choke," Mom warns.

I didn't even feel sick to my stomach until she said something about it. As the sharp pain crushes my stomach, this awful burning sensation takes over my private parts, and I scream out from the pain of it.

I feel the strangest sensation to push, but the pain hurts too much.

"Oh shit, oh shit! We are there, baby!" Mom hollers out herself. "Come on, pull your legs up, baby."

Mom's voice is mixed with excitement and fear all at the same time. Lacey tries to help me pull my legs up towards me, but my head begins spinning and I feel like my arms are noodles.

"No, baby, come on. The baby is trying to come out. This is where we start pushing."

I am overwhelmed with fatigue and just plain terrified to be honest. Just kill me now. Can I just die? Can someone just knock me *out? I heard people can pass out from pain, and this amount of pain has to be at that level. This is unbearable.*

Lacey jumps up, and I can feel her push up my back as she squeezes herself behind me. She shimmies down, and I am too exhausted to ask her what she's doing. She pulls my legs up for me up to my chest, and I lean my back against her front.

"I've got you. Come on! Let's push together, Meli! Come on!" I can feel the strength of her determination, and it feeds into my drained soul.

She lends her strength to me, and I can feel myself start to come out of the fog of pain that took me under.

I raise my head up and brace my legs.

"Good job, Lace, atta girl! Come on, Amelia, let's push. When you feel the next contraction, push with all of your strength!" Mom encourages me as she scoots down to get a full view of my private area.

I don't even care anymore. I just want the pain to stop!

A contraction starts, and I holler as I push. Lacey keeps her hands around my thighs and helps me pull them back as I push.

The contractions are on top of each other, one right after the other. The pain isn't stopping at all; I need it to stop! I barely am able to catch a breath in between. My breaths coming out in pants and raspy —my throat is dry, and my whole body hurts so much.

Please make it stop! God, make it stop!

"Come on, honey, push! That's it!" Mom encourages me as she pats my leg gently. "Come on!"

I push and finally feel an odd sensation slips through me, and my mom lunges forward. The pain stops, the pain stops! I sob out in relief this time.

The most angelic sound I have ever heard rings through the air. A soft little baby cry, and my sobs stop. I lift my exhausted head off of

Lacey, and I look down to see a baby in mom's arms. Mom is smiling as she softly coos at the child.

"She looks so much like you did, Amelia." Mom laughs, she actually laughs and is full of smiles as she looks at the little baby.

Then it clicks in my head. Mom said she. The baby is a girl!

"Here you go, honey." She leans forward and places her on my chest, and I look down at her. The little girl in my arms stops crying as she looks up at me.

Everything seems to just melt away as I hold her to me. A little girl, a sweet little baby girl.

I have a daughter.

How could I leave her like that?

How selfish could I really be?

I don't even feel like the same person from that night. How could that darkness take over everything so quietly, so easily?

A sob escapes my lips as I grasp shakily onto the white porcelain sink, my legs beginning to buckle underneath me. I can barely feel the sensation of warm hands gripping me around my waist.

The warmth on my back is an immediate comfort, giving my body permission to fall back into their arms.

Sobs escape my throat harshly; I lack all control as my body heaves from the onslaught of emotions that swirl like a hurricane through me.

"Shhh, shhh, I've got you," a deep murmur whispers into my ear as their hand soothes down my hair—almost fatherly like. "You are okay, you are safe."

My brain tries to decipher the owner of the voice, but my body is shaking so hard that even the person holding me struggles to keep his grip on me. I get pulled tightly into the person's chest and brought slowly down to the floor.

I can hear the way the cloth of their shirt frictions against the wall, causing a very low whooshing sound that surprisingly registers through whatever the hell this is.

What the fuck is wrong with me?

Barnette

My Broken Sleeping Beauty

I grip her tightly as her fragile body thrashes around in my arms. Jesus, she is going to end up falling or I am going to accidentally hurt her with my grip.

I push us back into the wall and slide down to the floor with her. I go slowly so as not to startle her, as I turn her so I can cradle her to me when we get to the floor.

Her body becomes jerkier and less thrashing once we hit the floor, and I cradle her tightly to me and bury her face into my chest.

God, I am so happy she didn't die.

A shuddering breath leaves me as I try to soothe her. All I can think about is to talk her through this.

"You are alive, you are okay. I've got you." Thank fuck she made it through.

They extubated her yesterday, and she has been in a deep sleep since. Almost like a sleeping beauty style, except my kiss would be the last thing she would want.

She looked so tiny in that hospital bed. I stayed up all night to make sure I was there if she woke up, so she knew she wasn't alone. Of course, she would wait to wake up when I go and get a cup of coffee at the cafeteria when the nurse practically chided me into keeping myself healthy too or I wouldn't be any good to her half dead. Why the fuck did I listen to her?

She shuffles in my arm and brings her face up to my neck, nestling herself against me. Her little hiccups are creating an almost tickle-like sensation against my skin.

When I walked back into the room and saw her bed empty, panic erupted through me as I scanned the entire room. I caught her in the bathroom staring at her reflection, and that terror quickly turned into relief.

I had taken a couple small steps towards her before I heard her begin to sob, the sound immediately wrenching my gut. Her entire body started to tremble as she attempted to keep standing. She began to sway, and I feared she was going to fall and hit her head.

As fast as I can, I stride towards Amelia to pull her to me, both out of safety and because of my own selfish need to hold her again. Seeing her intubated lying still in that bed as the fucking beeps from the machine systematically shrilled out has my nerves completely shot.

Sobs break out of her, and it shatters my heart. Her body shakes in my grasp, and I hold on as tightly as I can. She hasn't shed one tear in front of me the whole time she's been with me, and I never want to see her cry again.

I make a vow right then and there that I will do everything in my power so she doesn't feel like this again in her life.

"I'm soo... sooo...." she stutters out in between her dry heaves, tears streaming down her cheeks.

"Shhh," I murmur into her ear. "No need to talk right now. Just breathe. Slow, deep breaths." I can feel the wetness on my cheek from the couple tears that have betrayed my own eyes.

"What is going on here?" the nurse's high-pitched voice states out of panic as she shuffles into the room.

I don't mean to, but all my anger I was holding in snaps out of control towards her. She stands there in her burgundy-colored scrubs with her hands on her hips staring down at us.

"Get out!" I snap at her, not wanting her to interrupt this moment for one second. Amelia needs me right now, just me, and I've got her.

"Don't make me call security—" she begins when Amelia pulls slightly away from me enough to look at the nurse.

"I am fine. He's fine. Please, give us some space." Her voice shakes slightly, but my chest is tight as hell listening to her. She wants time with me.

The nurse just stands there, unsure what to do, before finally shaking her head and turning on her heels to stalk out of the room with a huff.

I breathe out in relief and put my gaze back onto Amelia.

"You're here," she murmurs, looking up at me with her bloodshot eyes.

"Of course." I am at a loss for words. I have so much I want to say to her, but I don't want to tell her everything at once. I swallow over the lump in my throat, the action of it drawing her attention to my neck.

"I almost died," she says quietly, her expression darkening.

"You did." I feel a hurricane of emotions run through me. Disbelief, anger, hurt, and the sadness of it all. "Don't you ever die on me again, do you understand me?"

I will not make it if this bundle of fire in my arms tries to extinguish herself again. Or if anyone tries to take her from me. Now that I have faced how much she means to me, I can't lose her.

"Will your plans get derailed if I die?" she whispers.

I blow out the anger that courses through me at her question; I feel the burning sensation rage through my chest and into my arms.

She can sense the change in my demeanor and goes to pull away, but I yank her against me.

"You are more than a *plan*, Amelia. You are worth more than the money I paid your mom, and you are worth more than anything I could ever try to achieve. I want you alive because I care about you. I want you alive because you deserve to be alive and experience life, and damn it if I want to experience it right along with you. I want you, Amelia. I want us, and you almost succeeded in taking that all away."

Emotion clogs my throat, and I don't even have the chance to clear it away for her to not hear it. I want an *us*, and finding her in that bed almost dead, someone might as well have carved my heart out of my goddamn chest.

Amelia starts to sob against me, and I for the first time allow my own tears to fall out right along with her.

"I didn't think you cared about me like that," she says, her tone muffled and raw.

Marisol's voice filters through my head, *"Just be honest with her. Don't hold anything back"* I take a deep breath.

"Amelia, at first, yes, I will admit I was using you. But getting to know you, how could I not fall for you and everything that you are? I admit I am not very forthcoming with my feelings—" To that I get a loud snort from the girl I hold in my arms, and I look down at her to find her staring at me with a big, goofy grin on her face. "What?"

"No kidding, mister." She rolls her little swollen eyes at me, and I can feel the frown spreading on my lips. "You seriously suck at the whole 'telling my feelings' and I mean that politely."

She chuckles, and I find myself holding onto that sound and wishing for her to continue.

"I will work on that, I promise, as long as I can continue to hear you laugh and see your smile," I murmur. She replies with an odd look that I cannot place. She just stares at me until an emotion I *do* recognize clouds over her: confusion. "Why do you look confused?" I ask.

"Because you are one confusing man, Barnette. What do you want with me?" she sighs, sniffling slightly.

There is so much I can respond with, but I just give the most honest answer I can provide her.

"I just want you to be my wife, Amelia, be my partner in this world." There's so much raw honesty in the statement, and I wish she could read everything I have to give and everything I want. I feel the heaviness of it in my tone.

She curls into me, and I embrace her as tightly as I can without squeezing the breath out of her.

"Please don't treat me like I am a fragile doll," she whispers. I hesitate for a moment at her words. She is so small in my arms, and what she just did to herself because of the war in her mind proves she is vulnerable.

Yet I can hear the plea in her tone; everyone has a breaking point in their life. She just happened to reach hers that night. I do the only thing I can think of to show her that I still see her fiery temper in her: I squeeze the ever-living shit out of her.

"Oof!" she squeals out in a deep voice as I crush all the breath out of her, not allowing her to inhale anything.

She finally starts tapping me repeatedly with her little hand, and I release her immediately.

"Mother fucker!" Amelia gasps. She coughs, and alarm bells ring in my ear thinking I may have squeezed her too tight so soon after she was intubated.

Fuck, did I hurt her?

"Shit Amelia I'm-"She laughs. She is freaking laughing.

"You are fine! I get your point, thank you," With that, she snuggles back into me. "But don't ever squeeze me that tight again or I will throat punch you." Her little fiery statement brings a smile back to my face, and every nerve on alert settles down.

She is back. Amelia is alive and back.

I pull her away from my chest and wipe her hair off of her face. There is so much I want to do with her and show her, but first I need to get her to see that I am a man worthy of it, too.

"Amelia, will you please do me the honor of going on an actual date with me?" I say softly.

My wife-to-be and I haven't even had an actual date, and that is the least she deserves. I did this whole thing wrong, and I know I did. Even if it is a hard pill to swallow.

"You want to go on a date with your fiancée?" I cannot read the expression on her face as she stares at me, and it bothers me how much I don't know about her.

"Of course I do; I want to know more about you," I say earnestly.

"If we are to be married, Barnette, happily married, and to be partners as you stated, then things have to be different. I don't want to be forced, I don't want to be told what to do and how to do it—I want to be asked and I want to be guided."

I stare at her in her small, faded blue hospital gown as she makes her requests. Furrowing my brow, I think back to what Marisol told me: that to have a partner, you need to treat them as an equal.

I haven't been doing that with Amelia at all. How could I have expected a partner out of her if I never gave her the chance to feel like she had a choice? She had no problem giving me sass, but when it came down to the bare bones of things, even though I did try giving up the reins a little, it was my way or no way. I did her a disservice by taking a part of her voice.

"You have my word." I can see her defensive barriers melt away at my words, and she sinks into me.

"I also need Andrea with me. Or at least communication. I tried to find a way to buy a phone, but you said I couldn't work…" she trails off.

"Now, wait a second, I never said you couldn't. I simply stated that you didn't need to. As for communicating with her, I will get you a phone. I just thought you had one." I try to reflect back on when we had this conversation; I know for a fact I didn't tell her no when it came to talking with Andrea, and I know I told her she didn't need a job because she doesn't; she has me.

"I can't afford to get her a phone either," she states, looking embarrassed.

"Then we will get her a phone too. It's just a phone, Amelia." I don't understand what she has to be embarrassed about.

She sighs loudly. "With what money? I have nothing." She looks at me like I am a giant idiot.

"Ours. It's not just my money, it is *ours*, Amelia."

Her eyes get wide for a moment at the statement. Then those beautiful hazel eyes turn into little slits and briefly, I am baffled by the turn of emotion and unsure what to expect.

I clear my throat and continue, "Also, maybe we should discuss if it is this important to you about her coming to stay with us. Maybe eventually when she is older if it will make you happy, but it isn't ideal while she is underage."

Her eyes go wide again, and I see a hundred different emotions go through them as tears start to gather.

But she eventually nods her head as if answering a question that is only in her mind, then looks back up to me.

"Then yes, when we get out of here and I can stand without

passing out, I would love to go on an actual date with you," Amelia agrees.

I breathe out a sigh of relief, not realizing I was fully expecting her to tell me no. Relief is as refreshing as a glass of ice water on a hot day.

"Can I ask one more thing?" she asks. I chuckle at her question; she acts like she was sitting here with a list of them.

"Anything you want." I brace for whatever she could fire out. It could be about my work, it could be about my life, the marriage; maybe it's about her sister moving in with us. My mind is going in a thousand different directions.

"Can we get off this floor now?"

My eyes widen in surprise. "Of course." I hold onto her as I scoop her up and get us off of the floor. "Anything for you."

As long as she's by my side, that is. I don't ever want to let her go again.

CHAPTER 24

Killer or Defender

Amelia

One Week Later

I TRY to adjust this ridiculous slit in the dress to cover more of my thigh. It rides up nearly to my hip, and I feel completely uncomfortable.

When Barnette left this on my bed, my jaw hit the floor. It was beautiful—no, stunning. I felt like a damn princess when I slid the black satin over my body. The silk was so soft against my skin, and it hugged me so tightly that there was absolutely no room for any undergarments. I felt sexy and wicked.

I looked into that mirror and even though I was still a bit on the thin side from my recovery from the hospital, the color did return to my cheeks, and I could see a spark back in my eyes.

It has only been five days since I got to leave the damn place; they kept me on a watch and wanted to make sure through numerous social workers that I felt safe leaving. I just know I am sick of Jell-O and I never want to hear those damn alarms again.

The guys have also been making sure I am not left alone for too long, and if they have something to do then Marisol is left to babysit. It wasn't until yesterday when

I lost my damn mind from being coddled like a baby that I explained to Barnette that treating me like this will spiral me out again.

I need to live, I need to breathe air outside of this house, and I need to be out of my head.

I haven't seen much of Dean and Derrick except for at breakfast and dinners. Apparently, a lot of things are happening out in their world of connections, and they have been busy following up on it.

Thankfully, it hasn't been awkward with Dean, but we also haven't talked about everything that happened, so I am just mentally preparing for that shitshow to come up.

I'm not ready to have that conversation with Barnette, so maybe just maybe, it will stay a secret.

Barnette did make good on his promise, though; he got me and Andrea phones, and I have been texting that girl nonstop. She has finals going on now that it's the end of the school year, but I promised her that once summer hits she will be coming to stay with me, and I am so excited.

I miss her so damn much. I didn't want her to see the bruises on me and freak out that something happened to me.

God only knows Lacey had to go douse the fire that Ramona started while I was in the hospital. She was already freaked out, but Lacey played the dramatic card, and we will discuss it at length later.

But I promised Lacey and myself that I would never do that again. Andrea needs me alive, not dead.

I stare back into my own eyes in the mirror and can see the

spark of purpose there. The spark that made me who I am, that gave me my steel backbone.

And with that combo, I feel bold.

I slipped the heels on gently; they look like they are worth more than the trailer I used to live in. Deep black, with a sexy red undertone. It gives that little pop of color, and I quickly go to find a matching lipstick.

Sitting in the back of the car, however, the boldness I felt looking into that mirror ebbs slightly as I begin to feel slightly self-conscious.

Barnette's hand overwhelms my own and stops it from fidgeting. He leans in closely to me, and I can smell the smokiness of his cologne; it's intoxicating. Now that I have seen his softer side, my feelings for him have gone haywire.

"You look absolutely stunning," he whispers, making butterflies erupt in my stomach. "And I expect to see those long legs in the air later with nothing but those heels on."

Motherfucker. I bristle at his confidence, but it doesn't stop the slickness that wets my thighs.

I turn towards him and murmur back, "The only place these heels are going is up your ass." He has the nerve to chuckle slightly.

"I am intrigued by the challenge."

Oh God, I am going to lose. I shuffle away from him, and he smirks as he keeps his eyes on me, devouring me on the spot.

His phone rings shrilly through the car a moment later, and he breaks our hungry stare-off to answer it.

"Speak." What a self-righteous asshole. Like a simple hello would be too difficult for him. I'm about to chide him before his body tenses up. "What? Now?" His voice is sharp.

Dean pulls the car over quickly and breaks so hard my body slams in the seat belt as gravity pulls me forward.

"On our way." And with that, he slams the phone shut.

"What happened?" Derrick asks, misplaced anger on his face as he tries to match Barnette's mood.

"Have to take a detour. Head to Parkens St." His jaw is rigid, and I wish for anything that I could have heard what was on the other end of that phone call.

"With Amelia?" Dean asks incredulously.

Now my curiosity is a raging inferno. Barnette looks at me with full intensity. I see a flash of emotions flow through his eyes, but it happens so fast it is hard to dissect.

"I can handle it," I assure him, trying to put strength in my voice even though I am not sure what I have to be strong about.

He blows out a frustrated breath. "I know you can, puppet. Stay close. We will keep you safe. Just some business that needs to be taken care of."

I smile appreciatively at him, reflecting on our last heart-to-heart. I told him I won't be the one to hide behind a veil, and I asked him to trust me. This *is* the trust. This is my test. I don't know what's happening, but while Dean peels out from the side of the road, I square my shoulders and straighten my spine.

We eventually pull up to a huge warehouse in the middle of nowhere. I thought the dirt road was never going to end; we passed fields beyond fields of cornstalk, and then dirt. The warehouse is gray and looks abandoned, but I know better than that. This place matters, and I was trusted enough to be brought along.

Should I be happy that this life that I was so terrified to be in now makes me feel honored to be entrusted into?

I must be backwards. Maybe being intubated gave me brain damage and altered my brain chemistry in some way to now accept this craziness.

A small touch to my hand pulls me from my thoughts. I turn, finding Barnette is inches from my face. A small gasp escapes my lips before I can swallow it down.

"I don't want you here. You know how I felt about bringing you in fully. I do respect you, though," he says quietly. I feel a delighted tug on my heart. "Some shit is going down. This is straight business. I would say stay in the car, but I would feel better if you stayed in between the three of us, understood?"

There was no room for debate. His tone is hot and firm, and for some reason it adds to my desire for him. This is not the time to be horny. Not the time!

"Focus." Shit, he noticed. I harden my glance at him and give him a little smirk.

"I will stay with you three at all times. I promise I won't stray," I retort.

He nods at my answer, visibly pleased.

"I will have to treat you like I don't give a shit about you in there. I know you still think I don't have actual feelings for you, but you need to understand that in this dangerous world, who I care about is used against me. I don't want *you* used against me. Ever."

Then he does the one thing I least expected: he gives me a soft kiss on my lips, and I am one hundred percent sure I am breeding a butterfly farm in my stomach. Damn it.

Dean opens my door once Barnette pulls away, and I don't have the strength to look at his face, not after the rare tender moment I just had with his best friend.

Shit, shit, shit this love triangle is getting a little crazy. Focus!

All three men flank around me as we walk in sync up to the warehouse. Barnette to my front, Dean to my back right, and

Derrick to my back left. I stumble slightly in the heels, and it ruins the badass picture I was imagining of us walking in all serious and in sync. I internally cringe as I hear Derrick give way to a slight snicker.

"I swear to God if any of you let me fall on my face from these ridiculous heels in the dirt, I will gut you!" I seethe.

None of these guys like to be threatened, but they must not take me seriously because I feel the tense air surrounding us lighten a bit with amusement. Which is irritating because that means they don't take me seriously, and I really don't want to fall.

The doors open as we near it, and I see four men immediately as we go to enter.

The stride of the team doesn't break, which informs me that they are friendly, so I relax my shoulders a bit as the tension tries to weigh itself into my muscles. Barnette turns left up the stairs down to a room.

Anxiety races through my bloodstream, and I am nervous that I don't feel scared enough or if it is okay that I am not wrecked with fear.

There isn't any yelling, no gunfire, no sound really. I look around the main space to see chests lined up in rows—and is that a tanker? Is there an actual tanker in here?

I spot a white board and a table surrounded by chairs. But my eyes keep going back to the damn tanker.

"Focus," Dean whispers to me so softly I almost don't realize he's talking to me. I look forward again just as we walk through the doorway to a small conference room.

Two men stand bickering with each other in low tones, both of them tall and in full uniform. Visible guns are strapped to both of their sides, and I glimpse the tops of knives sticking up from their black combat boots. Their heated discussion stops as we all enter.

"Boss," the one on the left begins, his red curly hair disheveled from running his hand through it. His sharp nose is scrunched, matching his pinched blue eyes. "I don't understand how they even got in the system when they breached the first wall, but luckily we stopped it there."

Breached what? I look over to the right where multiple monitors line the wall, half of them blacked out while the other half hold surveillance videos of different places. I have so many questions, but I bite my tongue. Now is not the time.

"Did they get anything?" Derrick growls as he stands even taller with his arms crossed tightly across his chest.

"Not enough," the man to the right responds promptly. His salt and pepper hair is brought to a tip in the middle of his forehead. His near black eyes are harsh and angry, but I guess to be in this line of work it isn't surprising to become that way. "Not much at least. They didn't get the important files, but they did gather some information on the Moscow file and the East Coast locations. We already called and told them to load up and relocate."

"Dean, call and make sure they're doing what they were told," Barnette snaps. What are the connections in Moscow? How far is his reach?

The one on the right points to me.

"We stopped them before they got the girl's file," he states. Barnette and Derrick tense up beside me, but I am too focused on the jab.

"This *girl* has a name, and it is Amelia in case that wasn't in my file," I snap before I can bite my tongue.

Why the hell do they have a file on *me*? Barnette looks back at me with a glare, and I give him a snarky smile promising we will have a discussion later.

Above all, I want to know what is in my file and why. Also, who would want information on me?

"Ooo, you've got a spirited one on your hands," the dark-headed one responds.

Spirited doesn't even begin to describe the irritation I feel in being talked down to and researched. Nobody respects privacy around here.

Which reminds me of the file I found before everything happened. They haven't brought it up to me, and I been too scared to ask about it. Maybe it's time to grow a pair.

"Pedro, Sam, this is Amelia. Amelia, the one on the right is Pedro, and on the left is Sam," Barnette introduces.

I cross my arms around my mid-section; I know they are strangers to me and haven't earned by attitude, but they could have come up with something better other than *that girl*.

They wave casually to me, reminding me they know so much more about me than I do them.

"If it makes you feel any better, Amelia," Pedro starts as he takes a few steps towards me, extending his hand in a friendly gesture, "that file was for their eyes only and completely top secret. We did not have access to it."

A wave of gratitude sweeps through me at the confession. My business was kept secure.

But that doesn't change that there *is* business. How much about me do they already know? The thought makes me uneasy.

"You have no idea how much I appreciate that," I respond, forcing a smile.

We shake hands for a moment, and I feel a deep sense of

safety around him. He is someone I believe I can trust, and if he is here and Barnette trusts him, then I can too.

"Moscow is moving. They will call back in an hour with more of an update," Dean states as he reenters the room.

They must have connections everywhere. If they have business there, I wonder if I will ever get to go with them if they need to follow up.

"This is becoming dangerous." Pedro's voice draws back to the conversation, forgetting for a moment that I should not be thinking of traveling.

Sam is talking to the guys, Derrick is already at the screens typing away, and Barnette is reviewing paper files on the table. I walk slowly beside Dean, who is standing there on his phone texting. I'm still trying to figure out what happened.

"This always has been dangerous; it is just that the stakes are higher now," Barnette replies. Why are they higher?

"So, what changed—" Sam begins just as a series of pops come echoing in. I hear glass break as the window to our left shatters into a billion pieces and something zips by my head. What the hell is happening?

Next thing I know, Dean is laying on top of me on the ground as hollering starts registering through the blasts. His face is flushed red, and his eyes are wide as he stares down into my face, and the terror I see scares me. It finally registers through what that sound is—gunfire.

"We've got to move. Amelia, you stay behind me, do you understand?" he barks in my face, and I just nod my confirmation. I feel frozen, like my blood is solid and a cold sweat slicks my skin.

"Move. Move. Move!" Derrick starts demanding.

"Cover Amelia. Get her out of here now!" Barnette snaps as he holds his Glock in his hand heading for the door. He takes one last desperate look at me. "Baby, this is where you run."

Then he rushes out of the room.

This is real.

This is the danger.

We are also on the second floor of this building with nowhere to freaking go but down into the chaos.

Dean yanks me up off the floor and pulls me tight behind him as we venture towards the door to get the hell out of here. He has his own gun drawn in front of him, and I hold onto his shirt like my life depends on it.

Well, it kind of does.

I try to take slow, deep breaths as more shots are fired and men are yelling at each other.

I do not see Barnette anywhere; he must already be downstairs. A whizzing sound goes above my head, and I squeal as Dean's ducking down causes me to follow suit as I clench onto him.

I look up to see the bullet hole in the wall. Someone almost shot me in the head!

"Watch it!" he yells.

"Get her!" I hear different voices ring out.

"Move, move, move," Deans grunts back at me through clenched teeth.

I just want to get the hell out of here! I straighten up on wobbly legs, the heels the least ideal running shoes, but I do not have time to take them off.

We start rushing down the stairs. Pedro suddenly shows up to cover the base of the steps as we descend.

It is hard to see where shots are coming from, but I can see the door to get out of here to the right.

Boom!

Everything shakes, and I am violently forced off my feet as smoke blinds my vision. I lose hold of Dean's shirt through the explosion, and I try to gather myself on my knees to crawl towards where I remember the exit to be.

Someone grabs my ankle and begins dragging me across the floor, and I kick out with my free leg in an attempt to shake loose. Smoke billows through the room, and I can start to see more than just the form that is dragging me like a toy, and it isn't someone I recognize. Terror suffocates me as I realize an enemy has a hold of me.

Stay calm, stay calm, stay calm, I chant in my head. He gives a hard yank, causing my head to slam back into the ground, and black dots overwhelm my vision.

I hear more grunts and yelling, but everything is distorted as I try to regain more stability. My ankle is released and slammed down to the ground, discarded as if I am nothing, and the man starts to laugh as he looks around us.

"Give it up, you fucking idiots!" he belts out, humor lacing his strange thick accent.

"Leave her alone, Richard, and keep this between us." I recognize Barnette's voice coming from somewhere in the fading smoke, but my head is still spinning.

"No, I don't think I like that idea." I look up to see who I've connected is Richard pointing a gun at me.

I take in his suede dark brown vest he has fitted snug over his navy-blue dress shirt. His shirt is tucked into his jeans, and he is wearing a massive belt buckle, slightly reminding me of a cowboy minus the hat.

"Richard, it would be in your best interest to let Amelia go," Barnette says slowly and calmly.

I am actually impressed he isn't losing his shit; *I* want to lose my shit. Finally, my vision stops swaying, and everything clears up around us.

The tension is thick in the air. Almost like gravity completely relaxed its control on the atmosphere and took a break from shouldering all the heaviness.

It is hard to take a deep breath; my chest heaves, rising slightly. Derrick is on the ground bleeding from his wound, and I can see the dark pool of it developing around him as he tries to apply pressure to it—his face twisted in agony.

Dean stands there with his hands up as the gun in the man's grasp stays trained at his head behind him; one wrong move and he is a goner.

My heart squeezes at the sight of it. Barnette has his own damn gun pointed at him from Richard, fucking Richard causing this whole goddamn mess. Barnette's face is in complete control, and not an ounce of emotion is bleeding through.

Did he know this was going to happen? How the fuck are we going to get out of this mess?

Richard starts laughing as he also takes in the scene around him. "Well, times have surely changed, haven't they?" His long back coat flaps around him as he gestures his other hand into the air as if making a broad statement.

Men like him irritate me. It's always a show to men like him, always a game.

"Long time, no see; I think the last time we saw each other was eight years ago when I caught you in the middle of that setup with Rebecca," Richard drawls.

Barnette cracks his neck as he turns his head to the side. I make a mental note to ask about this Rebecca later, because the way he continues staring Richard down tells me there is something deeper. "I think from the events of that night you would be treating me with a little more respect than you are now."

Barnette's veins in his neck enhance as he snaps.

"We may have called a truce that night, but consider it gone now. Coming into *my* place, causing a *blood* bath! For what, Richard? What is your endgame here?"

Richard turns his attention to me.

"Get up," he demands, gun pointed straight at my head. Fuck.

I slowly get up, afraid that if I move too fast, he will get trigger happy. My movement makes Barnette twitch from the corner of my eye; he is also nervous.

Richard yanks me the second I stand straight up and pins me against the wall beside him.

"Don't want to forget the little tidbit that I have your girl here with me now, do you? One would think that you didn't truly care that I have her cornered over here." Richard shrugs his shoulders dramatically and takes a look at me, then cocks his head to look back at Barnette. "One would think you weren't with her for *love* but for *title*."

Barnette's jaw flexes, the only sign that I know he is bothered by the words. What title is he referring to?

"Does she know?" Richard snaps.

Barnette eyes me before training his attention back to Richard. "I haven't told her yet." Told me what?

Richard laughs out loud.

"He figured, darling child,"—he looks at me like a wolf about to devour a sheep—"that because of who your daddy is that he can be force his hand into doing business together by marrying you."

"How do you know who my father is?" I ask Barnette, my confusion furrowing my eyebrows. Mom said she didn't know who he was by name.

"Uh oh." Richard does a little dance with his fingers. "You didn't even know who your daddy was, did you, sweet girl?"

"Shut the fuck up, Richard, I don't need you talking to me like a child," I sneer at him as anger starts to rock through me. This whole time, it wasn't that Barnette needed a deal or a wife; I never understood what he saw in me, but now it all makes sense.

His gaze locks onto me, but I can't help but replay the fact that he and I didn't go into this for love.

He doesn't know me, my dreams, my wants. I knew from the beginning there was a deeper reason, I just didn't know it involved *my* father. A father I didn't even know was alive.

"He is one of the biggest arms dealers and has a wealth of power, knowledge, and money," Richard boasts as if he himself was infatuated with the man.

My stomach sours at the thought that I have a dad, let alone a dad who is apparently up in the ranks of this crazy ass life while me and my mother suffered in a rundown two-bedroom shack with hardly any food on the table. Not one call, one visit. Was he ever even curious about me?

The thoughts swirl around my mind, and I can see Barnette trying to get my attention, but I can feel my throat squeeze as the pressure becomes overwhelming. What has my life become?

"Amelia, please—" Barnette's voice punctures through the mess of swirls clawing through my brain.

"Oh, Barnette, she doesn't want anything to do with you. Tsk, tsk. She just wants her freedom, right?" Richard looks at me and uses his pointer finger to lift my chin.

I jerk my head away at the sensation of it.

"Mmmm, feisty this little thing is, isn't she?" He turns back to Barnette and takes a step toward him. "Of course, you have no idea how she feels in the bedroom, do you? But your best friend here,"—he swivels slightly toward Dean, and I feel like the blood flow in my body comes to a halt—"sure does."

He winks back at me really quick, and I give it my all to keep every single emotion off my face. I can feel the heat of Barnette's and Dean's stares on my face, and I do my absolute best not to look at either one of them. How the hell does he know that?

"You and your fucking games. Don't you ever get tired of them, *Dick*?" Dean chuckles bitterly. Leave it to him to ruffle the feathers even more so.

Richard points the gun at Dean then. "Watch it." His stern tone echoes through the building.

Barnette takes two steps towards me, and Richard swivels the gun right back to him.

"Uh, uh, uhh, be a good little boy and stay where you are." Richard's eyes narrow, one of his brows raising in challenge.

I finally put my eyes back on Barnette and shake my head so that he does not take another step.

"Please, Barnette, just do what he says." My voice is so soft and low I almost don't recognize it. I do not want him to get hurt, let alone killed. I do not wish that upon him or honestly, any of them.

Even if this is all one big giant festival of using people and being greedy.

The endearment in my voice has caught all their attention. Richard turns partway toward me, keeping his gun on Barnette. He reaches out with his free hand and goes to tuck my hair behind my ear, and I jerk back from the touch.

"Does this little birdie have true feelings for her captors?" His tone is one of amusement and pity. I hate being pitied.

"How about you take the barrel of that gun and shove it

down your throat and give it a nice little squeeze on that trigger? Make us all happy," I snap out with venom of a darkness I didn't know I possessed.

I don't want them dead, and I don't want to die—let alone at the hands of a guy named *Dick*.

I lean towards him, letting the anger show on my face. "I am no one's captive, not even yours. I own myself." I let the words stitch themselves into me.

I am nobody's fucking toy, I am nobody's plaything, I am nobody's weak little girl who cannot take care of herself. I am me; I am my own person! The strength in the words feel amazing, like a blast of cold water pouring over my head, but I can immediately adjust to it. It feels right.

"You look just like your daddy right now. I bet he regrets not coming to see you again."

That word alone feels like a big cement brick just hit the bottom of my stomach. Again? What the fuck does he mean *again*? I have met him before? Does he know about me? This whole time, he knew about me.

"He has no idea she was born!" Barnette sneers. I try to focus in on his face, and on the deep furrow of his brows, but everything starts swirling.

"Oh, he does. Of course, Romona was supposed to… you know…" He makes a motion as if slitting his own throat.

I gasp out loud at the outrageousness of the whole idea. My dad told my mom to kill me. I become flush with the wall behind me as I try to battle the onslaught of dizziness making their way over me; he succeeded in what he wanted to do—distract me.

"That is a fucking bullshit lie, and we all know it!" Dean bellows, taking a step in our direction, his motion causing the man training a gun to his temple to yank back and smack him hard against the head.

A small drizzle of blood starts to trail down the side of his face, and the motion of it pulls me out of the downward spiral I was headfirst in.

"Then why didn't he kill me himself?" I demand from Richard. I step towards him and poke my finger into his chest to enunciate my words. My voice comes out in a yell next. "Why didn't he kill me himself?!"

Controlled anger and a little bit of pain has the fucking audacity to filter through his eyes.

"I don't know." Then he claps his hand loudly, causing my body to jerk as my shoulders scrunch in a startled motion, and he begins laughing like a maniac! "But we all know that bitch of a mother was never good at following the rules, so now it seems that the weight of it is on my shoulders."

I let the words sink in. I feel like a ship in the middle of the sea battling wave after wave, taking on more and more water. I just want to breathe; I just wish the sea could be a little calm, even if it is only for a mere few minutes.

Richard takes the gun and skims it along my temple slowly moving my hair behind my ear, then back down along my neck to my collarbone.

Anger pumps through me, causing me to tremble as he continues his petty ass games. I can see my slitted eyes in the reflection of his own, can see the tension in the tightness of my mouth and flex in my jaw.

"Such an angry little thing." He chuckles as his stupid gun slides down between my breasts. "And not quite the delicate bird I had imagined you to be. You have quite the temper."

"I don't fear death, if that is what you are implying" I grit out.

The gun stops in its tracks at the base of my sternum, and a glazed look starts hovering over his features. A chill rampages throughout my body.

"Now *that* is my kind of woman." His response rocks through me as I see his change of expression.

I realize now that this isn't simply just an execution: This is an act of dominance, and this fucker wants to use me to piss his dominance all over. I can see all three of the guys tense behind him as I steal a quick glance over.

Richard smiles. "How about a little fun first? We have quite the audience, and I am sure they will enjoy it."

I can feel a tight tether inside of me pull tightly. Fear wants to course through my body, dread wants to burden me at the thought of this man raping me in front of them. Taking a piece of me—but I have no more pieces to give. I will be nothing. Again.

I worked too hard to not be anything anymore. I refuse to go back to the darkness that nearly took me away, and I absolutely refuse to be at the other end of a pissing contest of a man who thinks he can do whatever he wants to me.

"If you fucking touch her—" Barnette begins, but Richard snakes his hand around my throat and shoves me hard back into the wall behind me.

The tether snaps sharply, and a hysterical laugh flows out of my throat.

Confusion gathers in his eyes as he stares down at me, obviously bothered by my hysterics. I grab at his hand gently as if it was a lover's caress. I only allowed one man to put his hands around my throat, and that was Dean. I refuse to let this dickhead take that pleasure from me.

"Why the fuck are you laughing?" he snaps as his face stays

only a couple inches from my own. The smell of his breath fills my nostrils, and it sobers me up. It fucking reeks.

"Because I liked to be fucking choked."

His eyebrows shoot up as I bring my knee up as hard as I can right into his balls.

His facial features twist as he lets my throat go to grab his sack, and I give a quick right-hand hook to the side of his face.

My entire body nearly spins me in a full circle in the process, but adrenaline is pumping full force through me and keeps me steady as I see red. Anger billows hot through me.

I hit him again as he began to raise his hand with the gun in it towards me, grabbing at his wrist and twisting it hard with my left hand as I take my right hand and stick my thumb right into his motherfucking eye, gouging it.

The soft squishy eye gives way easily to my nail as I dig in hard. Excitement fills me as he screams out in agony. He drops the gun, letting it fall to the floor and allowing his strength to be overcome by my left hand.

He desperately brings his right hand to my hair, yanking it hard to pull me off. I let him pull it until I can feel strands rip away from my scalp; I thought I would be overwhelmed with pain, but my need for vengeance is stronger.

I jump on him as I use my left arm to bring his head into my thumb and I rip that stupid eye right out of its socket.

He shoves me off of him as he grabs for his face, dropping to his knees like the little bitch I knew him to be, screaming in agony.

"What the fu—"

"Did she just—"

"Holy—"

I hear all three guys in the background murmuring as

everyone seems to be frozen watching the scene in front of them.

I don't hesitate as I take the three steps to pick up the cold gun off the floor. I don't hesitate as I lift it up to the crying man on his knees before me trying to hold his eye as blood drains steadily from the wound.

Nor do I flinch when I pull the trigger on the man who thought he was going to rape me. Let's see you try to take advantage of another soul again.

That shot forces everyone back into a flurry. Suddenly, sound starts reaching back to me in waves as I hear the men fighting and more shots ring out. I just stand there still holding the gun in my hand staring at the lifeless man on the ground.

CHAPTER 25

Victim or Defender

Amelia

THIS SENSATION IS NOT the nothing I'm used to; it is the calm of sweet revenge, and I revel in this feeling.

Something hot brushes against my ear, and suddenly I hear Dean's voice penetrate the calming fog I am in.

"Get the fuck out of here!" he yells. His presence dominates my space as his hands grab my face and force me to look at him. "Run!"

I look behind him at Barnette, who is watching us intently, his eyes widened as he sees the way Dean holds me, but he physically jerks his head to the left, indicating for me to go. I take one last look at Dean, turn on my heels, and get the hell out of here.

I shove through the doors, and the cold air embraces me swiftly.

My arms and legs start to tremble as I clumsily make my way to the black Escalade to the left of the building. The adrenaline melts out of me, leaving me weak and exhausted.

I just killed a man.

I am a killer.

No. No. I shake my head. I am a survivor.

He was going to hurt me.

I try to justify my actions to the angel and devil in my mind. A hard debate on my moral compass, but there deep in the pit of my stomach, I am sickened to feel powerful.

But I am a badass, too. What does that say about me? I knew I was all kinds of messed up.

Gunfire has ceased entirely by now. I hear nothing in the static of the night sky. I drop next to the car, not caring about the expensive dress I'm in. The blood on it will never come out anyways; what is a little dirt added to the mix?

I killed a man, but then the other nugget of information I was given tonight filters through to my attention.

I have an actual father, who has a name, and is still alive. I have a father who has enemies that want to kill me.

I look up at the sky and glare at the brightest little star I can find, cursing whatever god is up there looking down at me.

They must have a special interest in my life and all the ways they can twist it up.

Doors banging open capture my attention as I squint in the darkness to see who is coming out of the warehouse.

A heavy sigh of relief escapes me as I notice all three men that I know making their way towards me. Barnette is holding Derrik up, nearly dragging him, as Dean beelines in my direction.

I try to stand up, but my body is shivering harshly—and it isn't from the cold.

No one says a word to me or to each other. Dean bends down and scoops me up effortlessly, and we all get into the vehicle. The only sound is the grunts that Derrick is giving on any jostle.

I am placed in the back with him, and I position his head on my lap and try to sooth him as I rub my hand gently across his head.

"What are you doing?" he grunts, thrown off by the soft sensation. Mr. Wannabe Softie acting like he has never been shown a tender hand.

I roll my eyes at him as I snap down at him, keeping my eyes straight ahead on the dark road as we begin going full speed away from the building. "Trying to comfort you. Now shut up and take it."

I know I need the act more than him. The soft, slow movement brings me much-needed comfort, and I can feel my breathing calm as the time passes.

Barnette is speeding down the old dirt road, and I am assuming we're going to a hospital or to a doctor.

I can see how hard he is gripping the steering wheel, and I notice Dean is staring at Barnette's grip too. That steering wheel would have been dead if it was somebody's neck.

Dean clears his throat and turns fully to the side to face him, saying, "Barnette I—"

Barnette lifts a bleeding hand and immediately interrupts. "I already know."

A heavy brick lands in my stomach. Barnette now knows his fiancée has slept with his best friend, his right-hand man.

I can see Barnette look up into the mirror back at me, and we lock eyes.

But anger is not what I see. I expected rage at the very least. Instead, I see calm understanding and a small bit of hurt. My heart physically aches at the sight of it.

"I understand," he murmurs quietly as guilt cords around my

insides. With that, calm silence fills the car, and the only sound is the harsh breaths from Derrick on my lap.

The breaks eventually slam hard in front of a beautiful old-fashioned Victorian home on the outskirts of town.

The buzzing is still ringing in my ear, but I can feel Derrick's heartbeat thump into me as he lays still on my lap. His breathing has become painful to listen to as he attempts to stay in control of how much air he inhales and what energy he uses to exhale slowly. I peer up at the old cryptic home, biting my lip.

It stands with a purpose, and other than one calm fluorescent light coming from the downstairs right-hand window, it is dark. The vines that are delicately twisted into the side panels and the columns holding the front porch up are just barely visible in contrast to the shadowy evening. I would love to see this place in the daylight.

The double front doors open suddenly, revealing the outline of a man standing there hearing our intrusion of the squealing tires in his once peaceful evening, or maybe I am assuming too much.

This man does know Barnette, and by the way he grumbles low and quick into the phone, this isn't the first time Barnette had to show up here in a hurry.

I refuse to acknowledge the turn of events of this evening, the information that has been told and the actions that have been taken. No one has said a word in several minutes, and it is the small old man that hobbles forward who finally breaks the elastic band of silence.

"Where is the wound?" Immediately into business. I like it; it's something I can focus on.

Both Barnette and Dean pull Derrick off of my lap and carry him into the house as I quickly trail behind them. Pained grunts roll out of Derrick continuously, but he doesn't yell out once.

"At least he is still conscious, huh? That's good!" the man remarks more to himself than the crowd.

I slow my pace from them and take a moment to look over this doctor that they all deemed to trust. Shorter than them, he averages right above my height. His salt and pepper hair curls wildly, showing he indeed jumped out of bed for this. The heavy wrinkles in his forehead and around his eyes enunciate the stress on his face.

He must have years of experience in this field. He is pudgy in the middle, enough to show he enjoys his slice of cake, but he limits himself enough to keep in decent shape.

There is just something about him that makes me feel safe; I sense no danger from him or his home.

Walking through the door, the men have already barged in and have gone down the hall. I can hear their footsteps rumble through, penetrating the calm of the air.

The open foyer is rich in walnut with old black and white photos of various people framed in green and brown picture frames. I take a second to admire the photos; they are so unique. To think about living in a time where color wasn't an option…

"You are an awfully curious creature." I jump slightly and spin around at the unexpected female voice. "And what an awful mess you have on."

Her shiny gray thin line of an eyebrow shoots up at me, as if chiding me that I should have been more careful.

She is lean and slim, as one who cares about their appearance would be as she is propped gently against the bottom of the staircase. I didn't even hear her footsteps come down; she is so quiet.

She hugs the loosely tied pink robe tighter against her middle, her silk matching pink pajama bottoms hanging loosely underneath. I admire the small white slipper socks she wears;

how stealthy she can be in something so soft. She must weigh nothing more than ninety pounds soaking wet, yet the way she holds her head up and shoulders back tells me she is confident and will indeed attempt to kick my ass if provoked. I swallow the lump in the back of my throat.

"I was admiring the pictures," I say lamely. I have no other response for her other than what is painfully obvious.

I look at the young couple so happy and carefree, then other photos of children with smiling faces dancing or playing softball. It is a whole story of a wonderful lifetime on this wall.

"Why don't you tell me why you are so sad as we get you out of those clothes and into something clean and dry, okay, honey?" She takes my arm and gently leads me down the hall. This woman is definitely not going to take no for an answer.

I follow her into a room off to the side, and she pulls a plastic bin out from the closet. An assortment of different size clothes lay folded in it, and curiosity burns my tongue.

She doesn't say anything as she hands me a pair of gray sweats, a black t-shirt, and from another bin a pair of pink slippers.

"Bathroom is right there. Wash up and change into this. I will be here with hot tea when you're ready." With those parting words, she gestures for me to walk towards the door on the back left, and I do the smart thing and oblige.

The water in the sink stains red as I take the washcloth to my face and hands, scrubbing off the remnants of the night. This was the danger I was warned about.

Barnette's words come back to me, "*My world has chaos, blood, and greedy ass people.*"

He was right; greed taints them all.

I change into the new clothes and let the comfort of the soft, fluffy slippers bring happiness to my sore achy feet.

Greedy people who want me dead because of my father or want to have complete control of me because of my father. A father who has been dead to me all my life.

"Your tea is ready, honey." I hear her soft voice through the door, and I swallow down the sob that wants to escape my throat and channel whatever strength I have to hold it all together until I get back to the safety of my room.

I emerge from the bathroom, and the woman gives me a small smile from where she is sitting on her small beige couch. I shuffle over to her and take a seat beside her, gently taking the teacup from her delicate hands.

She explains, "I'm Mrs. Kettleson, but you can call me Judy. Mr. Kettleson, my husband, is who is taking care of your friend right now."

I nod my response, still afraid to use my voice.

"Did you get hurt?" she asks, furrowing her brows slightly.

Physically, no I didn't. My ankle and head are a little tender, but nothing of a serious nature.

Mentally, though, I am fried. But I shake my head in response slowly as I peer up at her, into her soft kind eyes.

Judy scoots over closer to me on the couch and puts her arm around me, tucking me into her small frame. For the first time in a long time, I feel like a small child in her mother's arms, as if those arms can protect me from anything in the world.

The comfort that overtakes me nearly overwhelms me, and I try hard to keep the stinging in my eyes under control. My leg starts to shake, and I focus on the warmth of the tea on my tongue, doing my best not to spill it all over me and her.

"Honey, are you okay?" Those words right there, those forbidden words have capsized my undoing.

The tears have broken through my barrier and rain down

my face. Mrs. Kettleson pulls my head into her shoulder as I freely weep beside her.

"It's okay to not be okay, honey, it's okay."

I feel horrible crying into a stranger. I have known this woman less than an hour, and she already broke down all my barriers.

But she allows me to cry without getting upset, occasionally patting my hair to remind me she is there.

"I'm so sorry," I am finally able to mumble.

"Oh, sweet girl, don't be sorry. Everyone cries. It is only human to have emotions. Can't fault someone for that." Her words are like a warm balm over raw wounds.

"We are complete strangers, though," I chuckle through the remaining tears, quickly wiping my face dry.

"Well, I am Judy, and you are…" she pauses as she waits for my answer.

"Amelia," I quickly respond.

"See? There not strangers, just new friends, and as long as you're my friend, you can sit here and cry for however long you want."

Where has this woman been all my life?

She smiles comfortingly. "Now honey, do you want to talk about what happened tonight? You looked so lost coming in."

I hesitate for a moment; how much am I allowed to share with her? Can her heart and mind handle all this information?

She adds, "Mind you, we have been a part of Barnette's life since he was a child. My husband worked for his father previously; I have seen, witnessed, and heard a lot in my day."

I dare not ask her age or what she has witnessed no matter how much my tongue stings to.

"There was a shootout at one of their bases, and come to

find out it has to do with me," I mutter. I don't know why I feel the burden of guilt weighing on me.

"Why you?" she questions.

"Because of who my father is. People want me dead or to have control of me because he's a big deal." I sniffle as I fight off a new fresh wave of tears. "I didn't even know I had a father. Like obviously yes, I had one, but I thought he was dead, to be honest."

"That *is* a lot to process." She purses her lips. "But their actions and their ways of doing things is out of your control; it isn't your fault they decided to go this way about things. You do know that, right?"

Yet, Derrick is still hurt and bleeding out.

"Look at me," she demands, her tone lending me the strength it holds. "What happened is not your fault. None of this is your fault."

Damn those never-ending tears. Hearing those words, hearing someone tell me what I needed to hear for years is like being filled with glue and my broken, shattered parts being put back together.

"Thank you," I gasp. She will never understand how deeply her words have affected me.

"Derrick is going to be just fine. My husband is the best of the best, and I am confident in that." She pats my leg and guides my hand holding the teacup back up to my lips, strongly suggesting I take a sip. I allow her to mother me. "As for everything else you are feeling and dealing with, one step at a time, okay?

"You can't battle the world in one day, but you can battle one issue at a time. Right now, I think it will be in your favor to discover more about this father of yours."

My heart seizes at the thought. The man wanted my mother to kill me; why would I want to have anything to do with him?

I think my distaste at the thought is evident on my face because she gives me a pointed look.

"He wants nothing to do with me," I respond bitterly.

"Well, everyone else sure does, and it leads to him, so find out why. Knowledge is what makes a dangerous woman. An ignorant woman already digs her own grave. Do not be foolish."

I will admit she slightly intimidates me, but her words resonate with me. She is right; knowledge is power.

"Finding out about him does not excuse what he has done or what he has not done," she adds, and I find peace in that.

I don't have to befriend him, or accept him, or even forgive him—I just need to find out why others want me to get to him. That thought leads me to Barnette, and I feel a tinge of betrayal blossom in my chest.

"Barnette used me," I confess, and it hurts feeling like a pawn in his game.

"Is he still using you?" She straightens out her bottoms, and the action has me following her movements like a puppy dog.

"Well, no. He says he ended up falling for me, though he admits he did use me in the beginning." I try to push out the words but feel overwhelmed as the angel and demon in my mind want to battle. What is truth or lies anymore?

"Barnette has always been a man of his word. He has been misguided some, and sometimes his big picture sways him off the good path, but deep down he is a good man. I am sure if he said he fell for you that he means it with his whole heart."

I ponder on her words for a minute. This is the second woman to inform me that this man has a good heart, and that's got to count for something.

"What if there are parts of me that maybe he won't..." I hesitate as I try to find the word that can summarize all of my conflicting emotions. "What if he thinks I am this worthy prize, and it turns out that I am too damaged for him? That I am not worth all this trouble?" I whisper the last part, hurting my own ears at the raw honesty of my confession. Everyone thinks I am either better off dead or some worthy prize.

"You don't think you are worthy of love, do you?" She gently pulls up my chin and has me look up to her. "You are just as worthy as any other soul on this Earth. You have a good soul in you—I can see it." She grips my chin tighter. "You deserve to be happy; you deserve to look at a wall of photos of snippets of your past and see the ones you love: your husband, your children, your grandchildren."

She sighs. "Baby girl, I saw the sadness the washed through you looking at my most precious happy memories. You deserve to have that too no matter what."

My lower lip trembles, and I am so afraid that I am going to have my third round of tears. Jesus, I am crying enough for every person in this house!

"I don't see a damaged girl in my hand. I see a girl who has had to be strong for far too long, and I think it is time for you to share some of your burdens, honey," she adds.

My burdens, my secrets, I have spent years keeping them locked up tight. The thought of someone else knowing them causes nausea to grip me in a vice.

"I killed someone tonight," I whisper.

She pauses at the confession, and her small lips purse again as she thinks about it.

"Were you defending yourself, or was it out of cold blood?" Does it matter?

"I was defending myself. I was defending *them*." Does that excuse what my actions did?

"A survivor. A defender. A heroine. Those are the words that should be chanting through your head. Yes, you will feel guilty for what happened because you are human. Yes, what happened sucks, but if at any moment in your life it is between your life or theirs, I expect you to defend yourself. Do you understand?"

She sees me as a heroine. I am not a killer, a trigger-happy fool, I am none of that. A kernel of purpose blossoms in my heart, and it feels so good.

Fatigue suddenly weighs over me and surrounds me like a strait jacket. I am surprised the guys haven't come to check in on me yet. At that thought, I hope Derrick is okay.

Biting my lip, I wonder, "How much longer until they send out an update?"

"Oh, it should be anytime now. How about I go check in on them, and you lay here and close those eyes? You look so tired you might just sleep sitting up." She chuckles as she pats my leg, slowly getting up and heading towards the door.

I look at the blanket beside the couch and pull it around me, the aroma of lavender and seashells filling my nose. Such an odd mix of scents, but it reminds me of that sweet old lady, and a small smile tugs on my lips.

I think about our conversation and get stuck on her reflection of me staring at her wall. She was right; I did feel some sadness.

I would have loved to have a typical family with proud moments up for everyone to see. Instead, it is like my childhood is stuffed in an album underneath a bed, lost and dusty for no one to see.

I lower myself down and curl into a ball. The adrenaline has long since worn off, and my body is feeling the toll that crying did to me.

Maybe, a few moments with my eyes closed wouldn't hurt. Just a few moments…

CHAPTER 26

Sacrifices

Barnette

I STARE at her curled up on their couch, slightly snoring the early morning away. Tonight did not go the way it was supposed to, but now the big secret of everything is out. The only thing is, chaos ensued.

I finally was able to pull myself from Derrick after too many close call moments. He was hurt bad, and we were extremely lucky the doctor here is still able to work those aged hands of his.

"You have a tough one on your hands there," Judy speaks up from behind me, and I glance down to see her eyeing me carefully with pursed lips.

"You're telling me. She has been a firecracker since she has come into my life," I chuckle, but she crosses her arms and raises one single eyebrow at me. Shit, I am in trouble.

"She is hurt and feels too damaged to deserve love. I hope you are steering her away from that mindset."

My brows furrow at the confusion I feel.

I try to keep my frustration in check. "I know she is going through some things, Judy, but I can assure you I am going to ensure I make up for my previous mistakes—"

"Mistakes happen, I agree," she interrupts me as she takes a peek around me to glance at the sleeping beauty in there. "It is up to you from here onward to let her know she is worthy of love. Barnette, she wants a family, she wants happiness, I know she has a dad, but what about any other family?"

I pinch the bridge of my nose. "She has a mother and a little sister that she loves with everything inside of her."

Judy straightens up and looks at me. "I suggest that if you want to reach her in any way, you ask her about her little sister and get to know the details. Don't lose this one because you are afraid to untie that tongue of yours and wear some of your heart we all know you have on your sleeve."

Dios mio, this woman has always mothered me right along with Marisol. I can't catch a break.

"Yes, yes, I will talk with her, I promise. Right now, though, I think I should get her home so she can rest comfortably," I retort.

She nods her approval and understanding, her mom rant over for the moment. I have a feeling that more is to come, but I will take this small win for now.

"Barnette," I hear her call out, and I pause mid-stride into the room. "Anytime that girl needs a shoulder to cry on or some advice from an old lady, please bring her too me."

This woman has always been too good for all of us; her kindness can reach the heavens.

"Of course." I give her a genuine smile to show my gratitude, then turn and swoop my little sleeping beauty off of the couch.

Dean and I drive in silence all the way back home. We have a passed-out Amelia in the back seat, and we will come back later for Derrick.

"Everything is going to complete shit right now," Dean finally breaks the silence. I look at him warily, unsure if he is about to vent or blow up. "They are coming onto our turf over this, Barnette. We need to deal with the actual problem."

"Amelia isn't a problem," I quickly input, my brows furrowing at his words.

"I didn't say her. The problem is people thinking she is easy to get to or kill. I know she doesn't want to be locked up at the house, but she needs to learn more defense techniques. Even though, after seeing her in action last night I never in my life would have thought she had the guts to do that, she still needs some training."

I am right there with him in the shock; she pulled Richard's eye out of his fucking socket. It was both grotesque and so fucking hot I could have bent her over and taken her there if it wasn't for needing her safe first.

Dean adds, "I'm sure Pedro wouldn't mind jumping in and showing her some moves."

My teeth grind together. "Nobody gets to be that close to her except us." Just imagining Pedro guiding her hips and legs into the correct stance makes me want to punch him in the jaw, and he hasn't even done anything.

Dean side-eyes me and gives me a smirk. "Oh boy, you *are* in trouble." He chuckles, and I try hard to keep my fist to my side.

She causes an emotion in me that I absolutely loathe, but I can't change the way I feel about her. I turn back and look at her laying there with a ringlet of her hair hanging over her eyes. I just want to scoop her up and hold her to me, but we will be home soon, and the time can wait.

"We need to talk to her about us." I clear my throat. I have no clue how she is going to respond to that thought, whether she will freak out or chose him over me. The whole idea puts me on edge. "Judy also mentioned we need to discuss her past with her."

That tidbit also puts me on edge; my stomach curls in on itself thinking about what she could have gone through.

"Honestly, Barnette, after her dad being thrown in her face the way it was, you need to be straight with all of us going forward." Dean's jaw is tense, the only tell that he is angry. "We all deserve it, and just expect her to be pissed off at you over it. Really all of us. She's going to be angry, and she has that right to be, but we all need to be forward and honest from here on out."

I already know she is going to be angry. Hell, I don't even know what I was thinking. I really fucked up the whole situation from the beginning.

I was so focused on the end game that I didn't even take into account the people I was running over to get to it. Now, Derrick is down, Sam is dead, and Amelia is being hunted. Was reaching for the top worth all of this?

I pinch the bridge of my nose and try to control the surge of anger radiating through me.

"Listen, it is what it is. We're in this now. Shit like this happens, life is fucking chaotic, but everything will work out," Dean tries his best to pep talk me, but I know this all leads back to me.

"Derrick doesn't know about Sam." I don't know how I'm going to tell him, either. He is loyal to a fault, and my actions led to his partner getting killed.

"We will tell him together, Barnette. He knew what he was getting into—everyone does. This isn't a safe world; there will be casualties." Dean's grip on the steering wheel is iron-tight, matching the knots in my stomach.

I know he will want to be a part of the interrogation process after Pedro gets what he can, and I will let him have it. But Richard is only the tip of the iceberg; we need to get a handle on this shit.

"I didn't know this was going to lead to all of this," I honestly confess. "Like, sure, there would be hiccups, but all of this? I know we can't grow without some sacrifice, but *she* is something I am not willing to sacrifice."

"Wouldn't it be easier to?" Her soft voice from the back seat has us both giving our necks whiplash as we turn to look at her.

"No," Dean responds first as I just peer into her soft hazel eyes.

She has gone through so much in such a short amount of time. I don't understand how she is not a complete and utter disaster.

"Anyone who attempts to touch you again will die before they even get a word out on what they want," I vow to her, not losing eye contact, so she can understand the truth to my words and my promise.

Her eyes slightly enlarge as she looks at me, taking in my words slowly. Tonight showed me that she is more than capable of protecting herself, but I don't want her to be at that point again.

"I need to know more about my dad." She speaks in a hushed tone, making me strain my ears to hear her.

"As is your right," Dean responds. I can feel the speed of the vehicle pick up, and I am sure he wants to get back to the house as quickly as possible. He probably wants to hold her as badly as I do.

"Are you mad at me?" Amelia can't look me straight in the

face anymore, so she peers down at her clasped hands in her lap as she shakes her small little leg.

She knows that I am aware of her and Dean, and though it did sting at first, I am not mad.

"Never," I swear. She looks at me quickly, confusion swirling through her eyes. "I am not mad that you and Dean were together. I get why it happened; I understand he is a lot easier to accept more than me."

I swallow hard. I have never been an easy one to love. Her eyes dart from Dean's in the rearview mirror, then my own and back to his.

"I… I like both of you." Her cheeks slightly tinge as she looks back down to her hands. I can't tell if it's shame or embarrassment, and her uneasiness brings a slight smile to my face.

"We both enjoy you too." My soft indifference causes her to furrow her brows, and a full smile takes over me.

"You aren't mad," she states, then looks up and matches my gaze, "but you aren't saying I have to choose either?" She questions, though by my small smile I am sure she can tell how I am thinking.

"We both want you." I rein in the growl in my voice, because every cell of me wants her all right now. "And I am not asking you to choose if you don't want to choose between us."

"You can have us both," Dean pipes in, but I can hear the underlying tremor, the unsureness of how Amelia would feel about having us both.

"Like marry… you both?" Confusion is written all over her.

"Well, date," no offense to Dean, but she will be my wife. I want her to be *my* wife.

"So, date both of you guys." Her confusion turns slowly into curiosity.

"Yes," we both say in sync. I give Dean a sidelong look, and he smirks back at me.

"We can revisit the marriage thing later," I add. I see relief and fear all in the same moment overtake Amelia. "Without the agreement being null and void. Andrea is always safe, and I promise you I never in my life meant to hold her over your head in that way. For that, I apologize."

Amelia's eyes are like giant green saucers staring at me, and Dean reaches over to pat my shoulder. They act like I've never apologized before.

"This is a whole other territory I am not sure of," she admits, looking between the two of us.

"Oh, puppet, don't worry. We will show you." I wink at her, causing a blush to erupt over her face and chest.

"A day at a time, darling," Dean adds. His gentleness is something I can't offer, but I watch the way she glances over to him like a little schoolgirl with a crush.

It is sweet and innocent whereas when she looks back to me, I challenge her with my gaze. I make her nervous and excited all in one breath. I fucking love it.

She stares off out the window as she adjusts herself in her seat, and I can see the wheels turn in her head as she tries to process everything.

"Are you okay?" I ask softly.

She defended herself beautifully tonight, and though I see the strength in that, I can also see the turmoil it might cause her.

"I will be," she answers, my strong resilient girl. "Will Derrick be okay?" Concern radiates from her.

"He will be okay physically. Mentally, though, he lost someone he cares about deeply last night."

She nods her head as she filters through her thoughts.

"Sam and him were partners?" My little eavesdropper. I nod my head, afraid my voice will let on to the hurt I feel for him. "I didn't know he was gay," she murmurs.

"Most don't other than those closest to him. That kind of news is sensitive and could be used against him," Dean responds.

He came out to us only a couple years ago, and that was a huge moment for us all. It didn't change him as our friend, nor how we saw him. Who cares about what he does in his private time? Seeing them together and the smile that would light up his face was all the confirmation I needed. I just want my brothers to be happy.

"None of you guys knew Richard was going to be coming for me tonight?" she asks, her voice coated in sadness.

"No, this was a surprise, and we do not like surprises." Dean's anger makes his tone cold and distant. Last night was the final straw anyone of us could take. A line was crossed, and war is coming.

We finally pull into the familiar street leading up to the house, and I am anxious to be out of this fucking car. I want a shower and to grab Amelia and pull her to me in my bed. She is sleeping with me tonight. I almost lost her yesterday, and that doesn't settle right in the pit of my stomach.

"What is so important about me?" she asks slowly. That is her favorite question lately.

I blow out a tentative breath. "Amelia, I know why you are important to me, but I do not know what the specific end game for you is for others other than greed. I will be honest, the news about your father stunned me, too. I truly thought he had no idea about you, but the fact that he does opens a whole network of questions, and I am not sure where to begin."

He wanted her dead, but not by his own hands. Then she

ends up living her whole life, but he just washed his hands of her. The whole thing is confusing even for me.

"I would like you to try to be open with us, if you can, about your past," Dean asks gently.

I already knew we were going to have to ask her this, I just wasn't ready for that look of complete fear that has taken over her face to come into view. It guts me.

He continues, "Maybe if we know about you and—"

"Ramona?" Amelia's fear turns into a mix of confusion. She is looking behind me.

I follow her gaze to the front of the house, and my expression swiftly matches hers. There on the front steps sits Ramona herself.

"What the fuck is my mom doing here?" Amelia demands.

CHAPTER 27

Can You Love the Secret Parts of Me?

Amelia

I JUMP out of the car before it is even in park and walk briskly up to my mother. She sits there with her hair in a messy bun on the top of her head wearing low rider jeans and a navy-blue t-shirt. Her eyes are rimmed red, and her cigarette is in between her fingers lit but unused. She looks lost and defeated, and that look causes my steps to falter.

"Mom, what are you doing here? Where is Andrea?" I look around for her but come up short.

I didn't even check my phone and realized I left my purse in the car. My blood starts to rush, and nausea churns my stomach.

"She's at a friend's house." She looks annoyed by my panic, but my shoulders relax heavily down.

"Did you need something, Ramona?" Barnette steps up beside me and asks. Mom doesn't even turn his way; she keeps her eyes on me.

She looks at me up and down slowly, narrowing her eyes.

"What's going on with you? Shouldn't you be dressed better? You look like a grandmother."

"This isn't about me, Mom, why are you here?" I try not to sound too annoyed, but her being here feels wrong, and her judgment ticks me off.

"You aren't going to come here and insult my fiancée," Barnette speaks through his teeth, and tingles dance through my body. He's defending me.

"Oh, shush, she's my daughter, my fucking pride and joy—" her voice gets louder as she stands up, ready to give the same speech I have heard over and over again. I no longer want to.

"Enough." My voice snakes out around her, causing her to stop mid-sentence.

"Excuse me?" Mom matches my tone, but I can see the shock in her eyes.

"That. Is. Enough." I am tired of her empty words, her theatrics, and her games.

Her lips create a straight firm line as she eyes me, then Dean and Barnette beside me.

"Ramona, you have one minute to tell us what you want, or we are going to have you removed." Dean crosses his arms as he stands to my left.

I've got two men at my side, and that gives me a surge of confidence. I am no longer that little girl who must play nice to get by. I am no longer that child who has to watch everything she does so she can eat.

But just as quickly as that confidence came, I think about Andrea and how she needed me to bite my tongue. Fuck.

"I was hoping since you all are so well off that I may borrow a couple thousand from *my* daughter," Mom drawls, and I reevaluate her.

I look over every exposed part of skin, how her fingers are

fidgeting, how she may show confidence, but her eyes are everywhere but me, and it hits me hard. She is on drugs again.

"It wasn't enough for you to give me up to get out of debt, but you couldn't even stay clean to make sure Andrea stays safe." I can hear the layered defeat in my tone. I don't know if I am hurt, angry, or betrayed anymore. Maybe it is all three combined.

Above all, I just feel defeated. Who is going to make sure Andrea stays safe? She'd be safer with me than her.

"I am clean." Her lies continue.

"Andrea is coming with me," I state plainly, having enough of this.

Neither guy moves nor says a word, and though the panic of my decision is felt throughout my whole body, I need her to be safe; I will deal with the consequences.

Mom immediately shakes her head. "No." Because she knows she can hold her over my head, but I have had *enough*.

"Does she have food? Are you even there enough mentally to keep a fucking eye on her, Mom? How high are you right now? What are you on now?!" I holler at her.

I asked her to keep her safe. Why couldn't she just do the one thing I asked of her?

"Don't be all high and mighty with me, Amelia! I raised your sorry ass. Look at what I got for you!" She throws her arms toward the house, and my blood begins to boil.

"Fuck you, Mom," I seethe. But Mom stills and stares at me with wide eyes. "Everything you got me?" My voice raises into a holler. "I had to struggle most of my life, I was made to feel worthless and dirty and fight for where I am now, and me being where I am at this moment is no thanks to you!

"So, fuck you and fuck your empty words. I am going to get Andrea, and you will *never* see us again!" My body trembles as the anger I have for the woman in front of me pounds through my body.

"Amelia, we can try to find a way to get—" Dean starts in, but I interrupt.

"I have every right to have Andrea here with me, every right!" I don't mean for my voice to be as loud as it is, but I am exhausted to the point where I want to sleep for a week straight.

"Andrea is fine where she is! I am your mother, and I am only asking you for a little bit of money, Amelia. The least you can do is help your mom out after everything I have done for you! Your dramatics have always been a little much, but today they are completely unnecessary. Grow up!"

Her arms sweep wide as she spins a hasty circle not only pointing to the house, but the yard and Barnette, and disbelief pounds through me.

Anger for everything she has put me through and everything she has done and disbelief that she cannot see what she has put me through. She takes no responsibility for anything!

"I almost died because of you!" I scream, even though I know it was her love for the drugs that was the cause for the domino shitstorm of my life. "Fuck you for making my life so shitty I felt like I am better off dead!"

"It's time for you to leave, Ramona, *now*," Barnette's business voice cuts through the air.

Normally, hearing that tone would have my stomach in my ass, but all I can think about is how much I need Andrea with me here, how much my mom has not been there for me the way I've needed her, and the hurt she has caused me.

"You have no right!" she yells, though her legs have already started drifting her down the remaining stairs and towards her beater Dodge neon.

"I will be there to get, Andrea. Have her pack her stuff. This is it, Mom. Enough is enough!" I shout back. She does not get to take anymore from me.

Mom angrily jumps and thrusts her car door open.

"You are not taking her! She is mine!" Mom fires back. She knows Andrea is her last leverage over me.

"No, she is *mine!*" I snap. A heavy weight shifts off my shoulders. It feels good to say it out loud.

"Over my dead body, Amelia, so help me you keep your ass here." With that, Mom jumps in her car and slams the door shut, taking off quickly. That bitch.

I turn to march up to the house. I need to wash the blood out of my hair, change, and then I am going to go pick her up.

Enough is enough. The guys follow quickly behind me.

"I understand that you want to protect your sister—" Dean begins as Barnette jumps in as well.

"I will call the lawyer and see legally what we can do."

Both men look ready to take on the problem head-on, but one little truth will make them realize I am in my rights.

I shake my head as I try to fight with the devil and angel in my head, that constant fucking war. Tell them the truth and risk my secret, or keep it hidden and cause more chaos.

Is my secret worth this much trouble?

"We don't need a lawyer, Barnette," I snap, losing my patience.

"Yes, we do, Amelia, because she is a minor—" he begins.

"It doesn't matter!" I yell. I try to take deep breaths but can feel the chaotic energy rain down hard on me. How can I get them to understand without having to tell them everything?

"We can take care of Ramona. I will send someone to get her in line," Barnette threatens.

"No, I don't want her hurt." I just want her to keep one damn promise to me!

"Okay, not hurt, just get some sense into her—" I glare at him.

"You just don't get it!" I interrupt. I need to shower and get dress, damn it.

"Then help us understand, Amelia." Dean gently takes my hand in his and pulls me towards him as he tries to comfort me. Will he be able to hold my hand like that after knowing the truth?

"You just don't understand. None of you will ever understand!" I shout, my voice rising in panic as my heart begins to race. Even to my own feelings, my own thoughts, to my own damn head, this never made sense to me either.

"Help me to understand, baby. Just try to explain it. Give us the information." Barnette's voice is soft, and it causes me to pause.

I look hard at him. I try to see through to every single vendetta he could have to hold any of this information against me. I try to envision every reason why he would want to know —what would he do with this information?

How will he hold it against me? Will he treat me differently after?

There are so many questions and not enough answers. My head starts to spin as I attempt to gain some semblance of understanding. How can I explain something that I don't even know myself?

He stares back at me hard. Then Barnette speaks, and his voice melts the last of my turbulence. "No matter what you say to us, what you say to *me*," he emphasizes, "I will never *see* you differently, and I will never *treat* you differently."

I feel heavy liquid honey cool down my fast-charged nerves.

Slowly, as if starting from my head and dripping down to my tiny toes, I can feel my pulse start to slow down.

"No matter what she has done to me or what she has put me through, a small part of me will always love her." My voice breaks. "I can hate her, I can disagree with her, but the little girl inside of me who just ever only wanted her mama will always love her. And for that, I can never be the cause of her suffering."

A small, shaky breath leaves me as memories from over the years start to play like a black and white film in my mind. It replays every moment. The good… and the bad.

"I was never good enough for her. No matter what I did. I could get perfect grades; I could keep my room extra clean and tidy. Nothing I did kept her away from those drugs. She loved those drugs more than she ever loved me." I gulp down the heavy rock of emotion that glues itself to the side of my throat. "How can a tiny bag of white powder, or a syringe full of disgusting amber liquid, be worth more to her than her own flesh and blood?"

Tears start to weigh heavily down my cheeks, but I pay them no attention. I don't even have the energy to wipe them away.

Dean leans into me by my side, the comfort of the small touch giving me the tiny amount of energy to continue to bare myself wide open. Barnette leans against the wall, listening without any emotion on his face, and I just pray to God they can't hear the crack in my soul as it begins to fall apart.

"I could be having the best day at school, or a report card showing my straight A's and I would be so freaking excited to run home and tell her about it. But I wasn't there. I was like a ghost that would pester her, and she would only be able to acknowledge my existence for the moment she needed to swipe at me. I just wanted to scream at her. Just scream at the top of my lungs, 'Mom! Do you see me?' I would question if she would know who I was, but then just like that,"—I snap my fingers in the air to emphasize the change of the moment—"she would do something to make me feel like the daughter she always loved."

I can feel the dampness on my cheek start to drip onto my chest. I go and sit down on the small couch in the foyer.

"The trips to the beach when I was little where she would build sandcastles with me and take me to the arcade and let me ride the spinning wheel attraction until I got sick to my stomach." I laugh a little, remembering the sensation. Snot, tears, and laughter—the perfect combination to how fucked-up I really am. "She would come in and whisper into my ear how much she loved me in the middle of the night while I laid curled up in my room and she would tell me that nobody else in the world would ever love me like she did.

"She would promise to take me places, or buy me certain toys, or buy me new clothes, but by the next day she'd forget about all those promises."

I finally swipe at the tears on my face, and the movement breaks Barnette from his trance. He takes a seat on the other side of me and grabs my hand between his palms. The warmth is almost hot because my hands feel like they are icicles.

"But she didn't love me like I needed her to; she loved me as if I was a possession she had to care for." I look at Dean, taking a shuddering breath. "I don't think she knew how to love.

"How can I hate her for not being able to love me if she never learned how? But then this is where my emotions start to fight each other. I look at Andie and I could never,"—anger worms its way into my voice—"never hurt her the way she did me. I could never choose my happiness over hers; I could never ignore her needs.

"I would never let a grown ass man walk into the safety of

her room and take anything from her!" I yell before I realize I am yelling. "Her innocence is hers! She deserves to be safe; she deserves to sleep without one eye open, she deserves peace of mind and not to be a fucking twelve-year-old girl pregnant because Mom was too fucked up in the other room to realize what was happening to her daughter."

My voice turns into a mumble. Both men tense up beside me, but neither one makes a noise. They sit there rigidly listening to everything I am saying.

I pull my knees up to my chest as the sensation of being exposed overwhelms me. I feel dirty all over again. Like a small child who never felt safe in her own home.

"I can't begin to wrap my head around how she doesn't even acknowledge what happened to me. We didn't ever discuss it. She asked once who it was that did it because she couldn't even pinpoint who it could have been. All those men were sleazy, and dirty. All of them, and she kept bringing them into our home!"

A sob escapes my throat as I think about how I would use all my strength to shove my dresser in front of my door every night so nothing would happen to me again.

Then when Andie was born, Lacey helped me go to the hardware store and purchase a lock to install on the top of the door so I could be at more peace that she and I were going to be safe that night.

"I hope life continues to haunt her the way those memories haunt me. The way they circle me around and around until they are going so fast, they take the breathable air out of the whirlwind and take my breath away!" I'm gasping now; I can feel the noose around my neck closing in at the words I am saying. "But I also hope she finds peace on this earth.

"I hope she can quit those god-awful drugs and she can

realize that she had something beautiful in her grasp and she was the one who didn't appreciate it. I want her to see that I have found my own happiness, I want her to know that I don't need her or her love!" I immediately quiet my voice, but the words echo through the room. "Even if I still want it."

That is the worst part; I want something she is incapable of giving. I want something that should have come naturally to her, and it didn't, but facing that fact hurts me deep in my bones.

A deep, sharp ache that pressurizes me inside to the point of wanting to explode forms, and I squeeze my eyes shut against it.

"You don't need her love," Dean whispers against my temple as he leaves a soft kiss against it. I open my eyes.

"She didn't deserve you. It is her loss not yours, baby," Barnette murmurs as he leans over to lock his gaze with mine. "It is okay to love her and hate her at the same time. It is okay to want her love and to be repulsed by it in the same breath.

"She is your mother, for Christ's sake. It would be abnormal for you to not be so conflicted!"

His words register slowly in my brain. The heavy fog is making it hard for me to process anything at the moment, even common sense.

I nod slowly as I process through everything. Like a paddle boat lounging lazily in the ocean, allowing the undercurrents to direct its path, I allow myself to just *feel*. I allow my emotions to *be*.

They are validated. They are real. It is okay to feel everything. I inhale a slow, deep breath.

"I can want her love, but I don't need it," I repeat. Both men nod. I stare at the two of them watching as their bodies slightly tremble, but their faces hold something other than merely pain or anger.

I try to wrack my head for the word, and it finally dawns on me what I see: admiration. They aren't disgusted.

Something blossoms in the pit of my stomach, and for a moment I feel worthy of being loved. I am worthy no matter what my mom, classmates, and strangers have said. I am worthy of being loved and respected.

"And you are one hundred times a better mother to Andie than your mom ever was to you. You are a wonderful mother," Dean states, and emotion clogs my throat as tears actually brim the bottom of his eyes. "I am so sorry. I didn't know she was your daughter. I would have never separated you two."

Barnette's body is rigid at the realization of what our arranged marriage did to my heart, to the meaning of my life. It was not him who I hated those first few months, it was the fact that I couldn't protect or love my daughter and the guilt tore me up.

Even though this lifestyle isn't safe for her, I also know these men would never let anything happen to her, and they showed that by accepting who she is to me.

By letting me bring her back with me here.

They helped make me feel whole again.

The only way I can show how much I appreciate that right now is to give them the truth no matter how much pain it brings me to relive it.

I take a deep agonizing breath as I allow myself to go back to that night, to the truth.

The fucking truth.

The stench of cigarettes invades my nostrils as I wander through the pathway of beer cans and red solo cups. The carpet sticks to the bottom of my faded pink Converse as I walk by a stranger sleeping in a giant lump on the floor.

Mom had another one of her rage parties. People are scattered around the floor, the couch, and some weird dude with dark brown dreadlocks swirled with bits of green and blue is curled like a baby on the coffee table.

I hid myself at Lacey's house for as long as I could. Her place was always my escape from my own home life.

You would never look at the two of us and think we would have become as close as we did, the rich girl down the street taking in the girl from the trailer park, but she never made me feel like she took me in.

Lacey always made me feel like an equal. She always tried to give me clothes that were from the boutique downtown or the mall, but it was a hard pill to swallow sometimes on my own. What was even worse was the way my mom would say I was trying to whore around in the fancy garb.

I didn't even understand what a whore was until Lacey's mom overheard me talking about it one day and Mrs. Carrington with her large brown doe eyes framed by light makeup and always perfectly lined light pink lipstick had sat me down and explained it to me.

She may appear as the rich housewife in her brand-name clothing and sweet-smelling perfume that would trail behind her, but she was one of the kindest women I have ever met.

At the end of her telling me what it meant and why people get that reputation, she had gripped the sides of my face and told me sternly, "You are not a whore. Not now, not ever. Do not ever let your mother's words taint the beautiful soul within you."

I cried in her arms after that. I am still confused on why my mother would think that way of me. I am only eleven.

Mr. Carrington came home late from work today while Lacey and

I were giggling at the TV. Right as he was walking by the living room, he demanded I go home.

Mrs. Carrington always had a soft spot for me and understood what my home life was like, but Lacey's father didn't care. Thankfully he was at work most of the time but catching me tonight after what seemed to be a long day had him saying hurtful things.

He stood there tall and steady; he was slightly on the skinny side but toned in a way that you knew he went to the gym multiple times a week. His suit was always sharp and crisp as if he didn't move around in it all day.

He held his black briefcase tightly in his grip as he locked his almost black beady eyes on me.

His words still echo in my mind.

"We don't take in trailer trash." With that, he had walked upstairs towards his room, leaving my soul dark and diminished.

Mrs. Carrington followed him immediately, anger defined tightly in the creases of her face, while Lacey cried and tried to tell me she was sorry.

Life doesn't give equally.

I learned that fateful harsh truth that night.

I make my way slowly around everyone and head into my bedroom in the back of the trailer.

Luckily, nobody is stirring, and I don't see anyone resembling my mother on the floor or table which means she is in her bed. At least, I could hope for her sake she isn't outside again.

I go to close my door when suddenly the bathroom door opens quickly, and a man stumbles out. Blood rushes to my ears at the sudden movement, and I freeze like a deer in headlights.

"Oh, hey, hun, I didn't realize there was a kid here." He takes a step out of the darkened bathroom into the dimly lit hallway, a step too close to me, but my stupid feet are glued to this spot.

"I live here," is all I am able to manage out of my mouth.

His features are cast in shadow, but I see the sharp angle of his nose and his bushy eyebrows as they stare pointedly at me.

His eyes are dark, which is odd against the soft smile that tilts his lips at me. It is hard to tell if he is drunk or stoned, because his stance is still, and his voice isn't slurred. No one leaves her parties sober, though.

"I can see that. You got home pretty late, though, don't you think?" Another small step towards me, and his eyes stray from my face, down to my feet, and back up.

He pulls something out of his back pocket, and my alarm bells are starting to sing loudly. Common sense starts to make its way through my frozen stature. I take another half step in my room and slowly ease the door shut.

"Well, I am very tired, so I am going to go to bed now," I say, trying to keep my voice from wavering.

He puts a cigarette to his lips and lights it just as I have my door almost completely shut; my arms feel like heavy weights. The door catches suddenly, and I look down to see his dark combat boot holding it open. My stomach drops; I know—I just know I am in trouble.

He tsks. "Now, those aren't very polite manners, this being your home and all. I came for a good time, hun, and see, I still need my good time."

I shove against the door with all my strength as he pushes through it with ease and slams it shut behind his back.

Shit, Shit, shit! What should I do?! My head starts rapidly shaking back and forth as danger signals through my whole body. I can't breathe right, I can't process any thoughts; I just know I am in danger.

I go to rush around him as I start getting some sensation back into my legs, but he catches me with ease and throws me onto my bed.

I inhale a deep breath as I go to scream, and the motherfucker blows smoke right into my mouth. I inhale the harsh chemicals and start coughing erratically as I try to push him off from being on top of me. Tears run down my cheeks, and lungs burn from the feel of the cigarette smoke.

"Get,"—cough—"ooff!" Cough. "Mo—"He blows another one of his inhales down my throat as he uses one arm to pin my chest down and the other to pull down my shorts and panties.

Any of my attempts seem to be nothing compared to his strength. Dread curls through me, clawing at my mind and any sense of safety I have left.

I can't escape this. I can't—

"Don't worry, hun, it will only hurt at first, then it will feel really, really good." He has the audacity to wink at me as I try to catch a clean breath. Smoke is completely billowing around us, and I feel like I am walking in a stinky hot fog.

"We don't take in trailer trash," echoes harshly through my mind from what Mr. Carrington stated just an hour before.

Trailer trash.

The man shoves himself inside me, and I feel myself split in two.

The tears turn into rivers, and between the coughing fits all I can do is sob as he continues to pin me down and thrust, thrust, thrust.

Trailer trash.

The world isn't fair. He takes the cigarette from between his lips and burns the tiny butt of it out against my arm. The burning sensation from it doesn't hurt nearly as bad as what I am feeling in my private area.

He tosses the butt to the corner of my room with a sickening laugh.

Why me?

"You are sooo tight! Uuuuggggh!" he groans out loudly into my ear, his voice deep and grinding.

I feel a hot sensation between my legs, and I am assuming he is finished by the way he just lays there holding still.

Did no one hear me sobbing? Did no one care about all of my coughs?

The man finally pulls out from me and gently smacks the side of my face as if he is comforting me. My face is soaked from every tear I shed. Dark spots fill my vision, clouding over the already shadowed room.

"Now that is how you take care of your guests, hun. I am beat. Now, I can get some rest. I suggest you do the same." He stands up and pulls up his jeans to re-zip and button them up.

I can't say anything. I don't even have any more tears to let go. My whole body feels numb except for the wet sensation between my thighs.

"I'd like to say I am the type to cuddle and say I will see you again, but I am not going to lie to you. I've got to get back to my wife at home. Thanks again."

He waves his hand goodbye as he slips out my door and closes it behind him.

A deafening silence rings through the air.

I don't hear anything other than his steps as he exits out of my home and shuts the front door. I curl into a ball on my side as my body begins to tremble.

I have literally nothing more to give. I can't even move.

I didn't have anyone to rescue me.

I am alone in this world.

Why did bad things happen to me?

"Shh, shh, you are okay. Come back to us." I can feel someone rubbing my arms up and down, and I slowly start to become aware of my surroundings again.

Thinking back to that night made me feel like I was stuck there all over again. It is soul-sucking and draining.

I blink back the remainder of my tears as I try to clear my vision and focus on Barnette in front of me.

"Hey there, you're safe. Okay? You are with us; you aren't back there," he tries to reassure me.

I didn't realize I had bundled myself into an upright fetal position until I finally released the tension in my arms that were holding my knees to my chest.

"He will pay," Dean's harsh tone comes from against the wall across the room. His posture is rigid with anger, but there is pain as visible as the naked eye can see in his gaze.

"I just discovered what his name was from your file," I whisper, and I can feel the thick coat of shame come over me.

"No, no, no, look at me, baby girl." Barnette pulls my chin up and has me gaze into his eyes. "You do not feel ashamed or embarrassed, you understand? We want to take care of him for his actions and what he did, not because of anything else, you know that right?"

I can see slight movement in my peripheral vision as Dean pushes off against the wall and comes to sit back down next to us.

"Absolutely. Amelia, I never want you to feel like any of that is shameful or embarrassing. What *he* did to *you* was wrong and downright one of the most horrific acts someone can do to another. He took *your* innocence; *I* am going to take his *life*." The truth in his statement radiates through me, and I feel the honesty of it in my bones.

"He deserves nothing less than to be executed from this world—slowly," Barnette seethes.

I take a second to look at the two of them. Neither one of them appear disgusted by what I just told them. Rather, they look angry and vengeful on my behalf.

We sit in silence for a few minutes, processing everything. A huge weight feels like it has been lifted from my chest, that burden of information I had been holding onto for years finally releasing me and allowing a fresh breath of air.

"Let's go get Andrea." Barnette jumps up, pulling my hand and causing me to nearly slam into him. But I don't care. I am so fucking happy right now, because I get to go get my daughter and bring her home.

CHAPTER 28

This Life Has No Mercy

Dean

I WATCH as Amelia texts away on her phone. She tried to call Andrea twice already and both times it led to voicemail, so now she's trying to reach her another way.

My mind attempts to grasp all the information I learned this morning. It all makes so much sense now.

Amelia's reason for being so defensive and secretive, and the reason why she got so upset that night when I asked about who Andrea's father was. Anger pours through me as I try to think of every fucking way I can make that pedophile pay for what he did to her.

I try hard not to let my anger show outwardly, but I want to kill every fucking person that so much as even looks at her wrong, so help me.

Ramona is a whole different fucking issue entirely; Amelia has a soft spot for that wicked witch, but everything has changed about how I view her.

The fact that she can even still talk with her or fucking have any feelings about her wellbeing mind boggles me to the point where I want to shake the hell out of her and knock some sense into her!

What kind of mother does that to their child? What kind of mother puts their daughter in a position to not only be unsafe and assaulted, but made pregnant by a monster?

He will rue the day he broke my girl.

"Breathe," Barnette mutters softly to me from the passenger seat. I glance at him and see he is eyeing the steering wheel that I am gripping to the point that my knuckles are white. "I am angry too."

His body is rigid, though his voice is steady. He, too, is feeling the wrath of this secondhand anger. He is more the calm before a deadly storm, but I am the mayhem that comes with it.

"Lace! Thank God you answered. I been trying to get a hold of Andrea. Have you heard from her?" Amelia's voice floats up to the front seat, and I can hear the concern thick in her voice.

She is worried about her daughter.

Amelia has a daughter.

If I had known, I would have pushed for her to come along with Amelia when we went to get her. If I had known, maybe none of this would have gone as far as it did, and Amelia wouldn't have lost herself so badly.

Damn! She was suffering right under our noses, and it could have been fixed just by picking Andie up!

"Whatever you are thinking, just know I feel the guilt too," Barnette whispers. Shit, he probably feels the heaviest of the guilt.

"What do you mean? Who's there?" Amelia's change of tone catches my attention, and I look up into the mirror at her. She is shoving her hair behind her ear and searching into the air with her eyes as if she can picture whatever is happening over the phone in front of her.

"Amelia, put it on speaker," Barnette demands as he too tries to make sense of what is happening.

I pick up speed, anxious to get to the trailer. Amelia does as he asks, and Lacey's voice fills the tight space.

"There is a grey sedan I have never seen before outside the trailer, Meli, and the door is wide open. I am going in right now —" I can hear her feet stomp on the trailer steps just as a high-pitched squeal of fear echoes through the phone and off the walls of the car.

My blood runs cold as the scream echoes again and I slam the gas pedal all the way down.

"What is it?! What's wrong?! Lace, is that Andie screaming?!" Panic is etched into Amelia's face as she stares down at the phone, holding it tight in her hands like it's her last lifeline.

"Get off of her now! Let her go!" Lacey's voice rings out, and Barnette pulls the gun from the glove box and racks one in the chamber.

"Andie! Andie, can you hear me? " Amelia yells into the phone. I take the turn harshly as we speed down the last stretch of road leading to the trailer park.

"Lacey, help me!" Andie's voice screams through, and I can see the color drain through Amelia's face.

I finally see the wall of the park, and I go as fast as I can towards it. I don't give a flying fuck if a cop tries to tail me. Bring it! Join us in what we are about to witness because it will be whoever is manhandling Andie at the end of mine and Barnette's barrel!

"Faster! Faster!" Amelia yells at me, pure terror radiating through her.

I turn into the park as the sound of scuffling is heard

through the phone. Believe me, if I could make this car go faster, I fucking would!

The mobile home comes into view, and two men both with black masks on over their faces are exiting the home. One of them is carrying Andie, and both have guns.

I slam the brakes and barely put the car in park before Amelia is out of the car and running towards her daughter. One of the men pull a gun up towards her, and Barnette is already exiting the side with his drawn up as well.

The guy holding Andie is easily six feet tall, and other than his exposed arms, he is covered in black clothing. I can barely make out his eyes through the mask as he holds a terrified, thrashing Andie in his arms.

She is fighting against him with the little bit of strength she has. He has the gun drawn to her head, and she winces as he slams it against her temple.

Amelia has stopped dead in her tracks, staring with horror at the scene unfolding in front of her.

I can sense Barnette by my side trying to strategically come up with a game plan that doesn't get either of the girls hurt, but time is not our friend here.

Time is what we need and do not have. The one gripping Andie gets into the backseat with her, holding her flush against his body and the gun cocked to her head, and the second man with the matching mask stares down Barnette and his drawn gun.

"You shoot and she dies." His Russian accent is thick and slightly muffled through the mask.

"This will not end well for you if she gets hurt," Barnette retorts with a clenched jaw. I can feel the tight tension in my own as I try to rein in some kind of composure to figure out a plan.

"Your threats don't scare me," he responds as the car door slams and the man who already entered the car jumps into the front seat and slams on the gas.

Dust picks up heavily from the tires, and Barnette shoots the man down just as he fires his own shot towards him.

Barnette dodges the bullet, throwing himself to the side, and as the second man falls to the ground the gray sedan gains traction and takes off quickly.

Amelia chases after the car as I run back to jump into the car to chase after them. Smoke is rising from the engine, and I connect that the bullet he fired may have missed Barnette, but it hit the engine of the car.

Goddamn it! I slam my fists into the car, anger and terror filling me as I realize Andie was kidnapped right in fucking front of us and there is nothing I can do right now.

I jump out as I see Barnette sprint down in the same direction as Amelia. I quickly follow, passing her slippers that were left behind in the dirt.

The dust starts to settle as I turn the corner and my heart drops completely. In the middle of the road, Barnette holds on to a now screaming Amelia, and this scream is one of nightmares.

A deep anguish of unrecognizable pain radiates through it, and I fear that scream will haunt my nightmares as long as I will live.

The look of utter lost and pain becomes her as she fights against Barnette's hold. I run up to them and drop down beside them, unsure of what to say or what I could possibly do.

Sobs escape between her screams, and she slumps defeatedly into his arms as if her soul was stripped from her body.

I look out towards the break in the wall that leads to the main road where the man took to escape with Andie. That motherfucker will pay for this. He will regret ever crossing paths with us and hurting Amelia.

I look at her and her defeated quivers that spasm through, and pain overwhelms me.

"He took my daughter," she cries out in agony.

Barnette rocks her gently in his arms and grabs her chin, forcing her to look at him. "I know, I know. Don't worry, Amelia, we will get her back, I promise."

That promise will be kept. I don't care how many people may die, or how many will suffer, we will get Andie back even if it's with my last breath.

Amelia shoves Barnette away and stands up with her bare feet in the dirt. She peers in the direction the car was last seen and stares out with a faraway look in her eyes. I rise to my feet slowly to stand by in case she collapses and am pleasantly surprised when she turns her attention to me, her eyes harsh, her mouth set firm. She wipes away at her cheeks, drying them, and straightens her spine.

"There will be hell to pay. I will kill that fucker myself for taking her." She looks at Barnette, who now stands next to me. "Now, where do we start?"

To Be Continued...

Author's Note

What a wild ride my main girl has been through. I swear, while I was writing this, I was emotionally going through it too. That being said, I have mentioned in social media posts how I put a little bit of me in every story I write, and usually I don't specify exactly what it is, but this time I will share a little.

In this story, I connect with Amelia more than I don't, and especially in regard to the ending—it hits close to home. What Amelia feels when trying to get to her daughter while she is being kidnapped, the pain, the screaming, the collapse when there was nothing else she could do, is a lot of what I went through personally.

That scene is in Dean's POV because it was too hard for me to write about it in Amelia's; it was easier for me to write it as an outsider looking in at that moment (though in book two, I do show more of her turmoil of emotions at the experience of it). My daughters were around one year old when some random man on street drugs decided to kidnap them. It was completely out of the blue, and I did everything I was supposed to by not parking on a main street and having my nana in the car with them, yet still my girls were taken.

The man watched from across the street as my nana had gotten out of the car to retrieve a bottle for one of my girls before taking the opportunity to jump in the driver's seat of the car and take off.

My nana had run into the building I was in (I was dropping off my BLS card for school), screaming in panic, and I ran outside to see my car at the light down the way. I took my sandals off and chased after my car with fear pounding through me. I wasn't fast enough, and he ran the red light and sped off with them. I was very blessed to have the police department in full force that day, and they found them a little over an hour later by an undercover narcotics officer. I was one of the lucky ones to be able to bring my girls home safely.

The trauma I experienced that day was like nothing I have ever gone through, and that was a whole level of torture I would never wish upon anybody.

Writing helps me overcome struggles I have faced, so yes, the ending here sucks, but life is shit, and I needed to heal that part of me, so it had to be written. I also chose to share this personal part of me so it is understood that what I write isn't always imaginative writing; sometimes, it is true experiences.

On a lighter note, I am so happy that you have taken the time to read my story! I really enjoy the world of these characters and when they first popped up into my mind, I never could have imagined I would fall in love with all of them the way I have! I have laughed out loud so many times with their banter and their little pieces that make up their personalities; I have an honest connection with them all.

Book two is well under way, and I hope you all look forward

to it as much as I look forward to seeing everything come together! I love it when things circle back and click together.

I cannot wait to see your reviews out in the wild, and I hope through the emotional turmoil that if this story resonated with anyone that you feel a little less alone. I am on social media and am always a message away. Life if too hard and full of shitty experiences to not have someone to connect with.

Thank you all for your support of an indie author!

Author Sierra Marie